D1584710

The Omega Line
The Search for a Viable Past
By M. Ambrose Forsyth

The Omega Line

See us at our Web site for many other fine books.
mlmranchpublishing.com
or
E-mail us at: mlmranch@hotmail.com

To all those who look beyond that which was, to that which might have been, and hear the sound of distant drums and the pounding of hooves.
And to Marie who believed that the past does not necessarily portend the future.

~Of another place~

Prologue

The Black Hills of South Dakota represents one of the oldest land areas on the continent. Far older than the adjoining plates that surround its perimeter, it is really an island within a continent. Scholars theorize that in a very ancient time the area was surrounded and eventually trapped between merging, more recently developed plates of dry land. These in turn, pushed by still larger landmasses, congealed into what is now known as the North American Continent. An area of extraordinary beauty, it also is the home of the richest gold mine in the continental U.S. To the scholastic world, however, its extreme antiquity is of paramount interest.

To all that have known them, the hills have always held a special attraction and a sense of the mystic. They were the preferred sites for young Indian braves seeking a vision for life direction. The Sioux considered it the land of the spirits and dubbed them *Wakan*, or holy. Their theft by the Americans was symbolic of the loss of the old way, the end of the people's journey down *the Good Red Road*.

At the heart of the hills sits the Valley of the Wind Cave, a solution cave stretching into the bowels of the Black Hills. A deer hunter who was intrigued by a strange noise coming from the ground discovered the cave in modern times. The hunter found a ten-inch opening through which the wind alternately advanced and retreated into the depths of the earth.

Many modern scholars advance the theory that the true opening of the cave was rocked in by unknown hands in ancient times. A new entrance has been cut in modern times for visitors to the Black Hills to view its wonders.

Another more ancient entrance lies undiscovered to the modern world . . .

Chapter 1

The old Lakota was wise. He knew that a man's heart, away from nature, becomes hard, he knew that lack of respect for growing, living things soon led to lack of respect for humans too.

Luther Standing Bear

Marion Penitentiary
Present day
Omicron Line

Beneath the guard tower a silent form waited without emotion. They would be out soon, of that there could be no question. The timing of the escape had been planned for weeks. As those plans were refined, they were passed along, without comment, to the Warden's office, where they were recorded and the proper individuals updated. It had taken a long time to get to this point – a point where the target's fear of a trap without the walls had been offset by the fear of death within them.

In truth, both fears were real. Very real! One way or another, the Indian was going to die, and the death itself, according to the most persistent or determined investigating reporter, would be found to be legitimate.

This wasn't the first time he had been asked to kill, mused the guard. The way things were shaping up in the country, it was important that some prison experiences ended this way. A message, if you will, to the friends of the dead man.

The autumn wind shifted slightly, blowing gently from the east as the American flag flapped directly over the guard tower. The shooter noted the shift without concern. His shot would be less than one hundred yards in the lighted perimeter. Wind alone would not cause a miss.

The guard lit a cigarette and looked again at the fence where the prisoners would come out. This method had been used before on a couple of occasions. The individuals behind the plan would offer a lifer, with nothing to lose, a little hope if he would convince the selected inmate that there was a plot to kill him within the prison walls. Show the targeted man that he must escape and then show him the way to do it. Sometimes it took a while for the fear to build, but the target usually took the bait. Then, with a high degree of precision, such things could be planned out, right down to where the wire would be cut. As the man left the hole in the fence, there would be a distraction, such as a noise or a movement, something to make the man pause for one wary moment. That moment was the one the shooter had been trained for.

"The moment when the tax payers of this country feed one less piece of trash," mumbled the guard.

A movement near the planned escape route drew his attention, forcing him back into the darkness to his rear. It was just as they had planned, smiled the guard. It was time for this Indian to die. In truth, his fate had been sealed before the thought of escape ever entered his mind.

Anxious hands carefully pushed back the ends of the severed wire as the wire cutters, smuggled in for the job, were laid aside. *Smuggled right through the warden's office*, thought the guard, as he slowly raised his rifle.

The lights clearly showed the emerging shoulders of a man with long dark hair pulled back into a ponytail. Behind him another man, this one not so anxious, watched and waited, staring into the darkness of the dark tower and its hidden predator.

"Stinkin' Red Nigger," muttered the guard as he settled the rifle comfortably into the notch on his shoulder. "I can't believe . . ." a movement in the bushes beyond the emerging man interrupted His whispered comment. *Right on time,* thought the shooter.

The now upright torso of the would-be escapee settled into the sights of the waiting rifle and paused, looking quickly in the direction of the movement. The deafening roar of the rifle split the stillness of the night as the accomplice, still inside the fence, beat a hurried, yet composed retreat back to the shadows.

The shooter had heard the tearing of the bullet as it had entered flesh and bone. The silhouette before him had dropped like a rock as the shell ripped through heart and lung, through life itself. The question of success was never in doubt.

Sirens wailed from all corners of the compound as spotlights jumped in rapid succession toward the area of the rifle report. Feigning an anxious voice, the guard was on the phone calling for back up. "Escape attempt in progress . . . man down . . . other convicts possibly outside the perimeter."

On the other end of the line, previously rehearsed verbiage from prison authorities flowed to the shooter as ground reinforcements were dispatched. The communications had to sound good to anyone who might ask questions later.

With the formalities out of the way, the guard walked calmly toward the fallen body. It was hard for him to repress a smile. *After all,* he thought, *this was one really dumb Indian, and now this was one really dead Indian . . .*

Something in the bushes to his right moved suddenly and with purpose. The guard halted and looked warily into the darkness. The decoy wasn't supposed to return to the scene. He was supposed to move away to give the impression of a possible outside accomplice to the escapee.

"Who the h-" A second roar split the illuminated perimeter as the guard reeled backward. Clutching at his breast with one hand, he reached his other hand toward the fallen rifle, now too far away, as strength ebbed from his body. Dying eyes looked now toward the sound of footsteps moving out of the trees, grew wide, and still!

Aged hands reached slowly toward the body and grasped a head of hair. A flash of light against a blade reflected back into the compound as hurried feet moved toward the scene of the escape attempt.

*

Powder River Basin, Wyoming Territory
1876
Omicron Line

Crazy Horse had left his mourning wife, Black Shawl, with his relatives and set out alone for the country where his friends had erected the death scaffold.

The village, now behind him, had seemed a place of great devastation when he had returned from a war party to the Crow. That morning, as he and his warriors had approached to within sight of the camp no welcome riders had come to meet them. When they rode in, the signs of mourning were everywhere. The father of the great Oglala fighter walked to meet him, taking the bay by the jaw rope and the sage hens from the warrior's hand. The weathered old face looked to the warrior son, the son of his great pride, and spoke the hard words.

"Son, be strong now!"

Crazy Horse could see that the old man was in misery, his hair cut in mourning, blood from self-inflicted wounds caking his torn clothing. "It was another of the white man's diseases brought to us by the traders, Son," grieved the old man. "One more hard thing they bring to the people."

Crazy Horse was off the bay then and headed for his lodge, where he would find his woman alone. Their little girl with light hair was gone!

Crazy Horse rode resolutely toward that place where they had told him the scaffold would be found on a little hill by a line of trees. He thought of the little one that was taken from his lodge. He remembered the time when the messengers had come from Red Cloud asking for him to come into the agency. How he had slipped from the council lodge as they talked to the other chiefs. They had found him with the light-haired daughter on his shoulders, running around the lodge of her mother, the little daughter yelling "pony, pony" to her smiling mother, then her falling to sleep in his arms as he visited with his guests.

Crazy Horse could feel the bay climbing now, moving toward that country where they had placed her. He allowed the bitterness to embrace him, to become him. How he hated the whites and the pain and suffering they had brought his people! How they would pay when the mourning was finished.

As he approached the holy place, he saw the playthings that the little daughter had loved hanging from the posts. A rattle made of antelope hooves strung on rawhide, a bladder filled with small stones, and a painted willow hoop hung in mournful silence. On the scaffold, tied on top of the red blanket that held his daughter, *They Are Afraid of Her*, was a deerskin doll. The beaded design on her cradleboard, the same as on the dress the little one always wore, was a design that came from far back in the family of her mother.

He saw these and his sorrow swept over him as he lifted his body onto the scaffold to be with her one last time. One who watched from afar reported that for three days the father lay beside the fallen little one, his cries of pain filling the valley, unafraid of his enemies, the Crow, in whose country he mourned.

In the months that followed, the United States Cavalry would pay dearly for the death of the light-haired little one. Miners encroaching on the holy land of the Sioux deep in the Black Hills would be found killed but un-scalped with an arrow in the ground beside them. That following June, Major General Crook, with fifteen hundred men, was defeated on the Rosebud, followed in a very few days by George Armstrong Custer and all of his immediate command on the Little Big Horn, most involved in those battles gave credit to the inconsolable grief of the light-haired one's father. It was said that after the death of the little one, her father could no longer love life and sought death with almost reckless abandon. It was said that with all the love he had once felt for his little one, he now felt hate for the whites, those bad hearts who had brought so much pain to the people.

After defeating every major force sent against him with stunning effectiveness, Crazy Horse, convinced that there was no other way to save the helpless ones of his band, surrendered at Fort Robinson, Nebraska, where he was assassinated the following fall. Holding one of his arms as he fought for escape was one of his best friends, Little Big Man.

The body was put in a pine box and placed on a travois by his parents, who slipped away toward the Black Hills, the sacred Paha Sapa of the people.

All those who subsequently searched for the body of the famous warrior of the Lakota came back empty-handed. The mortal remains of the most valiant fighter of a warrior nation... had disappeared. [1]

**

South Dakota
September 7, 1989
Omicron Line

In his classroom at the University of South Dakota, Hergin Rodgers stood before his third and final class of the afternoon. The subject of the day had been the Celtic tribes at the time of the Roman conquest. As he had moved forward with his lesson plan,

---

1 Correct as per Omicron Line, or the time line known to reader!

Rodgers had again noted the similarities between the Celts of the 360 BC through 52 BC period, and the warrior tribes of the American West. In truth, the similarities were glaring to even the most casual scholar, and he found himself digressing from his lesson plan to emphasize those similarities to his class.

The historian had noted that the comparison, and its subsequent analysis, created an interesting spirit in the classes that he had taught over the past many years. He was anxious to recreate that spirit in the students now before him.

It was a good thing, the scholar had thought, *that his white students had the opportunity to understand their own history. They, for the most part, were descendants of those warrior tribes who had conquered Europe and sacked the city of Rome itself in 356 BC.*

It was these Celtic tribes, eventually defeated by the armies of Julius Caesar in 52 BC, who were the ancestors of the European nations that had produced most of these Caucasian students. It was the ancestors of these individuals who first had the term "noble savage" coined to describe them by the Greeks.

As the historian spoke, the students of his class, as did their predecessors in other classes, marveled at the voice of the man before them. It had been this voice, as much as the vast historical knowledge, which had drawn each new group of students to his classes.

Each new class in its turn pondered the almost imperceptible accent that sculpted the melodious rise and fall of the historian's dialogue. The speculations had usually come back to French as the most likely influence. But still the picture was not so very clear as to make it a certainty. The influences seemed many fold and, in the end, were written off to the idea that the famous historian had lived in many countries during the years of his research and had picked up traces of accents from each of the studied peoples.

The professor stopped momentarily as if to gather his point. Beyond a veil, *that was no longer a veil*, he could feel the heat of battle, feel the beat of life and hear the voices of the long dead . . .

"Speak man, speak! We must know before you die. Tell us if our fate is as yours, or if there is yet hope."

The dying man struggled for breath as the leader of the horse held him in his arms and begged him answer. The wound near the heart of the man spoke of an end, very near now. Yet to have come so far with such a wound spoke of the courage of the warriors of the Keltoi and, perhaps, the fate of the same.

For three days, the horsemen had ridden without stopping. Servants rode in a constant circle, bringing fresh mounts forward from the following herd to remount the warriors who pressed on to the hilltop stronghold of Alesia, where the army of their greatest warrior chief awaited deliverance or death.

Day would be swallowed by night, and night once again defeated by day, before they could attempt to relieve Vercinegoris. If he could still be relieved . . .!

Returning suddenly, Rogers' focus came back to him as the students looked uneasily at each other. Then, with a voice schooled by the ages, he drove the point home. "For you Caucasian students, it must be with a certain sense of camaraderie that you look on your Indian friends here in this class."

Rodgers didn't have to look closely to see, or rather sense, the looks passed quickly back and forth between the two groups in the class. "The similarities between your two peoples are greater than you can possibly imagine. We have already covered the fact that the Celts, not unlike the Indians of North America, lived originally in moveable structures covered with animal skins. The people of the western plains called that structure a teepee.

"The warriors of the Celts were fabled horsemen and were considered by the 'civilized' peoples of the south to be the 'finest light cavalry in the world.' That exact phrase, along with *noble savage* and many others, was used by the descendants of these same Celtic warriors when they were displaced to the Americas, and found themselves face to face with the ancestors of the men and women of Native American extraction sitting here in this class today.

"It is not hard to take this further and note that the early Celts in war fought not under a single command, but to quote another phrase so often used relative to the American Indian, 'every man was his own general and sought his own glory'. Each victory was a personal thing, not at all related to the victory or defeat of the group.

"Even in this individual battle, the similarities increase. To kill an enemy was not a great achievement to the Celt in early times. To touch an enemy in battle, or to touch a fallen foe, was of far greater value. On this continent, it was called 'counting coup.' In both cases, this search for individual glory, coupled with the fact that the warriors of both civilizations refused to fight as a concerted unit, contributed greatly to the downfall and eventual defeat of both groups to more militarily correct peoples, who *had* learned to fight as a concerted unit and to be precise, and had come to kill!

"In the end, the Celts met Julius Caesar and the legions of Rome at a hilltop fortress called Alesia. Even given the fact that the Celts hit the seventy thousand troops of the Empire with more than two hundred and fifty thousand mounted and foot warriors, Caesar won the day on the strength of the concerted efforts and training of his troops.[1]

"Although several very significant attempts were made, the Celts were never able to mount such an effort again and were totally subjugated by Rome for the next four hundred years. For a hundred years or so, the people clung to their own culture and the way of the warrior that had been their life. However, the warriors had been defeated on the battlefield, and each year whittled at the culture of these men of the plains. In the end, their ways disappeared into the quagmire of their conquerors' culture.

---

1. *52 B.C. Modern day France*

"Fifteen hundred years later, a thousand years after the fall of the Romans, their blood, mixed with that of their conquerors, reemerged as the modern nations of Europe: Britain, France, Spain, Portugal, Belgium, and Poland, to name a few. Even the Germanic tribes, according to the earliest historians, were known originally as the Celts across the Rhine.

"There was a difference, however, that must not escape our review here. The nations that came out of these ashes had learned how to fight. Not to fight as their ancestors, as individuals, but rather as concerted fighting armies who would move under a single commander for the glory of the flag.

"Oh, and one other thing, these armies no longer fought neither for personal glory nor to touch a fallen enemy. No, these armies had learned what their ancestors had only too late come to understand. To win a war, you must kill."

Professor Rodgers paused a moment as he weighed the effect of his last words on the class. Yes, he was accomplishing what he had come to do. They were thinking! They were not there just to pass a class. He had made them think and, from here, he would make them understand.

"We have covered what the reformed Celtic and Celtic-mix nations had gained. Now we must know what they had lost. Somewhere in their long captivity and the dark ages that held them in bondage, physically and culturally, for a thousand years, the people had lost who they were.

"Among the old warrior tribes there had been a set of virtues that ruled their lives. Bravery, of course, was one of these. A warrior race, or any people, could not long survive if their hearts lacked that critical attribute.

"The next, however, was strongly associated with it and, in many ways, created the other. Fortitude was defined not just as the ability to withstand the rigors of nature and the elements, but also as a personal point. It required the ability to show reserve under emotional stress. The blatant and often vindictive expressions of anger in our society have left many a marriage, family, community, and in times of historical insanity, even nations destroyed. The ability to control our emotions and not to express them in anger, criticisms, and pain to our fellows is a virtue to us lost.

"The ability to push negative emotion aside and give to the world an expression void of it accounts for the stoical terminology used so often in reference to the Native Americans of the past. It is this same virtue, enumerated and practiced both in the emotional and physical training of the young Celtic warriors, which made the Roman scholar Lucretius refer to them thus:

'. . .this race of men from the plains were the harder, for the hard land that borne them, built on stronger and firmer bones, and endowed with mighty sinew, they were a race undaunted by the heat or cold, disease or famine. For many years, among the beasts of the earth they led their life. None was yet the driver of the curved plow; none yet could turn the soil with iron blade, nor bury a new shoot in the ground, nor prune the ripened branch from the tree . . .[1]

The class now was visibly stirred as Rodgers, the master teacher, moved toward the analogous end. "These indeed are great virtues shared and honored by both groups, the Celts and the Native Americans. There are two more virtues that have commonality in these great and ancient people. Does anyone know them?"

---

1. Circa 365 B.C.

In the far rear of the lecture hall an elderly, stocky looking Native American man rose to his feet. Rodgers felt a sense of exhilaration as he began to speak. The man, obviously in his late sixties or seventies, spoke with a pronounced accent, as if English was a second language, learned late in life. "The remaining virtues of the Lakota are two that the whites have long forgotten. As I speak, they are also forgotten by the Lakota; they are *generosity* and, most important, *wisdom!*"1

The two virtues spoken by the man rippled through the historian to his roots. In the distance, his thoughts fell on drums pounding out their hypnotic rhythms as the bodies of the dancers wove a pattern of memory into a lurching mind.

As the class filed out of the lecture hall, Rodgers made a special point of turning his back, working on erasing the board and shuffling the papers so recently placed on his desk by the departing students. He could feel the old man's continued presence and he knew that he had not left with the others. And what's more, he knew that this moment was essential to, a *beginning*.

He knew they would try again!

---

1 *Bravery, Fortitude, Generosity and Wisdom, the four virtues of the Sioux.*

Chapter 2

The historian must have some conception of how men who are
not historians behave.
Edward Morgan Forester

Rapid City, South Dakota
Present day
Omicron in transition

Snow had begun to fall quite heavily as Special Agent Daniel
Banyon and his partner pulled into the parking lot of the Rapid
City Public Library. The night itself had a bitter feel to it, thought
the agent.

"When this snow stops, it will get cold," he said out loud,
"very cold."

The younger agent nodded his agreement without speaking as
the two men moved quickly toward the old building in front of
them.

Banyon was the ideal agent prototype, and everyone in the
bureau knew it. The younger agent, Keller, knew also that it was
looked on as an honor to work with the man. The senior agent
was in his early thirties, athletically built, and he had won a
reputation as a, no nonsense, can-do individual. Originally
recruited by the bureau for his weapons skills acquired in Special
Forces, it was soon understood that he was a do-it-all personality
who could work well in a team, but preferred to work alone. The
senior spent most of his time alone and, despite the
encouragement and teasing of his fellow agents, had always found
the women he met to be lacking. He had the haunting feeling that
there was someone waiting for him, but his work was too

demanding to devote any time to that kind of search.

When he had arrived in South Dakota two months previously, he had imagined a short stay, a quick investigation, and, at the worst, turning the hot potato case over to some local agents as he returned to Los Angeles. It hadn't turned out that way at all, as the case had mushroomed into something that threatened to strangle Banyon and all others who touched it in the snows of a South Dakota winter.

It had occurred to the senior agent that his career itself was on the line, and he had redoubled his efforts in what had proven to be a vain attempt to reintroduce some order into the investigation. The only clue of any value that had turned up was the absolute predictability of the fact that every trail would turn up *empty*. In and of itself, this had proven to be the most solid lead that the agent and his team had discovered in two months of pursuit.

Banyon and Keller paused just inside the lobby of the library to kick the snow from their boots. Beyond the desk of the head librarian, in a prearranged reading room, sat the history professor they had come to meet. The man himself was an enigma. To the senior agent, he represented everything he had grown to hate in society. *In the real world,* thought the agent, *things were clear; things were explainable. Maybe not at first glance, as this was a world of deception – deception and evasion.* But the man he had come to meet was beyond these parameters, beyond the facts that so purposefully surrounded a proper life.

In so thoroughly investigated a case as this one, rehearsed the agent, the life of every individual was researched, regardless of his or her apparent importance to the case. The bureau took a smug pride within itself that it knew everything about everyone. By the end of an investigation, the bureau knew what each person had done, when he did it, and with whom. As a case grew, the life of every associated individual was reduced to paper and carefully reviewed by the investigating agents.

So it had been in this instance – until they came to Hergin Rodgers. His professional life was an open book. Following in the footsteps of his father, he had begun his teaching career at the University of South Dakota. There, seemingly beyond explanation, the relatively young Rodgers had stumbled upon a great deal of hitherto unknown critical historical knowledge. This knowledge, reduced to book form, shocked the world of academia to its roots. Within five years of receiving his doctorate, *the Great Professor*, as his students called him, was acclaimed by many as the most knowledgeable historian of his time, or of any other time, according to some.

All that was fine, but predictable within the realms of chance, thought the agent. It was, however, when the search reached into his earlier years that the professor officially became the focus of the investigation.

An adopted son of Professor Clinton Rodgers and his wife, Claudia...

Estimated age at time of adoption: 21-years-old.

Estimated age? The note had sent the agent team back to birth records to find actual age and name of birth parents, only to find nothing whatsoever. Suspecting deception, or even tampering with official records, the bureau had set its best men to unravel the mystery.

Another dead end!

Normally, the investigation would automatically turn toward such apparent misinformation, pursuing the trail of those who had fled before they were pursued. Suddenly, however, the origins of one man became very insignificant indeed. Even if the pursuit of a past for Professor Hergin Rodgers had been of critical importance, as Banyon suspected it was, the bureau's ability to follow that trail, or any other trail of significance, suddenly fell into doubt...

This was not their first meeting, yet this one should prove to be different, the agent thought. This time it had been the esteemed professor who had requested the appointment, not the F.B.I.

In the past, Hergin Rogers had been cool, if not evasive, as the agent had asked questions about his contacts on the reservation. These questions dealt mainly with people in the radical Indian movements that the professor had been known to champion in his many published books and articles.

This time, however, when Banyon had answered the phone to the sound of an anxious, worried Rodgers, he concluded that finally one of the world's foremost historians on the subject of the Lakota Sioux was ready to give him something he could use.

What had caused the change in the professor, the agent did not know, but he could guess. He had told the historian on their last meeting that this day would come.

"These people are hiding a killer," he had told Rodgers. "When hiding a killer *in a glass house*, you can get very nervous – nervous enough to want to get rid of anyone who might be standing too close to that house in worried times."

He remembered the professor's quick look of irritation at the agent's reference to the historian's latest book, *In a Glass House*, which dealt with the overbearing presence of the F.B.I. on the Pine Ridge Reservation.

"Hello, Professor," the senior agent smiled, as he reached over a small conference table for Rodgers' hand. The professor reached slowly but firmly in response. Banyon smiled inwardly. This was the first time in their interviews that Rodgers had taken the agent's proffered hand.

"How can I help you?" Instantly he regretted his flippant manner. Irritation on the face of the historian confirmed his concern.

"How can you help *me*, Special Agent? I thought that it was you who were in need of help."

After weeks of verbal abuse and evasion from the man before him, the senior agent had a hard time letting it go. "Well, I just thought that maybe things had changed in your world," he smiled back.

Rodgers appeared tired. The deep gray eyes revealed a weariness that was difficult to hide. Sighing inwardly, the great scholar rose and walked away from the table. "Mr. Banyon, things *have* changed in my world. They have changed a great deal. Unfortunately, I am not talking about change along the superficial lines that you are suggesting. The problem goes far deeper than that."

Rodgers stopped at a rack of books and stood as if pondering the titles. *Looking for something that is not readily apparent*, thought the agent.

The historian spoke again without looking at the agent. "It has changed a great deal in your world also. You just haven't *...chosen to talk about it yet."*

The agent had been down this road with the scholar before, but this time he decided not to be led. "I'm really not that interested in the niceties of your philosophical junkets, Professor. I have a murder to solve and an escaped prisoner to bring into custody. There is excellent reason to believe that the same man committed both crimes, but frankly, I can't seem to come up with enough information to determine that. If you could *please . . ."*

To his immense irritation, the senior agent could see that the professor was not listening to a thing he was saying, and, in his suddenly ceasing to talk, could discern no difference in the scholar at all. The professor had simply shut him out, as if he didn't exist.

He stared malevolently at the enigma before him. The man he was speaking to obviously bore no relation to the voice that had called him on the phone not an hour before. The change was incredible, he had to admit, but he still had an investigation to complete and had wasted enough time on this snowy evening. He turned toward the door and started to leave.

"Mr. Banyon, before you leave, I do have one question," said the professor.

The agent slowed slightly, turning toward the professor, who was still pondering the rack of books. "Well, join the club, Rodgers; we have a lot of them!"

The historian appeared to completely disregard the comment, and went on as if the agent had not spoken.

At his side, Keller looked on apprehensively. What ever transpired between these two, he knew that his place would be as an observer only.

"What did . . ." the scholar paused for a moment, as if weighing his words, "prison and court records show about the predisposition of your prisoner to commit murder?"

The senior agent turned somewhat ashen as the words dropped meticulously from the professor's mouth. Instinctively he knew that the great scholar already knew the answer to that question.

But how could he?

"Actually, you don't know, Mr. Banyon! You don't have any records at all, do you? They have somehow, *disappeared*. In fact, the only way that you can prove that Leonard Sharpfish even existed is from the *memories* of people, inside prison and without, who saw or knew him."

The silence was deafening.

"Am I right, Mr. Banyon?"

The agent could feel the sharp intrusion of the professor's eyes as they bore into him.

He knew, unbelievable! How could he possibly know? The scene of *the great professor* before him, uttering the exact details of the most closely guarded secret in the history of the bureau, became blurred as the agent suddenly noticed a point that he had missed before. Hergin Rodgers had changed!

It had been less than a week since he had last seen Rodgers, yet the change was pronounced.

"I don't know why I am even wasting my time talking to you, you think that . . ." He trailed off, his face a picture of frustration.

The agent stared at the hands waving expressively before him. They were darker than they should be. They held the darkness of a summer tan or long exposure to the sun. Banyon glanced out the window of the library at the snow continuing to pile up on the steps.

"Frankly, I thought that we had agreed to never contact you again," said the professor.

"Wait, now, wait just a minute," the younger man interrupted, "We? Who are 'We' and what is this about contacting *me*?"

The interruption had halted Rodgers, but the specific question had pushed him back into deep thought. The investigator thought for just a moment that he was about to get the first straight answer he had ever received from Hergin Rodgers. As the scholar began to speak again, he realized that he would not.

"Have you spent much time, *in this life*, studying the history of the Lakota people, Mr. Banyon?"

*

The Black Hills Dakota Territory
December 30, 1876
Omicron Line

"The snow is falling heavier now," thought the elder Black Elk as he moved his pony a little faster through the mounting drifts. He had always been amazed at the buffalo as the bad storms blew in about them. In good weather they would always run at the approach of a mounted hunter. All of a sudden, with the beginning of falling snow, they could no longer smell well, and settled themselves in to eat the dried grass beneath the white surface. They became almost as docile as the white man's spotted cattle that he had seen on the Platte many years before the war with the whites had begun.

Still, he reminded himself, the people in camp were hungry and he needed to get the meat now burdening his pony back to the helpless ones before the snows forbade passage.

On the edge of the herd, he could see one remaining Lakota sitting on a raised log, watching the milling animals, his pony close at hand. Black Elk rode toward him to ask if he needed help and to remind him to hurry.

After approaching to within a few yards, he recognized the bay hunter of his nephew, and his desire for return to camp became greater. He could see him clearly now, watching the herd as if they were all his very own and he could somehow protect them by his presence.

The elder Black Elk rode up to the motionless figure, seemingly without being noticed.

"Nephew, it is time to go. The helpless ones will worry with so many of the warriors out and the bluecoats very close."

"The blue coats will not come for a while yet, my uncle. This weather will hold them in their camp for a few days. Then they will come, and we will fight them again."

Black Elk slid off his pony and walked closer to his nephew leader. Indeed, he was the one they all depended on to know these things. He was seldom wrong. That was the reason the camp of Crazy Horse had grown so much after the snows had begun to cover the land. The people felt safe when he was around. The bluecoats had never defeated him in battle and, at least in times past, this had always brought happiness and hope.

Something had changed, however, and the people now saw that the past summer of victories had brought only sadness and fear to the Lakota. They pondered that maybe the free life of their fathers would end soon. Many thought maybe it was time to go in and try to walk the crooked road of the white man.

Sitting Bull and the Hunkpapa had gone north, to the old hunting grounds around Fort Peck. Some said that they would even go so far as Canada, the Grandmother's country. Sitting Bull had invited Crazy Horse and his people to go along. The other head men, the last of the hostile Oglala leaders, had wanted to go, but Crazy Horse had protested, saying that they were better off to die in their own land.

They were camped in that warm country near the Tongue River, about eighty of the white man's miles from its confluence with the Yellowstone. The scouts brought word daily that the soldiers under the Bear Coat officer were camped at that confluence and were preparing for war. Most believed that, given their lack of ammunition and warriors, Crazy Horse would have his way concerning where the people would die.

Still, they would not leave him. He was one of the last and perhaps the greatest of the remaining Lakota warrior chiefs, one of the last to offer hope that somehow the Good Red Road of their fathers could be found again. The life that most of them knew would soon be gone if the powers that guided the path of the people did not intervene.

As the limping Black Elk led his horse forward, he found a small fire that the snow and wind had hidden from him before.

Crazy Horse could see the worry on the face of the old warrior and thought of their first battle together, when Crazy Horse was just a lad. The people called that fight the Fight of the Hundred Slain. It was there that the elder Black Elk had been crippled by a white man's bullet. *Never to walk without a limp again in this life*, thought Crazy Horse.

Not one bluecoat had left the bloody hillside where they had sought refuge from the encircling Lakota. Crazy Horse looked with unbridled admiration at the aging warrior that now stood before him.

Crazy Horse showed no signs of leaving, and the elder Black Elk spoke again. "Can I help, Nephew? The snows are getting heavy."

The warrior turned back toward the fire. "Uncle, you have noticed the way that I act, but do not worry. There are caves and holes for me to live in, and perhaps out there the powers will help me. Time is short. I must plan for the future of my people..."[3]

Black Elk was long gone into the blowing snows when Crazy Horse mounted the bay hunter and headed into the hills to find shelter for the night.

The parting words of the elder Black Elk hung in his ears. "The old ones say that a part of our people came from the cave in the Paha Sapa; that they came from another world, not like this one, and they were wise. Maybe there is wisdom there for you too, Nephew."

The warrior knew that the old man was right. In previous nights he had slept *in that very cave* that many called *the womb of the people*. In it he had sought and found the answers that were so terribly needed. The answers, which would bring death to the people...

Turning into the blowing snows, the warrior raged against the powers that led the Lakota toward their graves. *"Wakan-Tanka, must it be so? Must we die to find <u>the Good Red Road</u>? I am a warrior, born to leave my body on the prairie for the people. There are many of my brothers with me who will fight to give the people life. Is it not enough?...Why must the innocent ones also*

---

[3]   *Scene and conversation correct as per Omicron. <u>Crazy Horse, the Strange man of the Oglala,</u> Mari Sandoz*

die...?"

The voice of the strange man of the Oglala faded off into the rising snows as the wind wailed through the naked trees. Snow gathered heavily on the buffalo skin draped over his shoulders as the great warrior squinted his eyes against the growing blizzard, hoping to see the silhouette of the Black Hills, the Paha Sapa of the Lakota, in the direction of the dawn star. Maybe if he returned to the cave again, maybe if he pleaded with the Wakan man who had instructed him there. Maybe there could be another way to seek the Road.

No! He knew that there would not. The wisdom of those of the cave went beyond the understanding of those in his world. He knew there were purposes he could not understand, and that if they were to succeed he would have to do as he was counseled.

Crazy Horse pulled the bay to a stop. He would not return to the cave until he could do so as directed by the Wakan man. The bay turned almost on his thought and headed west, back toward the camp on the Tongue where the last of the free Oglala awaited his return. He would go and help the people prepare to fight. If the powers had decreed that the people must die to live again, then he would help them to die with honor.

**

_____

Rapid City, South Dakota
Present Day
Omicron Line

_____

"Have I studied the history . . ." Banyon slowly sat back down in his chair and stared blankly at the professor.

"I used to listen to my grandmother talk about the old days. The stories have stayed with me to a certain extent. I know the history of my own people, if that's what you mean."

Rodgers smiled inwardly. "You have Lakota blood?"

"That's what I just said, Professor. I may not look it, but my mother was half Lakota. It wasn't by mistake that the bureau sent me here. I not only have the blood in my veins, but I can also speak the language. That's partly because of my grandmother who raised me, and partly at the bureau's insistence. They like us to develop the natural talents we have. They thought that with all the trouble in years past, an agent who could understand the native language would be of use.

"But yes, to answer your question, Professor, I do know a bit of the history. I even went so far as to read some of *your* books."

Banyon could see that the historian was barely paying attention, but was impressed at the change that he perceived in his face. It seemed almost that he had been mentally transformed since his first acknowledgment of his Lakota blood. When the scholar came out of his thought process, he was a man with a purpose.

"We will try again!" said the historian, barely over a whisper.

Then, appearing to remember, he turned to the agent and grinned, "Your grandmother, as you remember her, was not your grandmother at all, who she was, you can learn, if you would like."

Banyon interrupted him roughly. "How could you possibly know anything about my grandmother?"

The agent sat motionless, but churning inside as he realized that the interview had turned dramatically and inexplicably out of his control. With one sentence the historian had swung direction into his own hands, and he knew somehow that it was all part of a plan!

"What kind of a trick is this?" demanded the agent.

The professor was instantly on his feet and seemed genuinely angry. "Your grandmother, as you call her, was a wise and valiant woman, well versed in the ancient histories of the people. You dishonor her by your ignorance."

The steel gray eyes of the historian bored into those of the shocked agent. Suddenly softer, the historian spoke again. "Do you have any clue who she really was, or, for that matter, who you really are? Any clue whatsoever?"

Agent Banyon felt his own anger pouring through his blood unlike any time since the war. He was losing control, and he knew it. Slowly, very slowly, he worked himself back one step at a time. His mind, so carefully trained, yet so unpredictable and faulty in his perspective, struggled against a tangible *confusion*.

"We came here to listen to what *you* have to say, not vice-versa. You think that it is important that I know more of the history of my people. Very well, I'm ready to listen – go that direction if it helps my investigation. As for my family, however, or what I do or do not remember, that is not relevant to this case and I would like you to drop the subject."

The professor looked at the agent through calming eyes while his face betrayed an inner metamorphoses. Purpose and reason, man's ancient allies, gained momentum against anger and fear, the oldest of his enemies.

In a distant past, he could feel the pounding of a million hooves as they galloped toward their death, galloped toward a destiny that he could not save them from. In the pounding rush of that great army, he could hear the singing of doomed men, defying fate in the search for glory.

"It is *their* courage that will lead us again," he mumbled to himself. "It is *their* vision that will give us light." The fading voices of his past told Professor Hergin Rodgers that "a beginning" was close at hand, and, turning back from what had made him, he refocused on what he would make!

His voice was soft at first, almost a whisper. "In truth," he started, as he seated himself back on the padded library chair, "most of what we know of the past before our own time is fiction. The history that we pride ourselves on is usually little more than an outline of what happened, and sometimes not even that. Often, it is no more than fabrications made up to cover the real story for reasons that have escaped us since that time. That's why you can't keep the average school child awake during a history lesson. The whole thing is disjointed, fed by distant perspective and faulty memory or just plain deceit. The only constant we have is what is written on paper, contradictory and impossible as it so often seems, it is still all that we have. We must use it as a lever to lift the veil of time and surmise what we can of what is really there. The written word, along with scarce physical remains, becomes the only evidence to succeeding generations who have no choice but to accept them for what they say or imply. Those evidences become 'the truth' by the sheer lack of opposing voices, which are lost in the dark recesses of time and death. Nevertheless, the general details are somewhat correct and do paint, at least, a hazy picture of what really happened."

The professor could see the agent's attention was superficial, his fingers tapping impatiently on the table. "Your investigation is an excellent example of this principle," said Rogers. "Would you tell me what you can about it?"

"My investigation" the agent responded, "How is my investigation an example of your theory? Dr. Rodgers?"

It was the good professor's turn to now act impatient. "Simply because you have followed exactly the same pattern, everything that you have released to the press, to be reduced to writing, is a lie, a fabrication, intended to deceive and to tear at the very fabric of history."

Banyon's mind reeled as he rose to his feet. The historian *did* know!

"Stop it, stop it!" he heard Rodgers yelling distantly. "I'm sick of this! We don't have the time!"

And suddenly, the agent could see it, this same scene, this very moment played out to its last detail in his mind. Mind? No, deeper than that – a different consciousness. But he saw this scene not once or twice, but many, many times, hundreds maybe.

Slowly, from a deep fog, he began to find a focus. Around the scenes themselves there was a light. A light? No, a voice really, mixing that which was, with all that was sensed, combining to create pure knowledge. And words, words that beckoned, yes that throbbed with life:

A good nation we will make live . . .

The words of Rodgers filtered through to the receptive mind, yet he had heard them before.

"Yes," a voice whispered, *"many times . . ."*

"Stop it, do not go there!" yelled Hergin Rodgers as he reached for the confused agent. The scholar shook the agent's shoulders in a desperate attempt to make him hear. "We'll never make this one happen unless we stay focused here. This is reality. This is the only reality that will save us."

Keller was on his feet now, concern showing openly on his face.

Rodgers stopped abruptly and Banyon, as if from a foggy distance, could see that the scholar's fist, hanging at his side, was clenched. Whether in rage or in frustration, he was uncertain.

"We're close now, Dan, don't you feel it?"

The younger man felt an inner peace, so unknown in his life, so elusive to the boy without parents in a land without a heart. He had built walls to protect himself – walls to keep out all those who would hurt him and his grandmother. Walls, he also knew, to protect others from him. He could hear the words of the historian as they breached those walls, filtered through the sheer mass of rock and mortar and, in a place of pain, sorrow and hopelessness, found him.

The words had changed somehow. They were quiet, even gentle. They were the words of one who understood. "Come back to us one last time, my friend, and we may win."

Agent Keller continued to stand although the scene had noticeably calmed.

Suddenly the eyes cleared, Agent Banyon was back, and the historian saw "awareness" fade within the inner him. Rage brought the professor's fist crashing to the desk before him. It

31

would have to be done as it had always been done. Step by step, Line upon line.

The historian's voice was calm, in spite of the desperate anger that had eclipsed his hope of an easier path to a critical beginning. "Tell me about your investigation, Agent Banyon. Please tell me a truth that your grandmother would be proud of. If you're concerned about telling me something that I shouldn't know, then restrict yourself to what the newspapers have said up to now."

Everything from the agent's training screamed a warning; this was a compromised position. Something was terribly wrong and, in his weakened mental state, he found himself in the presence of a man who may be an enemy. Still, deep within, a fading voice told him that all would be well. More, it was time for the truth – that the truth was critical.

The agent began slowly, carefully fighting residual confusion, aware that he would probably be called on any diversion from the exact facts. "Leonard Sharpfish," mumbled the agent as he sat back in the cushioned chair, "escaped from Marion Penitentiary in November of this year. A guard was killed in the escape, and before reinforcements could arrive the body was scalped by someone, either the convict or an accomplice outside the prison. The escapee is still at large with his accomplices and is assumed to be hiding on the Pine Ridge reservation here in South Dakota where he has friends to keep him hidden."

"Okay," interrupted the professor, fighting back his impatience. "Show me that what you have just said is historically correct."

"How do you mean?" queried the agent.

"Well, we're in a library. There are newspapers here right up to this morning's editions. Prove to me that what you have said is true."

The senior agent pushed back in the library chair and stared blankly at the professor. "You know that I can't. I don't know how you know, but you do."

"I know because I'm a historian," retorted the professor, "a man whose life is wrapped around things that are written down, things that are supposed to have happened. And frankly, Mr. Banyon, what you just told me never happened!"

"What do you mean it never happened?"

"I mean you cannot document it and so it didn't happen. You don't have a single written report, you don't have a prison record, or an employment record for the guard who was killed. For some unknown reason, all the trial records that landed Mr. Sharpfish in Marion have disappeared, as well as any written reports relative to him being there. Not a single newspaper story printed at the beginning of the case can be found, and no one can explain what happened to them. Your agency is in the biggest turmoil in its history over this thing and their best man, i.e., *you*, hasn't got a clue. As far as you can prove, the incident never happened, and what's more, I can tell you as a fact . . ." The Professor paused for just a moment to allow the reeling agent to refocus his attention to what he was saying. " . . .those people never lived, in this life, and except in your memories, they are gone forever!"

The agent sat erect in his chair now. The eyes of the two men locked, seeking understanding.

"How do you know this?" asked the agent finally. Rodgers got up from his chair, walked back to the rack of books behind him, and removed a hardbound volume with his name indelibly written at the bottom. "Do you know anything about the death of Crazy Horse, Mr. Banyon?"

It was this way of changing subjects between two sentences that had always annoyed the agent to the extreme. It was almost impossible to follow the historian from one moment to the next. Yet he had learned that the best way to get anything from the man was to go along with his line of thought, to become part of the scene that the scholar saw before him.

The senior agent smiled slightly, shaking his head and motioning for Keller to sit. "No, no, Professor, I don't. Just that he was killed in some kind of arrest attempt in Nebraska. The old Fort Robinson, I think."[4]

"Very good! In fact, I wrote a review of the many versions of his death a few years ago, endless eyewitnesses, endless variations on the same theme. The only thing that *all* the witnesses could find in common was that he was killed at Fort Robinson in front of a large number of both Lakota and white witnesses. All that was left to us that was supported by *all* those witnesses was that he died in the Adjuncts office after counseling his father to 'tell the people not to count on me anymore.' These are the only facts on which all parties agree and can be accepted as historical fact relative to the time line we refer to."

The agent interrupted, "The time line that we refer to? What the . . ."

"Shut up, Mr. Banyon. I am trying to tell you the answer that you have been seeking. Just shut up long enough to allow your mind to work. Allow who you are, for once, to override what you have been trained to be!"

In spite of the relative coolness of the room, the agent could see tiny beads of sweat on the forehead of the scholar as he slid the brown leather-bound volume toward the agent.

"Mr. Banyon, since my book on the actual death of Crazy Horse, which used to appear in multiple copies in this library, has disappeared as completely as your records on this case, maybe you would oblige me to read a reference made in the last chapter of my *Biography of Famous Western Chiefs*."

The agent pulled the proffered book closer and fixed his eyes on the paragraph indicated by the professor. "*What became of the*

---

[4]   Correct as per Omicron, readers line

great Lakota warrior, Tsunka Wakan Witko' (Crazy Horse), after that time is purely speculation. His death will remain a mystery. He was last seen during the battle on The Hanging Woman on January 8, 1877." Banyon looked up from the text "The battle of what?"

"The Hanging Woman," Rogers responded. "It was a relatively minor skirmish between Col. Nelson Miles, in command of the second cavalry, and the combined Oglala and Cheyenne camps on the Tongue River. The only thing notable about this fight, *in this line*, was that it was Crazy Horse's last formal fight with white troops. However, he most definitely was there, and was one of four warriors who stayed at the rear in an attempt to keep the troops at bay as the rest of the band escaped into the snow. History, as we know it in *Omicron*, has him surviving the battle and surrendering at Fort Robinson the following spring where he was assassinated in the fall."[1]

"In *Omicron*?"

"Yes," responded the professor. "In *Omicron!*[2] In the time line that you are aware of in your conscious mind. The line that we currently live in!

"What your investigation is uncovering, Agent Banyon, is that something has happened to change our conscious present. Not only are things changing and disappearing in this present, but in recorded history as well."

Rodgers took the book back with both hands, his thumbs seeming to caress the leather binding. "How many Lakota do you think live on the reservation…?"

"Well, I don't know exactly. Maybe twenty thousand…"

"The morning paper says less than five hundred," retorted the scholar.

---

[1] As per Omicron Line

[2] The time line known to the reader

The agent knew better than to doubt Rodgers or the facts he quoted. Too many people had disappeared for him to doubt the possibilities now.

"If you go just a little further in this book than where we just read, you will start to find the names of *other* battles in various places. No other historian in this line has ever heard of them. It is clear that what happened on the Hanging Woman has had far reaching consequences. Many battles followed, but all unwinnable battles, it seems, for the Lakota, at least.

"The bottom line is that they decided to fight. More correctly said, they decided to fight to the death, and the five hundred Lakota left out there are testimony of the outcome. There is one person who might shed some light on this. His name was His Horse Looking. If you want to join me in the morning, I'll take you to meet him."

The eyes of both men remained locked momentarily as the professor ceased to speak. Banyon had seen this behavior before from the celebrated historian. The conversation was over, and there was little that he could do to change that fact. He would go the direction that the historian would lead; something in his instincts told him that there was something to gain there for them all!

When the arrangements for the following morning had been completed, and the agents had left him alone, the historian leaned back in the padded chair and closed his eyes. He could hear the voices tugging at him, could feel the light ...

Time had been the enemy *then*, an enemy without mercy – not that the Keltoi had ever asked for mercy. Still, every warrior knew that all battles could not be won, and one battle must be the last.

Just as it appeared that the wounded man would answer nothing more in this life, the flame rekindled for a moment. Words poured raggedly into the ears of those who watched.

"Caesar builds two walls, one to trap the army of Vercinegoris, one for those who come."

Chapter 3

Every advantage in the past is judged in the light of the final issue.
Demosthenes (384-322 B.C.)

Hanging Woman Creek at Confluence with Tongue River
1877
Axial point: Omicron Line

Crazy Horse stood on the edge of the bluffs overlooking the Tongue River, looking north on the camp of the night before.

On his return, he had told the people that Bear Coat's soldiers would attack them at any time, and they should be ready. In the first fight, the warriors had stood in front of the oncoming soldiers and held them as the innocents had retreated. The directions of their leader had prepared the hostile band, and casualties were light on both sides as the lower camps retreated up the Tongue toward the Hanging Woman – toward Crazy Horse. The second attack had come two days later, and the warriors again had stood to fight as the people retreated toward the main Oglala camp upriver.

The soldiers continued a dogged, though careful, pursuit. The ammunition among the people grew less with each shot. Now they were together on the eighth morning since the arrival of the white troops. As the night fled before the light, the air was filled with a morning mist and the feel of impending snow. Crazy Horse had moved everyone to the bluffs in the darkness, telling them," to be ready", as the soldiers would come before the light.

The headmen of the hostile Lakota and Cheyenne camps were gathered together, close to Crazy Horse, at a high point on

37

the south face of the bluffs. They had sat in council the night before and had been stunned at what they had heard from the Strange One.

"The people could run, that is true, they have been running for months. But run to where? With armies moving through the snows in all directions, this is one of the best places left to them, one of the last."

Weeks before, they had sent a delegation of chiefs under "Sitting Bull the Good," the Oglala, to attempt a peace with the Bear Coat officer, only to see the eight headmen cut down by Crow scouts as they approached the soldier place. Now it seemed that there were no answers left to them, only paths, and they, in fact, lead nowhere.

Crazy Horse was a fine warrior, from a family of holy men, but to put the future in the hands of one man alone was not their way. However, as the events were fulfilled as he spoke them, they had begun to believe, and now accept, what the powers had advised their Strange Man in the cave of the Paha Sapa.

The day rising before them showed a desperate people, too tired to run and lacking the united vision to continue, there was nowhere left to go. This was the last piece of land left to them and, if the powers had so advised, they would fight for it. This last time . . .

He Dog moved closer to his cousin friend and they spoke in hushed tones.

"Those two have always been close. Closer than brothers, really," the elder Black Elk thought aloud as he watched them at the highest prominence of the bluffs. "If there were only one that would believe in Crazy Horse with his life, He Dog would be that one."

As He Dog moved off, a certain sense of anticipation rose in the bosom of the old fighter. It had always been his desire to find a warrior's death. Yet now that death was upon *them all*, he wondered at the course chosen by his nephew leader. How can a man's death be an honorable one if there was no one left to sing the songs, to recount the deed? A warrior gave his life to protect the innocent ones, not to . . . *help them die.*

On the valley floor, the soldiers began to come out of the fog. They came in formations at first. Then, seeing no resistance, made every indication of making camp. Big fires soon sent the smell of coffee and fresh bacon through the bluffs to where the hungry people waited.

The chiefs had made the decision that there was indeed no future for them, that the road of the white man would bring slavery to the Lakota. The people had said they would follow the counsel of their Strange Man; that they would rather die fighting than become the dogs of the whites. Their leaders, after trying all they knew how to do to gain an honorable peace, finally agreed. It was not known how the future would be for the Lakota who had gone into the agencies to live off the grudging charity of the victors. Their wise men said they foresaw a day where the Lakota would live in little wooden boxes like the white man and there, without the buffalo, they would starve.

"A people without hope, a people without vision, living out their lives and finding the grave without joy," the powers had told Crazy Horse. He who had always loved them and protected them with his own life, he who had pled with the powers in their behalf, saw that it would be so.

Yet there were whisperings that seemed to have come from within the council tent. Whisperings of something else said by the Strange One, something about *a rebirth!* If the hearts of the people were good in death, they would gain something unknown. In that unknown, there would be the seed of hope. The people had always depended on good men to direct them, to tell them what they should do. Yet each individual had to be the one to make the decision to die.

The stories told by their old men talked of a time when another race of red men had been beaten by the whites, had become slaves. Knowing that all was lost, they had refused to plead with the powers for more children. They had refused to bring more children into the world to be the slaves to the whites. So it would be with them! But they would die as a free people, in the land that held the bones of their fathers.

The morning mists had been pushed back before the winds of the upcoming storm. The soldiers broke camp and started to fire the wagon guns at the bluffs where the people had gathered. Crazy Horse had told them they must wait, that they must not run.

The whites would need to come closer and climb the bluffs to get to them, and then they would give them their fight. When they were through, there would be fewer whites to tell the tale of how the last of the free Oglala had died![1]

*

Black Hills of South Dakota
Present Day
Omicron Line

Snow was falling heavily as the Blazer driven by Hergin Rodgers turned toward the Black Hills. Banyon had slept very little during the night and had spent most of his time at his terminal, researching what the professor had shared with him the evening before. He now tried to act mildly interested as the scholar recounted the historical gaps relative to the Sioux, their principle events and leaders. As they drove the historian attempted to suggest how these events could affect the agent's investigation.

---

[1] Attempted Omicron - Omega transition

Yet none of it was new to him, and the very telling of it brought only more anxiety to the seasoned veteran. In truth, the capture of Leonard Sharpfish meant almost nothing to the agent or his directors. One missing convict mattered very little in comparison to the overall problem that faced them now.

Across the country, reports continued to flow in at an ever-increasing rate of *disappearances* or *kidnaping*. They were all the same confused pleadings from friends that had suddenly seen those whom they loved or associated with cease to exist. The pattern was predictable after the first few cases. The report would always be from a friend or business associate. Never had a call been received from a blood family member. As these incidents had grown numerically, the bureau, with the help of local law enforcement, had attempted to investigate. In every case, there had been no one to speak with who was any blood relation to the missing person. This was not a disappearance of an individual, *but of families*. Families, who a few days before had lived and played in a neighborhood, maybe for generations, *now were gone!*

The words of the professor, relative to Leonard Sharpfish, had become the verbalization for the whole mess, thought the agent. *"You don't know, do you? You have no records at all. They have somehow disappeared. The only way you can even prove that these people existed is in the memories of their . . . friends."*

The only solace that he had been able to find in his inability to solve this case was that he was not alone. The best law enforcement minds in the country were poring over all available information in an attempt to discover how tens of thousands of people's lives could possibly come to an end without any written record left behind.

There was only one clue of any real value that was left to them. The disappearances had all begun the night that Leonard Sharpfish had escaped from the Marion Penitentiary. That night officials had raced to find prison and personal records to help in his recapture. The files were not empty; they were gone – as if they had never been.

The bureau had originally thought this had been a covert attempt by the Indian extremists to cloud the trail of the escaping felon. Then, as the other disappearances came to light, it was assumed that the trail was being further clouded by a decoy attack on the official and legal database of the country. The best computer minds in the law enforcement world turned to search for the point of attack, but to no avail.

The trail, however, always ended at its point of origin, the night of the Leonard Sharpfish escape. All subsequent trails led nowhere. Except for the ever-growing list of missing persons being filed from all over the country, the past seemed to hold its secrets in silence.

The special agent returned his attention to his traveling companion. "So how long have you known this 'His Horse Looking' individual, Professor?"

A look of extreme irritation touched on the face of Hergin Rodgers. "Is that the way they taught you to interrogate a source in F.B.I. School, Mr. Banyon? You're working on the most extraordinary case in your career! You think running things by the book will give you the answers? How I relate to His Horse Looking is not important, it's how he relates to you that will gain us something – if it even makes a difference now!"

"What do you mean if it makes a difference now? It seemed to make a big difference to you when we talked last night, Rodgers."

"When a man is faced with few options, Mr. Special Agent, he often will take the best that is offered while he awaits another. We are playing out what seems possible now – right or wrong, I couldn't say yet. What other possibilities might be presented, I cannot know."

Agent Banyon tried to look as casual as possible as he looked into the side-view mirror and, to his satisfaction, saw nothing. He knew Keller still had them in sight and that he would be his ace in the hole if things went wrong.

Hergin Rodgers looked steadily ahead at the opening morning. "He's still back there, don't worry!"

**

Hanging Woman Creek
January 8, 1877
Five hours beyond axial branch - Omicron Line

Nelson Miles knew he had a victory, the victory that had eluded Custer and Crook and all the others who had tried to beat the hostile Sioux and Cheyenne under Crazy Horse. They had tried and failed. He would be remembered as the one who had ended the string of humiliations handed to the United States army by the allied tribes. There would be those among the do-gooder eastern press who would criticize him for the tremendous loss of life. In fact, he himself was surprised that it had gone this way. The hostiles had never stood a chance and yet, instead of running off as they should have, they had stayed and fought.

"And fought well," Miles murmured out loud with more than grudging respect. The warriors had died like men, and when they were gone, the women had refused to yield. Many had picked up the weapons of their fallen mates and had carried carnage into the ranks of the already battered troops. The order had been given to kill any *individual* attacking with a weapon and, in truth; the troops had no choice in the end.

Miles had been told that a few small groups had escaped, dragging the bodies of their dead. "Let the poor devils go," Miles had answered, when asked if they should pursue. "They have nowhere to go and no one to receive them or lend them aid. Most of them will die in the snow. The rest will struggle into the agencies when they can. Whatever else we may say of this day, we will say that this is the end of the significant Oglala resistance.

Sitting Bull and his Hunkpapa are all there is left of the Sioux fighting men."

"That's quite a lot," responded Miles' adjunct officer. "They say he has over eight hundred warriors with him, seasoned veterans every one."

"You're right, Lt. Baldwin, and if they fight and die like these today, it will take two thousand men to gain a victory."

"Maybe they will go to Canada like we have been hearing. It would be nice to not have to worry about them again," said the young officer.

"No, they'll always be a worry," responded Miles. "If we have learned anything, it's that these people put a big value on the graves of their ancestors, on the ground that holds their bones. Just one generation of bones is enough to make the ground holy under their feet."

The Bear Coat, as he was known among the Indians, looked out over the carnage of the day. He was a veteran of the Civil War and had seen battles where thousands had died. This constituted little more than a small incident in the history of warfare. Still, to the history of the plains this would be called the greatest defeat the plains tribes had ever sustained.

They had gone into the fight expecting that Crazy Horse would just retreat in front of them. The troops would make his band miserable by the constant need of defense and, by the end of the winter, force them into the agencies.

It had been a surprise when the warriors had opted to fight, and the troops were stunned by the ferocity of the attack. The Hotchkiss guns sought to decimate the defending Indian force and allow the troop's time to prepare to push them from their position on the bluffs. Still, the warriors had held on with an unreasonable tenacity, and soon the fighting was hand-to-hand as the troops were forced to scramble up the ice-covered slopes in the face of fierce resistance.

Lt. Baldwin, standing beside his commander, knew that the soldiers had barely eluded defeat. At one point they were about to order a retreat.

Still, Nelson Miles was an officer unused to the concept of retreat and chose to stay the course. The fight had lasted less than two hours, and ultimately the big guns were the deciding factor. Crazy Horse's warriors had been barely defeated, at a cost of almost half of the attacking army troops, more than Custer had lost the year before on the Little Big Horn.

Both officers standing on the conquered bluffs knew, however, that the old battle axiom would hold true again.

"Casualties are counted against you in a defeat, for you in a victory."

Miles had said earlier that this would be remembered as the greatest victory in the history of the plains, and he was right. *Yes*, thought the young officer, *the Sioux had been provided with a very holy site today.*

A great number of *would be ancestors* had left their bones in a snowy hell. Perhaps more importantly, as the ripple roiled through the fabric of time, there would be no descendants to mourn them.

"Keep searching for Crazy Horse's body," Miles had ordered. Yet they would be unable to identify any of the fallen warriors as the famous Oglala fighter.*1*

---

1 Scenes form Omicron-Omega conversion attempt.

***

The Black Hills of South Dakota
Present Day
Omicron Line
Omega Insertion imminent!

Rodgers reached for a book sitting on the seat beside him. Handing it to the agent, the scholar turned into what appeared to Banyon to be an open field. The blazer continued without undue roughness toward a mound, covered with snowy pines, less than fifty yards in front of them. The agent had been suspicious when Rodgers had refused outright to allow him to drive that morning, and subsequently had watched very closely as they had entered the Black Hills and headed toward the Wind Cave area.

Looking closely at the lay of the land and convincing himself that he could find the place again, Banyon's eyes turned back to the book handed to him by the historian. It was the *Biography of famous Western Chiefs* from which the professor had asked him to read the night before.

The agent thumbed quickly to the back page and continued where he had left off the evening before. "...*last seen at the battle of the Hanging Woman, where his band was destroyed by the troops of Col. Nelson Miles. A thorough search of the bodies by the victorious troops could not discover the remains of the famous Lakota fighter. It is assumed that he was one of many of his people who were left unidentifiable by the Hotchkiss guns of the attacking troops.*

"Oral tradition passed down among the surviving Sioux tells of his body being brought to the valley of the Wind Cave in the Black Hills of South Dakota for burial."[1]

Rodgers had been right earlier. The special agent was used to asking fairly stock questions. This, however, left him without the appropriate question to proceed.

The blazer pulled into a tree-lined clearing at the north end of the mound and stopped. Banyon quickly reread the last passage in the biography as he stepped out of the blazer into ankle-deep snow. At a distance, he could see an Indian man and woman standing at the entrance of what seemed to be a cave or a large hole at the summit of the mound. The woman was supporting the man, as if he were hurt in some way. The agent observed there was something odd about the way the man was dressed, even about the way he walked that seemed out of place.

There was a familiarity in the features of the pair that, as the distance closed between them, momentarily stunned the agent into inaction.

His mind clearing, the agent reached suddenly for his service revolver. The man in the cave pushed the woman to one side and, without hesitation, lowered his rifle and fired.

Banyon could feel himself instinctively beginning to jump behind the blazer just as his body was involuntarily thrown backwards. The deafening sound of the rifle followed instantly, and the agent knew that he had been hit hard. Writhing on the ground behind the blazer, he felt another murderous jolt hit him, and he turned to see smoke coming from a revolver held by

---

1 Other sources and lines call out, Porcupine Creek and more prominently Wounded Knee Creek.

Hergin Rodgers who had fired at him from almost point-blank range.

He seemed suddenly to see clearer than he could before. There was Rodgers, lowering his gun and looking up at the couple in the cave. Tears were running down his face!

Banyon could clearly see himself lying on the ground with his lifeblood beside him.

Chapter 4

Death borders upon our birth, and our cradle stands in the grave.
Joseph Hall (1574-1656)

The Black Hills of South Dakota
January 16, 1877
Omicron Line – Eight days beyond Axial Conversion

He Dog pulled at the pony, forcing him through the drifting snow. His thoughts had been those of a dreamer since he had left the battle site five days before. In that day he had witnessed the death of everyone he loved. In the heap of bodies now prowled by the conquering whites lay not only his wife and children, but also the remains of his parents and friends. All that were dear to him were gone, and he alone was left to breathe the morning air with nostrils fouled by the stench of death and despair. He never would have believed something like this could happen.

They had always known they would eventually be defeated by the white troops. That possibility had been the companion of the Lakota warriors for many years. The whites had more guns and ammunition. They had more men. Surrender had always been just a matter of time and terms.

It was the giving of the innocent ones to the rifles of the troops that left him in this state of unbelief. Never had he envisioned that he himself would leave his people in a time of need. Never would he have left them, if it weren't for his vow to his brother friend.

Crazy Horse had made him promise with his life that he would do this, though if he had known the circumstances in advance, as he knew them now, he would never have made that promise. It had seemed innocent enough when the commitment was extracted – a vague possibility.

"I will be killed in the battle with the Long Knives," Crazy Horse had said. "Pull my body from the fight and, without waiting, take me to the Wakan cave in the Paha Sapa. You must promise me that you will not stay to help the others. Time will be very short, and you must bring me to *the cave* without hesitation."

He Dog had promised, though he doubted he would see the day. He had fought at the side of his brother friend endless times and did not believe that the soldiers could kill him. His medicine was too strong for their cowardly ways.

Yet he had been wrong, and as the pony pulled the laden travois behind him, he knew that somehow this was what his brother friend had envisioned. He Dog was proud to honor him this last time.

Still, it was difficult to understand. It seemed almost like Crazy Horse had brought death upon himself, throwing himself into the battle with the whites. Drawing their fire to his attack, neither seeking nor taking cover from the withering fusillade that eventually found him. Taking no thought for his life was not like the great warrior. He knew that the people needed him and that his loss would be *an* end for them. Maybe with the decision to die fighting he had felt that there would be no people left to protect. In that, he had been right. Only with the death of the Oglala hostiles would the one they called their "Strange One" feel free to go to the land of dreams. The death of the innocent ones was the only release for him.

As he approached the cave, He Dog could see movement inside. It was nothing new to him. The old men had told him the stories from his birth, the stories of the mysterious cave and the spirits that moved within them. As a child, he and his playmates had ridden to the cave and watched for hours. There was always movement within. It was as if the place was a living thing, breathing in that which sought its darkness, breathing out that which it had changed in its depths.

The old men had said that in an early day, men had come out of the caves and had become part of the ancestors of the people. These men were wise and they were of a lighter skin. It was said they had come from a dream world, a place very far from the world of the Lakota. Who these men were, they had never known. They knew only that they had brought wisdom, and their blood mingled now in the blood of some of the families of the Lakota – the blood so recently spilt on the ground by the Bear Coat's soldiers on the Hanging Woman.

This had been a place of fear and wonder for the small boys, but He Dog was beyond fear now. Indeed, death was something to be desired. This last promise he would fulfill to his brother friend, and then death could take him in any way of its choosing. The pony, pulling the travois, was exhausted and hesitated at the mouth of the cave.

"It is enough," said He Dog aloud and allowed him to slow before the entrance. The haggard warrior led the pony to a nearby sapling and tied him. Working without thought, he untied the travois, pulled it into the cave entrance, and gently placed it next to a small fire.

He Dog was surprised to smell the smoke of the fire as he broke the entrance of the cave. Why had he not smelled it before, and who could be here living with the spirits of this place? He stood for a moment, waiting. There was no movement, no tracks on the ground, and no sign of fuel to feed the fire.

A faint, weary smile crossed the face of the warrior. It was only right, he thought, that a man like Crazy Horse who had lived such a strange life should be left in such a place. It had been his last wish and, somehow, nothing about his brother friend would surprise him now.

He had been a great warrior for the people, but deep within, he had always been a holy man, as had his father and his father before him. They were of that group that had been with the Lakota since the time of the emergence from this very cave. A lighter skinned people, a *Wakan* family.

"Until the next fight my friend!" whispered the exhausted warrior as he turned and walked out into the storm.

The snow was falling heavier than before, blinding He Dog with the constancy of its attack. The pony was nowhere in sight, and He Dog was surprised that such a tired animal would have the strength or the inclination to break away.

A sudden light in the distance diverted his attention from the search for the pony. It was a strange light and seemed to move toward his position. Still there was no fear in a man to whom death would now be a privilege. Whatever this strange thing was, it had something to do with his brother friend's request. Whatever awaited him now, he knew, would somehow be part of that request.

Nothing that Crazy Horse had ever done had brought anything but good, even if, in this case, that good was death.*1*

*

Wakan Cave, Black Hills
Womb of the People, Place of Emergence, Valley of the Wind,
Center of Time

The smell of smoke filled the air as consciousness slowly returned. Banyon's eyes began to focus far before his mind. Still, what he was feeling was familiar. The place and the dreams that

---

1 Scene from Omega line failed attempt.

had come with it were one in his memories. She was the constant in it all. Caring for him, encouraging him to move forward, to win in spite of what his body was telling him. It had always been this way, his dreams had said. *Always* she had been there watching, pulling him along. The confusion was massive however, difficult to penetrate in the fog. One minute she was young, his ever-capable companion in the great fight. Next she was old, teaching him, firm in her discipline, demanding that he try harder, that he try longer, than those around him. Telling him over and over that he must prepare himself for what would come.

Then there was the confusion that had always been there, always haunting him. For that also she was the focus, the one that would take him by the shoulders. Sometimes she was the young woman, the companion, and the friend. Then she was the old woman, face concerned, worried beyond his understanding, telling him that he must return to her . . . again . . .

Her memory was mixed with where he was, and his pulse quickened in anticipation of seeing her again. But as his mind reeled into focus, he knew that this time ...she was not there!

This was a damp place walled in gray limestone. By the sound and smell there was a fire burning, warming, yet not large enough to offset the cold that went bone deep. Off to his left was a cleft in stone and in its inner recesses Banyon thought he could see a series of leather bound books. Some appeared to be of very ancient origin, while others seemed to be recently bound.

Banyon had seldom really thought of life after death. When he had, he had not believed it to be anything like this. The ground beneath him was warmer than the surroundings and gave some degree of comfort. As his eyes focused further, he could see the fire as though it came out of the distance. Then, suddenly, it was right in front of him. It was a campfire, feeding on dried wood and bark. It was not large, but it burned with an intensity that told him it had been there for a while. Whoever had started it could be close, but the agent was not yet conscious enough to care whom that person might be.

His thoughts, though still in a fog, told him he had nothing to fear. If he were dead, then he could not be hurt again; if he was not dead, then he was dying and nothing anyone could do would either help or hurt him further.

Still, the question of who started the fire was persistent, sown like a spring seed sending roots into a foggy consciousness. In spite of all he might say, no man wants to die alone.

Banyon hesitated to move, afraid of the pain from the ghastly wounds that he had seen earlier. Such wounds he had witnessed many times before during the war, and he knew the tremendous pain that could come upon a man who was unfortunate enough to survive them beyond the first few minutes. The initial blessing of numbness would soon be gone, he thought, and pain would have its day.

Concentrating in the extreme not to move any part of his torso, the agent moved his right hand toward the area of the chest wound. Touching gingerly, expecting torn, tender flesh, his hand advanced a fingertip at a time.

"It's not there anymore, my friend," sounded a voice beyond the fire. The voice was not familiar, but the tone was reassuring.

Banyon moved his hand further, faster. The voice was right, there was no wound! He fought to sit up, waiting for the pain. There was none. Strong hands reached to help him to a sitting position. Dizziness was followed by a sense of nausea. His eyes began to focus further. It was a cave all right, or a tunnel of some sort. Across from him, an Indian with a long ponytail was feeding the fire. The agent's vision, though clearing quickly, was still not sufficient to make out the man's face.

In truth, however, he was much more interested in the fire and its comforting warmth than in the identity of his companion. The flames soon had the desired effect as he felt cold muscles coming back to life.

"I appreciate . . ."

The Indian turned toward the agent's voice, and Banyon froze.

"Would you like something to eat?" Leonard Sharpfish asked.

The agent didn't move. All information he had received up to this very moment told him that he was in the presence of a killer, a madman responsible for the death of two lawmen and ultimately the death and mutilation of a prison guard.

Something deep within him suddenly found humor in the situation. Whatever the convict in front of him might do could hardly compare with the *death* that he had already experienced today . . . or thought he had.

"How are you, Leonard?" Banyon smiled.

Sharpfish smiled back, answering with his own friendly questions. "Are you feeling okay? Would you like a little food?"

"Sure, whatever you've got. I'd appreciate it," responded the agent.

As the former inmate cut him a slice of meat, he noticed that someone had taken his clothes. He was now dressed in tanned buckskin, fringe at the arm and chest. The color, a kind of doeskin, made his outfit very unlike the buckskin leggings and shirts he saw regularly in Rapid City and on the reservation.

The recovering agent felt a warming within. Whoever was responsible for this, with the man by the fire being the most likely suspect, they obviously had meant to take care of him and intended him no immediate harm.

The convict smiled broadly as he handed the agent the strip of meat. Banyon had heard that he was the amiable type. It had seemed hard to believe; with the rehearsal of his crimes, yet those were the reports that came back from friends of the escapee interrogated during the investigation.

He received the sizzling flesh gratefully and pressed it to his lips. The juices alone entered his mouth and brought strength.

"What is this? It's good!"

"Its *Pte*, buffalo," the convict smiled back.

"It's not like any buffalo I ever tasted," the agent responded. I've eaten enough buffalo burgers at the burger joints. It always tasted a little . . . disappointing; I guess would be the word. Not like this."

"Yea, I know what you mean," the young Lakota smiled. "This is the real buffalo, the kind that grows strong on grass from over a thousand miles of prairie. It makes the meat juicier, I guess."

"Over a thousand miles, that's some buffalo! Must have made some park rangers kind of crazy," returned the agent.

There was a twinkle in Leonard's eyes that made the agent a little uneasy. The uneasiness moved back to the first words he had heard when he regained consciousness. "It's not there *any more*?"

For the felon to know that the wound was not there *anymore*, he must have known that there had been a wound. If there had been a wound, then that whole scene outside of the cave was real, and if it was real, then . . .

" . . .then what?" Banyon said out loud.

Still, in the midst of the uneasiness and confusion, there was something in the situation that amused the agent. At least, he guessed that it was amusement. *It might just be relief*, he said to himself. Now that he thought about it, it did seem awfully good to be alive.

"Wherever this is, it's good to be here," he murmured.

Sharpfish stared a brief knowing moment, "You got that right," Leonard's smile never dimmed "beats the heck out of the other option." He handed the agent another handful of meat.

"You both look pretty good to me," entered a voice from the entrance of the cave.

Banyon stiffened. That was the voice he had heard right before a bullet had ripped half of his chest away . . . or he thought had ripped his chest away.

"How are you feeling, Dan?"

The recovering man didn't answer but looked in the direction of the voice. Beyond the fast approaching Rodgers he could see horses tethered near what he perceived was the entrance to the cave. With them was the silhouette of a lone man.

The agent could feel his senses clearing with the perceived approach of danger. By the smell, the horses had been there a while, waiting for the storm to abate, or some other objective beyond Banyon's immediate abilities to comprehend.

Rodgers moved around the small fire, reaching for one of the cooked pieces of meat, sitting down beside the former inmate. "I asked how you were feeling," repeated the historian.

"How am I supposed to feel?" responded the agent. "It seems like you are the one pulling the strings here. First you make the decision that I am to die, and then I guess you decided that I was to live. You made the decision that I would have terrible killing wounds, and then somehow you decided that I wouldn't? I always knew you were bad news, and now I find out you do a pretty good job of being bad dreams also." He felt dazed, this new experience having thrown him completely off balance.

Deep within, the agent could almost hear a quiet, yet calming voice . . . clearly his own. *"Maybe considering the circumstances the regular line of threats may not be appropriate,"* the voice counseled.

The agent swallowed deeply, fought for control, and then spoke again, calmer now. "Possibly . . . could you tell me what this is all about?"

Rodgers chewed thoughtfully on a piece of meat and seemed, at least to Banyon, to be amused. "I will tell you, with all sincerity, that which I believe you can physically handle at this time," chewed the historian. "What is happening here will be very difficult to relate to your current memories. In fact, any attempt to tell you too much, too soon, may very possibly be a threat to you. I can tell you that you *will not* accept verbally the facts of the current situation, but will have to experience them yourself, *as you always have before.*"

The agent interrupted weakly. "Before?"

Rodgers nodded his head. The agent could sense that, beyond their current conversation, another concern seemed to be haunting the historian.

"Please," the scholar was almost pleading now, "Listen very closely . . ."

Rodgers reached to retrieve a leather bound book from beneath his coat, and, taking a deep breath, spoke purposefully.

"When we leave this cave, we will not return to the time that you have been accustomed to. As I have told you before, and for future reference, we will call that line, or future, *Omicron*. Having left *Omicron* to its inevitable conclusion, we will find ourselves in the year 1877 A.D. As we move toward our destination there, I will explain what I can of what our intent is and how we are able to accomplish this. It is best and possibly critical that you don't try to understand all that is happening all at once. You will gain full comprehension soon enough, hopefully not too soon, as the events unfold before you."

Rodgers held up the book and looked at him as a father looks at a troubled child. "Your only hope of surviving this situation is in this book. It is the only tie you will have with me and *possibly* the only way I will be able to help you. I have come to this cave with you, and with others before, and in coming we have attempted to change the future. Not just to change, to improve the course of what may come, to find, if we use the terminology of the Lakota, the *Good Red Road*. We have sought to effect changes that would put things right that now are decidedly wrong.

"You see Special Agent Banyon somewhere along the path of the history of our people, there was an *error* made. I couldn't tell you exactly what it was, although I can tell you now where and when it happened. Whatever the error was, we are given the opportunity to change it, to make over.

"We have taken that opportunity on many occasions before this attempt, knowing that our cause was urgent, but we have failed over and over again. We have done things that seemed to make sense, and the outcome has been disaster. We have not done things that seemed wrong, or prevented such things from happening, only to find that such omission was irrelevant to the outcome.

"I know that you don't understand, and I beg you not to try to at this juncture. We believe now that for us to succeed, I have to be in the future while you and Leonard work at the *axial point*, the point where the lines branch and that which is new is created. I will report in this book the facts of what will happen, and as I know them, so may you."

Banyon's mind was swimming. His confusion seemed to have found new depths, swirling through what seemed to be an endless labyrinth of conflicting and irreconcilable facts. Still, he could feel his anger growing amid the chaos of his thoughts. It became stronger with every word from the apparently crazed historian, seething and roiling against all that could not be, but had been or could be.

"You are crazy Rodgers!" exploded the agent, "certifiably and unquestionably out of your mind. I don't know what you expect from me, but you can forget it. I can tell you one thing as an absolute certainty. When I get away from here, I will hunt you like the crazed animal that you are, and I will see you in jail for what you have done here. Assault on a federal officer, aiding and abetting . . ."

Rodgers flew to his feet and grabbed him by the back of his shirt. "We do not have time for this! Now get up! Get up, or I will drag you!"

He could feel the arms of Sharpfish grab him also as he was drug quickly toward the entrance of the cave. Almost between breaths he was at the cave entrance, with Rodgers holding him in an iron grip from behind.

"Look! Look you stupid fool! What do you see?"

The agent looked out at a scene of shocking wonder. The trees, so recently covered with heavy snow, now basked in the harsh glare of the summer sun. The ground was covered with the brown grass of late summer and, almost at the entrance, birds sang in a tall pine tree.

Suddenly Rodgers was pulling him back into the cave again and then, just as suddenly, pushing him back to the entrance where the agent froze in shock.

Before him, the snows of a harsh and unmerciful winter hung on the sleeping valley and, in the distance, the lights of traffic moved slowly and deliberately along an invisible highway. Banyon's eyes stared uncomprehendingly at the spot where the birds had so recently sung in the stately pine.

"No birds," he mumbled; and deep within him, his own voice spoke that which was unbelieving in his reeling mind.

"No pine!"

Again, the agent felt himself being jerked backward into the cave, and just as suddenly thrown toward the entrance.

The valley of the Wind Cave lay devoid of vegetation, no trees, no grass. The mountains, ragged and forlorn in the distance, moaned as the wind gave voice to a vision lost, gave substance to a time long forgotten, and murmured with an inner voice of a time yet to come.

"We can show you more if you want, Dan," started the almost reverent voice of the great historian.

Special Agent Banyon shook his head. "It is enough!"

The historian nodded. He himself had never truly lost the wonder of what was before them. "Now, my old friend, my friend of so many battles on so many fields, come back to us!"

The numbness that trembling man felt was only partially physical now. What he had seen at the cave's entrance could have been explained away under the blanket of hallucination due to his recent experiences. But deep inside, he knew that it was not a hallucination, but was inexplicably very real!

There was almost no other explanation for the occurrences that had been his obsession for the last three months. At a crucial juncture in the investigation, one of his fellow agents had posed just such a possibility…

"It almost seems like something in the past is changing. These people who are disappearing are being drawn into the reality caused by that change, i.e., that they, because of something that changed in the past, do not cease to exist, but rather, they never existed at all.

"No. That's not right," his confused colleague had started again. *"It's almost like these people did exist, at one juncture, but then something changed, like a junction in a railway station. These people were not killed, they were not kidnaped, but rather just went someplace else."*

Banyon remembered sitting in the situation room at the bureau field office, expecting to hear laughter at such a ridiculous scenario. There was no laughter, only silence. His fellow agents had spent too much time in the field studying the bizarre realities they were faced with to discard any possibility, however impossible it seemed.

The speculation and extrapolation of the possible scenarios introduced in that room in the following hour now led him back to the summation of his thoughts. Those thoughts invariably blended to form a singular question, vocalized as he was helped back to sit by the warmth of the small fire.

"Who, and I mean this quite literally, *in hell,* do you think that you are?"

Hergin Rodgers walked to the little shelf of books and brought out another leather bound book. He opened to its very ending and sat down by the fire across from of the agent. Banyon could make out a single word on the spine of the book. *Omicron!*

Opening the volume to a section toward the end of the book, he placed it on his lap and took up the answer to the question, seemingly without thought. Indeed it appeared as if he was responding to a question he had been asked many times before, as if the asking itself was a necessary step in the progression that must be made in his world.

"Your question is astute and concise; in fact, it is that question that has told me, in previous attempts that you had a

61

handle on what was happening. The full explanation is more complex than we will deal with right this moment; however, you have a right to an answer to your question, or at least the beginnings of one.

"You, of course, are correct in your assertion that anyone in his right mind would not deal arrogantly with history. Neither should they steal the lives of tens of thousands of people for their own political agendas, however noble or correct. Only with the most compelling of motives should a man, or a group, given the opportunity that we have, deal with the past with intent to change the future.

"A person, or set of persons, so depraved as to believe they had such a right, would make the trail of chaos, and brutalities, throughout the history of our race seem tame and humane by comparison and would certainly deserve history's most sincere condemnation.

"But, you will remember, I said that our cause was most urgent, and it certainly is, by any standards."

Special Agent Banyon felt the pull of the historian's eyes as he was drawn helplessly toward them. In his life, he had never heard anything that had sounded so wrong and yet rang so true as the historian's explanation wove fantasy into truth and truth into dread.

"Let me read to you the end of the time line you see as your own. That line that, as I have said, we refer to as *Omicron*."

Lifting the open book from his lap, Rodgers began to read.

"At the beginning of the 21st century, the fragmented remains of the old Soviet Union, after years of failure in their attempts to adjust to a free market economy, were hit by a series of catastrophic economic setbacks. These related directly to the worldwide recession that began on the heels of huge increases in the cost of petroleum and worldwide strife. Fighting to keep their own economies afloat, the western allies could ill afford to subsidize the fledgling free economies. Before the century entered its adolescent years, Russia and most of central Europe were starving.

"Frantic to provide food for their starving masses, the leadership of these countries covertly offered what they considered to be obsolete, but still fully functional, segments of their nuclear arsenal to those who could pay.

"Aware of the proliferation of access to nuclear weaponry, and unwilling to begin another series of confrontations with belligerent governments, the United States rushed forward with the completion of its 'Star Wars' missile defense technology. At the earliest possible moment, the United States activated the system which experts deemed impenetrable to transcontinental ICBM's.

"Under its perceived umbrella of protection, and fighting its own internal financial struggles, the United States turned a deaf ear to cries for help from unstable democratic nations in the Middle East and Central Europe.

"At a crucial juncture in international events, from deep within a desert fortress inside the former borders of Iraq, a militant Islamic terrorist organization fired twelve multiple warhead ICBM's at the United States mainland.

"Confident in the invulnerability of its borders, owing to its sophisticated anti-missile system, the leaders of the United Stated chose to wait it out. The first nine ICBM's to enter the U.S. territory were destroyed by the Star Wars system, then, unexplainably, catastrophically, the system failed.

"Bereft of high level leadership after the initial strike, and uncertain exactly who had attacked them, surviving military leaders unleashed a massive nuclear assault on the Arabian Peninsula. The area was left unfit for human habitation for a hundred years.

"Lacking Arab oil, the major surviving western economies were thrown into a massive, convulsive, economic depression.

"Lacking fuel for transportation of foodstuffs, the entire world began to starve."

Rodgers continued to ponder the remaining pages. "How much further do you want me to read?" asked the historian? "It gets worse, I promise you!"

Banyon stared at the book as if it were a poisonous snake.

The scholar looked at the agent in deep concern, momentarily afraid to say more, yet at the same time afraid to stop. "I repeat," he started softly; we would not be as insane as to play with the past, save to prevent just such a scenario. Maybe now you can begin to understand why we have to do this!"

The agent measured his fragmented thoughts carefully before he spoke. "No. No, I don't! If what you have read in that book is true, then now is where we must deal with it, not the past. We need to spend our time here in the present trying to get someone to listen, trying to warn whoever can do something."

"Listen to what?" asked Rodgers. "Shall we tell them we can read the future in a little book? Shall we tell them that the scenario I just shared with you will happen if we don't change our ways? Maybe carrying signs saying something like '*The end is near*' at public events would help. Or maybe we could tell them we know all of this because we have played out several time lines hoping to change history and, having failed, have decided to do the right thing and turn it over to the politicians and the bureaucrats to deal with."

Banyon could feel his chin dropping to his chest. He could hear the voice of the historian as if it were coming through a deep fog.

"Whatever you believe, or think you believe about the time you remember, I can tell you, as a voice literally rising from the grave itself, that what I have just said is true! It is true, and we can change it if we have the courage . . . and the knowledge to know what to do!"

The historian and Sharpfish moved unexpectedly to help him to his feet and then to walk to the horses where the stranger waited.

"Just be quiet for now," the professor whispered.

Banyon's mind was still foggy, but his eyes managed to focus momentarily on the man with the horses. *Where had the Indian been when the historian and the convict had drug him to the opening before,* he found his mind asking? The professor's words, however, rang a louder warning knell deep within him. The man was carrying a rifle!

The stranger moved toward him, purposefully replacing the historian at his side. He felt himself being lifted into the saddle by Sharpfish and the man.

As the agent adjusted him self in the saddle, the professor walked swiftly to his side and stuffed one of the leather bound books into the pocket of his fringed jacket.

"Read this book, old friend. Read it now and commit it to memory. Every last seemingly insignificant detail may be important. After the surrender I will go and you will have to make this happen without me. You will see that I have told you the truth. Then watch!"

The agent looked back quickly at Hergin Rodgers climbing on his own horse behind them. "What surrender?"

"The surrender on the Hanging Woman," replied Rodgers.

Banyon shook his head in unfeigned confusion. "Where will you be? I mean later . . ."

"Hopefully, I will be in my office writing a book," came the response.

Crazy Horse had felt a growing sense of confidence as he lifted the white man into the saddle. If this was he who was supposed to be found, then there would be another chance, a chance not only for the people to survive, but to survive with honor. Now if he could just keep this soft Wasichu alive long enough to make the attempt, then another option would be open to them.

It had been a hard thing for him to trust these men. Even as they had sat with him when he awoke in the cave, he had fears, questions about the truth of who they were and where they came from. Yet the words they had spoken had been proven correct, and indeed, after the battle, he had awakened as they had promised, just as he had after dieing at Fort Robinson. He did not remember that death, but the men in the cave had told him he would not remember a future that would never be.

If the powers had decreed that the people would have another chance to find the *Good Red Road*, then there was something very valuable to gain. The problem, as the men had said, and as he him self was so very aware, was in knowing which road would bring them to the promise.

"Every move might be the wrong one," the white man had said, "and the road missed."

As the horses filed out into the waiting valley, a scene of winter wonder awaited the agent. The trees, full of leaves moments before, now stood in their winter sleep. The valley lay quiet and snow laden. Banyon looked toward the spot where the great pine had sheltered the singing birds. A small sapling rose ever so tenuously through the drifting snow...

It was a beginning!

Chapter 5

The future is a world limited only by ourselves; in it we discover only what concerns us and, sometimes by chance, what interests those whom we love most.
Maurice Maeterlinck 1864

I believe that the future is only the past again, entered through another gate.
Sir Arthur Wing Pinero 1855

Drainage of the Tongue River, West of the Black Hills
January 1877
Omega Transition

The stranger led them through the deep timber to the divide and headed west. The four men and their horses traveled until light began to dim. The stranger led them into another cave for the night. This one was not as big as the first cave but provided sufficient shelter for the travelers and their horses. Banyon thought he was correct in his assumption that the stranger was the "His Horse Looking" that Rodgers had been bringing him to meet.

He slept fitfully during the night. As he awoke from his dreams, he could see Rodgers and the other men talking around the fire.

"We have to watch him for the confusion. It may come at the wrong time. It may rip his very fabric. If that happens, we're lost. We at least have to get him to the girl. She can call him back where we cannot. He will come to her if the damage is not complete. If it is, then we will see if he can find his way through it or if he will be permanently lost. I still believe the girl is the one that can bring him to where he must go. She has trained and prepared him for years in spite of all our doubts."

The agent watched warily during the following day as the convict and the stranger rode in front of him in single file. How did *they* know about her . . .?

They traveled along snow-covered trails, moving at a hurried pace, thought the agent. At every juncture in the trail the stranger moved decidedly without hesitation. There could be no question, thought Banyon they were on his home turf. He moved like one who was a part of the earth itself.

At first, he had not been impressed by the buckskin dressed Lakota. He was a small man, almost boyish in his appearance. His hair was parted in the middle, and a single feather protruded from the back when his head was uncovered. His face, marred by a scar extending from his mouth to the outside extreme of his left cheek, showed very little emotion, and the brevity of his questions to Sharpfish and Rodgers was that of a man well acquainted with command, yet someone not at all accustomed to saying a lot. The Indian was one of those rare individuals, to whom listening had become a tangible, aggressive activity!

On the second day they stopped to rest the horses under the cover of a shallow cliff edge. In close quarters the agent could hear the historian speak to the stranger again. The Indian listened, seemingly lost in thought.

…"so what we have learned is that if we do not fight, we lose everything that is dear to us. If we do fight, we die and there is no future for our children," said Rodgers. "But I think more importantly, we have learned that the question of what will happen if we do fight has a predictable and catastrophic answer.

Of the many roads we have chosen and could yet choose, these two are not acceptable. It is our plan that we try something altogether different. A whole new path must be opened to him, one whose ultimate effect we can gauge only as it emerges."

The warrior's gaze moved now to Banyon. His chin moved upward toward the half-frozen agent. He assessed the white man as one would assess the conformation of a new horse. He guessed that he was roughly his own age, in his early thirties. Tall by white man's standards, but not as tall as the average Lakota; his hair was dark brown, lighter than the Lakota, mused the warrior, but not lighter than his own. The eyes however, were not those of the people. They were blue and penetrating. Eyes, he observed, that had undoubtedly seen battle and, in recording its rage, had gained something hard of their own. They had gained the cast of a fighter!

"With this Wasichu, we will know?" asked the warrior.

Rodgers appraised the former agent intensely. "We will know some things, other things he will tell you from his own mind. These things we cannot know now, although we may wish this were possible. When the time comes, if he can understand what is given to him, he may be our only hope. Our biggest concern is to keep him with us, to keep him in this path. There are too many things that can take him, too many significant memories that could tear at his mind and destroy him, in a web too complex for us to penetrate."

The Indian's gaze was long and hard. If the agent had previously thought his features those of a boy, he did not now! There in front of him was a man filled with anguish and its companion, anger. Whatever he was, he was not a child, neither was he someone to be trifled with. *In any time,* he thought, *this one would be called a warrior!*

The following morning, the man that Banyon referred to only as *the stranger* led them back into the snow as they pushed hard out of the shelter of the Paha Sapa and down into the drainage of the Tongue. Before the sunset, they found shelter in still another cave, this one barely adequate to shelter both men and horses. After the fire was built and they had eaten, Rodgers sat pensively beside him.

The former agent chewed ravenously on the meat fresh off the fire and pretended to pay little attention to the professor. Rodgers at first seemed irritated, then amused as he poked a stick in the fire. His manner seemed almost childlike. "You just never seem to be able to figure out who the enemy is, do you Dan? I'll tell you what – if you will just be so kind as to give me fair audience, I promise that after this is over, if you desire it, I will take you back to the cave and you can return to your old life."

Banyon's continued silence could not mask the dogged confusion that had blurred his thoughts since the beginning of this odyssey. Rodgers seemed somehow to understand and gave him some room to verbally respond. When nothing was forthcoming, the professor started again.

"There is a great deal to be accomplished here, and somehow you have to come to grips with what has happened to you and help us to see that this is done right. You have an important task in this line, and that's a lot more than I can say about the life you left behind."

The agent stared at the professor with a coolness that belied his inner sense of confusion and curiosity. Slowly, he began to speak. "What do you know about my former life, as you call it? For all you know, I had a fine life there . . . until I ran into you, that is."

Banyon could feel his temper rising again as the scholar continued to play with the embers of the fire. The agent knew the anger was putting him at a disadvantage in this situation. He had been trained to deal with extraordinary circumstances. Even before he joined the bureau, his grandmother had taught him that above all he could ever learn he must find the way to control his own mind. *Control*, she had reasoned, *would give him the advantage*. Reaching back to that which she had so freely given him, he found something that was solid. From there he started to speak.

"But . . . putting all that behind, I have to acknowledge that there is something very compelling in what you have told me about what you intend to do and your motives behind these actions. So, how about we start this new partnership by telling me what it is I've been chasing these last months. Whatever has been going on, I know now that you are a part of it, if not the instigator."

Rodgers began to chuckle, but amid his obvious enjoyment of the comment, the former agent could detect weariness. "I guess you are right, Mr. Banyon, you probably do have a right to know what happened to your world. I know that it would only confuse you more if I told you everything, but the one thing I can tell you is that for you that world does not exist anymore. But also in a very real sense it goes on just the way you left it, less one F.B.I. agent and ten or twenty thousand other people who, in the reality that will be yours, never existed and may not ever exist!"

"So you think that leading me with riddles will somehow make me understand, Professor?" asked the agent, feigning a cheerfulness he had not found within himself.

Rodgers dismissed the comment and continued. "A group of people, Mr. Investigator, came into this country very early on. They didn't stay long, however, as they were on their way back to the south, which was their traditional homeland. This area around the Paha Sapa, or the Black Hills, as it translates, was occupied by other tribes who encouraged them to move on and since that was their intent in the first place, there was no conflict. The group was not very numerous, yet as it had always been, and would always be, they were warriors. They camped near the valley of the Wind Cave while they hunted to refill their provisions in preparation for their journey south. One day, while a group of hunters was looking for buffalo, they came upon a group of light skinned, strangely dressed wanderers."

"Wait a minute," interrupted the agent, "about what time period are we talking about here?"

"Oh I can't be precise, maybe one thousand years before Columbus, maybe much more. There is some evidence to support a date of around the time of Christ."

"So these were white men fifteen hundred years before Columbus?" glared Banyon.

Rodgers hesitated momentarily, staring benignly at him. He seemed to be pondering and weighing what he would say next.

"We have a long way to go…! Well I tell you what, let's just start with saying they were just a lighter skin color than the group that found them. But who they were, now that's the question I have spent several lifetimes trying to make relevant. All most historians know is from oral histories, and that is very sparse.

"Basically, it came down to the fact that they came out of the cave, and they brought great wisdom to the world they entered. They married into the group, and their descendants were lighter skinned than their contemporaries were in successive generations. More important than whom these men were, was the question of where they were from or when!"

"So you're saying that these people came through the cave like we did?"

"Exactly! The concept of people coming out of a cave or a hole in the ground is one that is very common among the Native Americans. The Hopi, the Navajo, Apache, the Algonquin, and the Siouan peoples are all examples. The descendants of this particular group became a family of holy men and warriors and, at times, have produced great leaders among the indigenous population."

"Anyway, the people, augmented by this group, continued south and eventually arrived at their home country, called by most the Good Red Land. History assumes, from what we can glean from the oral traditions, that this was someplace in Mesoamerica and, given all we have learned from the excavations and investigations in that area, *as well as other sources,* it was without question the greatest center of civilization and learning on the globe at the time.

"The population was a mix of many races and backgrounds, and others came later, leaving important cultural and scientific contributions. All were assimilated and became part of a rich folklore heritage. But in every case, the knowledge of that society was retained by the *Keepers of Learning*, as their contemporaries had dubbed our group. What that world was like then and who were the active players is largely lost. Archaeologists have tried to patch a history together based on their findings, but there was too complex a social structure and too fluid a power base to allow for much more than supposition.

"There were people in that country from very diverse parts of the globe. The concept that this was a new world, discovered by Columbus, is as preposterous as the 'world is flat' theory that was so prevalent in his time. Theirs was a mix of cultures not unlike our own country. There was a strong Middle Eastern influence, as well as a smattering of influence from the Orient. These differences made the culture strong and, *for a time*, invincible to its enemies. Again; much like ourselves…!"

The professor stopped talking abruptly, lost in thought.

"Somehow I believe you are going to tell me that, this *"group,"* as you call them, are the ancestors of the Lakota," the agent said.

"That's right," replied Rogers warily, searching the agent's face as if hoping to find something that was not yet there. "We believe they were the ancestors of all Siouan speaking peoples. The Sioux, the Crow, the Assiniboine, to name a few, all of the Siouan and Macro-Siouan language family including much of the Iroquois League."

"So how did they get back to this part of the country?" asked Banyon.

"Well, again not unlike us, the differences began to show as each group thought more of his own history and people than that of the group. Civil war was the result, and the empire was weakened, both militarily and culturally."

"So what happened?" pressed the agent.

"The same thing that has happened throughout history," continued the professor. "It is as predictable as the dawn. Thinking so highly of their superior culture, they took no notice of the, *barbarians at the gate*. A very dark skinned people from the North invaded in force. This particular group was a Uto-Aztecan speaking variety and fought with large war dogs that, along with their superior numbers, allowed them to conquer the weakened empire.

"The survivors made their way to the top of the mountains and called for all men *who would not be slaves* to join them. Individuals of a variety of cultural backgrounds heeded the call and they determined to cast their lot together and find a home for their people. Their traders had told them about the Father of Waters, or the Mississippi, as we call it, and they headed for it. It was a huge armada. Everything went, their women and children, their animals, and everything they could carry from their old homes.

"They were led by the Black Tortoise clan, or the *Keepers of the Books and Learning*. These were the ancestors of the Lakota and other Siouan speaking people.[1] Their genealogy was diverse and complicated their knowledge amazingly comprehensive. In their veins ran the blood of the ancients and of many diverse cultures, as well as the blood of those who came out of the cave.

"Anyway, we'll have to continue this later, its time to get some rest. Just remember," smiled Rodgers, "this time, we are the ones who came out of the cave. At this juncture our decisions will determine whether this great culture, or ours in a later time, will continue to exist or whether it and we will become extinct. The one thing we do know is that the future, as we knew it in Omicron and other lines, was unacceptable to *them* and we also

---

[1] <u>Deecotah, the last high priest of the extinct Elk People</u>, Walter Pidgeon

know that the same future is unacceptable to us as well. The next few months will determine the fate of millions in many generations.

"Don't forget," smiled the historian, "we're supposed to be wise and, maybe more importantly, we are supposed to be looking for something specific; something that will give them and us a chance in a future that, at least for now, is not yet born."

"I appreciate the history lesson, Professor, but it still doesn't tell me what happened to thousands of people in my time. Where did they go?" asked the agent.

"In the history as you currently know it, Mr. Banyon, the Lakota of the Crazy Horse band fought an insignificant battle with Nelson Miles' troops on the Tongue River, and the following spring surrendered to General Crook at Fort Robinson. The result ultimately was the death of Crazy Horse and the subjugation and virtual imprisonment of the Lakota people and the destruction of the culture. That is the history of Omicron, based on what happened in one scenario. There are, however, many roads that a people, or a person, can take in their history. It is known now that the road the Lakota took in surrender was disastrous.

"Powers that are far beyond your understanding determined to correct that decision and attempted to put *us all* back onto the Red or the Good Road"

The historian seemed grim for a moment, but soon began again. "The decision was subsequently made to fight to the death at the battle of the Tongue to see what difference that decision would have on the future. The result was what you saw, the virtual disappearance of the Lakota as a people. People who had lived in the future, as you knew it suddenly had ancestors, both Lakota, Cheyenne and white, who, instead of living to reproduce, were killed in a hopeless series of battles. These people, the would-be descendants, simply ceased to exist."

"By families . . ."

"Yes, by families. The numbers disappearing in Omicron as it started to change to a new line were exponential in comparison with those in the fight itself. Still, there was something more, something that we cannot know right now." The professor paused, "That we may never know, that is what happened after the fight."

"Why can't we know," interrupted Banyon. "Wasn't there a book on your shelf to show what happened?"

"No, responded Rodgers, "that will be an aborted line, a line that we will not allow to continue by our presence before the *branch*. We will stop that line from continuing by what we do here.

"What we do know is enough to stop the future that it portents. It would have required more than just the elimination of one band to decimate the entire Lakota population. That's the problem when you start changing history you don't know the effect of a decision on down the line. The decision to fight brought disaster to the Lakota, and in the end, did not change the overall outcome of the nations."

The younger man wondered if the Professor, so deeply lost in thought, could even be aware of his continued presence. Mechanically at first, as if from a great distance, he returned with words equally mechanical. Somehow he could sense a worry, better said, a fear, couched in every word.

"It has been determined to try again, to attempt to find a combination that will work. At this juncture, we will make a change."

"At this juncture . . .?" the agent started.

"Yes," retorted Rodgers, before he could continue.

Banyon looked at the ground beneath his feet. A thought had begun to form in his mind as Rodgers spoke, and now it had taken substance.

It was the woman, in a log cabin. The surroundings spoke of extreme poverty and need, but there was something else. Her eyes! Yes, the eyes were a deep brown, and there was in those lovely, longing eyes a glow as she stared intently at a boy. He thought she was about to say something, but suddenly she turned toward the door, and he could hear her words as she moved toward a light beyond . . .

"I must go, Grandson . . . If you see me again, then what we did here will count for something . . .!

The warrior walked into the cave covered with snow. The agent had noticed that his complexion was lighter than the other Lakota of his acquaintance, the eyes leaning from a light brown to almost a gray.

Banyon nodded toward him. "Who is he? Who is he really?"

"He is historically known as Tsunka Wakan Witko', *the Crazy Horse.* His Horse Looking was his name before he was given his father's name of Crazy Horse. He, like us, has stepped backward to create a new future!"

"Why didn't you tell me his name correctly in the first place?"

Rodgers smiled broadly. "Well, take just a second and remember where we were. Remember what you knew about your reality and the world around you. Imagine what you would have thought if I had told you that *Crazy Horse* might help us?

"Still, that which is most vital to us now is the truth. The truth is that Crazy Horse may be the only one with the heart and the influence to go the distance we must go. In the end, he may be the only one who can control the Lakota, make them see that the road we seek is for them also, not just for the whites."

*

Hanging Woman Creek at its confluence with the Tongue River
January 7, 1877
Birth of Omega line imminent

Four days later they entered the camp on the Tongue. It was

early in the *Moon of Frost on the Lodge* (January), and a storm was coming quickly. The activity level indicated that the village was preparing to move. In the distance a column of soldiers was approaching a lower camp, and the sound of gunfire began to define the primordial wilderness as the warriors formed a line against the whites to give the innocents a chance to move upriver.

The guns continued throughout the day as the terrified women of the Lakota herded their animals and children up the river toward the looming bluffs.2 The talk in camp that night was hushed and covered the future of the people and the strange men that had been brought into camp by Crazy Horse.

The next morning, as the troops approached the assembled Indians on the bluffs, there was a pause as a warrior moved forward under a white flag with a message for the whites written in the historian's fine hand.

Lt. Baldwin hurried back to his commanding officer, Nelson Miles. "They say they have white prisoners, Sir."

Nelson Miles covered his eyes against the wind and tried to make out the top of the bluffs. "What do you think, Lieutenant?"

"I don't know. Somehow a flag of truce and an offer of prisoner release is not what I expected. It might be just a ruse to get the noncombatants out of the way."

"Go to the bend of the river with my field glasses and see if you can confirm what they're saying. We'll stop our advance until you report. It's not my opinion that these Indians are going anywhere. Either they came to fight, or they've something else in mind. Maybe these prisoners, if they exist, can give us an idea of what they want. In any event, if they really do turn the prisoners over to us, bring them to my tent immediately."

"Yes, Sir," responded the Lieutenant.

Nelson Miles turned easily on his heel and walked briskly toward his tent headquarters. He had missed the opportunity of his life when the Oglala chiefs had come down to negotiate

---

2 *Omicron-Omega Transition point*

surrender the month before. Miles could still feel his chagrin when he received word that his Crow scouts had charged as the headmen approached the cantonment and shot the men dead.3

The officer that took Crazy Horse's surrender would gain quite a feather in his cap. *In many ways, accepting surrender would have been better than a military victory,* thought Miles, *especially with those bleeding hearts in the east having the ear of Congress as they did.* He could show himself as a voice of moderation in a situation that many believed called for one.

Still, there was the other thing, that unthinkable memo that had come down from the war department the month before. The politicians had made it clear they would not tolerate another defeat like Custer's or Crook's. It was held as a certainty among the officer cadre that another such defeat would cause Washington to pull the funding for any future operations north of the Platte.

On the bluff, Crazy Horse stood next to Rodgers and Banyon as the troops backed off through the blowing snow toward the valley floor.

"Whatever happens now is all new to you," said the historian in a discreet undertone. "What you're seeing now is a complete rewrite of everything your history believes happened here. From here on you play it by ear." I will tell you that others have been beyond this point; they found only defeat awaiting them. They did however come back with certain information that may be of assistance to you. I will make these events available to you as I can!

Turning to the warrior chieftain beside him, he looked deep into the hard grey eyes. "This may be the chance we were looking for. Don't forget that when the time comes you must be ready, and somehow you must control the young men. This is not the

---

3 *December 1876 Yellowstone-Tongue Confluence. Future Ft. Keogh, future Miles City Montana.*

time to be divided. That is what they want most. I will do all I can on the other end."

Turning back to Banyon, the scholar stared intently, "you'll have to make it on your own soon. I know that you will miss my company, but your fate is out there somewhere. I don't know a lot more about what happens from here than you do. You'll have to figure it out on your own. I can give you a little advice, though. If you go out there and tell these soldiers that you are from a different time and were brought here against your will . . . Well, you're a smart boy. I'll let you figure it out on your own.

"This is your life now! Find a place for yourself here. I repeat, there is nothing back there for you . . . find a place for yourself and be ready. You were brought here with a purpose, of that you can be certain. I didn't really want to say this, but I figure it's your right to know. What the Lakota will attempt to do in the next period of time may affect you more than you can know."

Banyon stared at the historian. "In what way…?"

Rodgers moved closer, staring directly into the eyes of the former agent. "Many times in life our path is already chosen for us by history. It is because of it we exist. In spite of our desires, we must follow that path. Altering it too dramatically, we threaten to destroy that which may have created us."

"Wait a minute," the former agent started, "I'm trying to understand, I really am, but you speak in riddles. In what way may this affect me?"

"Well," responded Rodgers, "you are part Lakota. Let's say for a minute that your great-grandfather and grandmother are here with this band. If they are and you were born in *Omicron*, then we know that they survived in that line."

The younger man nodded, waiting for the scholar to begin again.

"What if, because of what we do here, things change, and they who are meant to survive do not?"

The former agent thought, just for a minute, that he could detect a smile on the face of the historian – a very amused smile.

A movement down the hill caught both of their attentions. A group of blue-coated soldiers were working their way up the bluffs toward them under their own white flag.

Rodgers' voice lowered as the first of the blue-coated men topped the ridge and moved toward them. "The day will come when the knowledge in the book will cause you to act. Act quickly and creatively. Probe into what might be, and be assured that with your every move we will learn more of what we must do – or not do. Act until your mind or I myself tell you there is no further need, in which case you must stop the cycle!"

The flashing gray eyes of the historian seemed almost to roar with intensity as he repeated, "If it is *right*, if we move toward that future, you should know it in your mind. If it is wrong, you will also know that. We will learn from our errors, like any thing in life. By our failures, and those of others before you, we will gain direction!"

Banyon was so shaken and confused by the seemingly unintelligible instructions that he felt unable to speak.

Out of the growing storm, the first of the blue-coated soldiers came into shouting distance. "Are you men all right?"

The question jolted him back from thought, to find the historian staring worriedly into his eyes. His whisper was penetrating. "Are we? Tell me, my old friend, are we all right?" probed the scholar.

The former agent could feel the clarity rush over him, probing, absorbing, and finally convincing. He stared back into the eyes of the historian, and between them there was understanding.

"We're just fine, Lieutenant," yelled Rodgers. "Please signal your commander that these people do not want to fight anymore. They are ready to surrender at this moment."

Lt. Baldwin looked away, at the armed warriors lining the bluffs to the northwest and the southeast. "How do we know this isn't a trick, Mister? Too many good men have died at the hands of these Redskins in this last year. We're not ready to take chances with them again."

"Lieutenant," the historian's vision seemed to clear for a moment. Then he continued, more slowly now. "Lt. Baldwin, isn't it?"4

"Yes," the officer responded, somewhat taken back.

"The man walking toward you is Crazy Horse. He is here as a pledge of good faith for the behavior of his people. He says to tell you they do not want to fight you more. He gives you his Winchester as a sign of his word to you, and he asks that if any of his people attack you, to kill him with that gun."

Crazy Horse moved toward the Lieutenant and the small group of blue coats, who now joined him at the cliff's edge. The Strange One of the Oglala raised the Winchester above his head, looking first at the confused soldiers and then slowly moving it toward the warriors on the bluffs.

On the Hanging Woman there was peace as the people waited on the future!!

**

———————————————

Confluence of the Tongue and Yellowstone Rivers commonly referred to as "the cantonment." Future site of Fort Keogh, Dept. of the Dakotas
Col. Nelson Miles Commanding
January 19, 1877
Omega Line

———————————————

Rodgers had told the former agent that the text of the book would change. He had told him that he must study quickly and

———————————————

4 *Lt Alex Baldwin 2nd Cavalry recently returned from campaign against Sitting Bull and Hunkpapa Ft Peck country.*

purposefully, committing every detail to memory. Memorizing against the day that the text would be different from what he had known. The change itself would be almost instantaneous when it came, and all that he had memorized would be lost to print. It would be in the comparison of the two that the long-term effect could be told.

The new text, however, would tell him as precisely as possible about the time line in which he now lived, that line dubbed *Omega*. It would not only be his defense against unforeseen events, but his barometer of things to come that might be changed to effect. Since the surrender on the Hanging Woman, Banyon had spent much of his time alone with the book.

His conscious mind still fought against what had happened and why it had happened. Nonetheless, the facts were before him. With the dawn of each new day came acknowledgment of the world around him, and with acknowledgment came acceptance.

On the day of the surrender, the officers of Bear Coat Miles had questioned them extensively as to how they had come to be with the hostile band.

Rodgers had responded for them both, explaining that they were miners from the Black Hills mines and had been taken prisoners by the Crazy Horse warriors. They had been brought back to the Hanging Woman to act as interpreters so that the surrender could be accomplished without the loss of blood.

Nelson Miles had studied them closely as the questioning continued. Without waiting for a break, he had interrupted quite forcefully, asking, "How exactly does it happen that you two speak such excellent Sioux?"

"We're squaw men, or at least, have been before we went to mining. Banyon here had his woman killed by the Crows last fall. He is trusted since his woman was an Oglala. Some of her folks are here with Crazy Horse. My woman was a Yantoni Dakota and I left her with her folks when I went prospecting last fall."

"Last fall?" pressed Miles. "You thought that right after the death of Col. Custer and his men, along with the defeat of Crook and his men at the Rosebud, that it would be a good time to go prospecting deep into the heart of the Sioux holy land?"

"Sure did, Colonel, and we were right about it in the end. You see; Sitting Bull and the Hunkpapa, they have been staying over in this here country and Crazy Horse and this group, well they have been runnin' up and down country being chased by the whole United States cavalry.

"Truth Col., the hills were real peaceable until Crazy Horse came along just eight days past. Dan here knew him being that he had that woman from his band. Truth Col., I thought he would kill us sure. There have been a lot of deaths in the hills last month or two. Whoever does the killen doesn't skulp em, neither. Just shoots an arrow in the ground next to the dead man. Anyway, Crazy Horse recognizes my Pard here and come in for a talk. He settled him down an' we agreed to come along to see if we could help."

The former agent remembered how shocked he had been when Rodgers had begun to speak. The old trapper accent and lingo had flown from the historian as if he had been born to it. The picture before him suddenly focused and he saw, for the first time, what Nelson Miles and his officers had seen. The Hergin Rodgers of this time was, to every eye and ear, a very common example of a trail worn squaw man. Dressed in buckskins, covered by a bulky settler's jacket and cap, he blended in every way with the other men in the Indian camp and the scouts attached to Miles' command. Even the smell of the historian's clothes spoke of endless campfires, both recent and long forgotten.

Holding up the sleeve of his own jacket before him, he had little doubt that his own clothing, almost completely ignored in the turmoil of the last few days, was equally authentic.

The talks had gone on deep into the first night, with Banyon, at Rodgers' insistence, translating for Crazy Horse and his chiefs everything that was said by the pony soldiers of the Bear Coat.

By the time the talks had ended that first night, he knew that two things had been accomplished without any room for doubt.

Colonel Nelson Miles had been thoroughly and permanently convinced of the truth of the past that Rodgers had woven for them, and Crazy Horse had found a new weapon that he esteemed of great worth in his dealings with the whites. That weapon was Banyon! For the first time, the warrior chieftain had someone who could and would tell him not just the words, but also the heart of the pony soldiers. Deep within the greyish eyes of the Strange One, the former agent thought he could see something new, something that he had perceived only the lack of in the days past. He thought he saw *hope!*

The decision was made to break camp on the Hanging Woman and return with the troops to the cantonment at the Confluence of the Tongue and the Yellowstone[1] where further talks would be held relative to the future of the band.

Before the troops and their captured adversaries left the next day, Rodgers explained to Miles that after they arrived at the cantonment and everything calmed down a bit, he had a desire to return to his diggings in the Black Hills.

At his request, Crazy Horse would send along one of his chief lieutenants, one of his closest friends, a young Indian of about Crazy Horse's same age named He Dog, to allow safe passage for Rodgers to the hills.

He Dog had treated the former agent well since they had met the few days before and always seemed to be at hand when he had a need. He Dog himself was a shorter individual than most of the Lakota on the Hanging Woman, yet he was heavily muscled and gave every indication of being a fighting man of impressive

---

[1]   *In Omicron the United States Congress allocated funds the following Feb. to build Ft. Keogh on the site of the cantonment. The site is found in present day Miles City, Montana.*

abilities.[2] Banyon had noticed that he and Crazy Horse spent a lot of time in those first few days talking privately. What they were talking about, with so many immediate concerns facing their people, he couldn't know. The possibilities were many and the future uncertain.

However, he could feel that the friendship was strong between them, and that Crazy Horse was making specific requests. He Dog seemed displeased at the prospects implied by those requests. Still, there was an understanding that the shorter man would do what he was instructed to do by his brother friend.

Banyon had remained largely silent, except for his translating duties, and was not surprised to hear Rodgers explaining to the officers that the former agent, now called the *young interpreter* by the whites, would be staying behind when Rodgers returned to the digs.

Nelson Miles seemed quite enthusiastic at the prospect of the white man staying with the hostiles as he, in his turn, had recognized the squaw man was a valuable asset in the army's ability to control its newly acquired wards.

Of course, there were other interpreters among the army scouts who were pressed into service at varying times. These, however, were somewhat unstable in their approaches to translations, and, on more than one occasion, had been known to translate the words of either side to best suit their own needs or agendas.

On the morning of the 19th of January, the army and the surrendered band arrived at the cantonment. Rodgers and He Dog prepared to leave camp the next day. Crazy Horse was there for one final conference with He Dog and, although not pleased at whatever had been decided between them, He Dog had put on a

---

[2]   *He Dog died on the Pine Ridge reservation at the age of one hundred years and four months. Probably Crazy Horses' closest friend, he was considered a living repository of accurate information on the pre-surrender Lakota. (Omicron line)*

86

good face and seemed resolved to accomplish what he had been asked.

Rodgers had spent all the available time he could, away from what seemed to be a long series of responsibilities, talking with Banyon and Sharpfish individually.

The former convict, by all appearances, looked no different from any other Indian in the camp, other than it soon became apparent that he spoke English fluently. The English abilities of the young Indian would soon become the talk of the cantonment and villages that would be established across the river. Only Rodgers offering a very well rehearsed story line settled the growing fervor for explanation. A missionary couple from the east, he said, raised the young man, after his parents were killed in the early stages of the war along the Platte. Coming of age, he had found no place for himself among the whites and had returned to his own people. This explanation was readily accepted by the whites and gained Sharpfish a bit of popularity among the Indians. The Oglala received him as a lost son, one who had shown an uncommon amount of good sense in his choices to date – in spite of a poor start.

As they traveled toward the cantonment, Banyon had been aware that he was not invited to the one-on-one discussions between the former convict and Rodgers, but was given the chance on numerous occasions to observe them from a distance. Rodgers was continually drawing maps, maps of excellent detail in the dirt. On one occasion they had failed to erase completely one of the maps, and the former agent had examined it, though with little result. If he could understand at all, the historian was trying to give instructions to somewhere some distance from where they were. To a 20th century man, accustomed to street and highway references as the only true guide to a specific location, the challenge was great, as his references must be made by mountain ranges, streams, and rivers.

As Rodgers saw him watching on one occasion, he waved him over. As he approached, he heard the end of Rodgers' explanation. "Nothing we have done here will affect their situation whatsoever. They will still be there on the same date. Sturgis will be faked to the south, and the people will escape over the pass. In leaving, they will stop here," pointing to a spot in the map on the ground.

"There they will leave a badly wounded warrior before they head back to the valley. You must be there on that date. Remind them about the Assiniboines and tell them that time will be the factor. They must get to Sitting Bull and back before the last day. That is, of course, if Sitting Bull is still where he would be in Omicron. What Dan and Crazy Horse do here may change that. If it does, you must adapt to the new situation. If he still is in Canada, the difference between success and failure will be a matter of only about four hours."

As Banyon arrived, Sharpfish smiled broadly at him and made his exit. The former agent had to admit that the young criminal had shown himself to be as good a friend as he could have expected from anyone in his present situation. He seemed to be constantly looking toward his needs and was ready with a smile and agreeable conversation at every turn. Whatever he was supposed to have done that gained him a place in Marion Penitentiary was certainly a charge very suspect in his eyes!

"Why don't we all meet together?" asked Banyon as Sharpfish walked away.

Rodgers let the comment go without remark and, with a hand signal, reassured the former inmate that he should go on. "Please don't question me on this. There is a job Leonard must do that if you were aware of it, may cause you to act differently than you would normally. Let him attempt what he has been prepared and trained to accomplish. It is enough that you succeed at what is before you without worrying about Leonard."

"Is Leonard's job, as you call it, tied in any way to what I'm supposed to do?" pressed the former agent.

"Everything is related," responded the historian. "Still, there are specific junctures where you will have to operate separately, and the possibility of each of your successes is limited by factors that we cannot imagine at this time. If you were to count on his success and he was to fail, or vice versa, the entire plan could collapse in on us and frankly, our window of opportunity, is short. How short, none of us know. It could be any minute, it could be months, but it is soon."

"What is this window of opportunity? Why is any of this so time critical? If we fail, why not just go into the cave again and return to try and get it right?"

Rodgers seemed troubled for one of the few times since they had left the cave. Since that time, the scholar had seemed to be filled with enthusiasm in almost every aspect of his being. He rushed from one conversation to another, always happy, encouraging, and the center of attention, as he told stories that left both the troops and the Indians in riotous laughter. Each story was told in the respective languages and geared to the knowledge and culture of each group. The man seemed driven with a mission of happiness and hope. Banyon had heard the term 'joy' used in his life, but had never seen the personification of it until now. Hergin Rodgers seemed a man filled from head to toe with a pure love of life, and it was infectious.

"Well," Rodgers began his reply, "I wish I had a better answer for you as to the why of it, but the bottom line is that the cave is an intersection of time, a crossroad in space where the time lines converge at varying points for reasons that we don't understand. The tribes have assumed that this was a permanent thing, having to do with location. I can tell you, however, that while the cave has formed here before, it has not remained constant. The corridor, if you want to call it that, has been right where it is on many occasions. On others, it has not. We know that it changes locations, or disappears altogether, at uncertain intervals. Circumstances make us believe that in a relatively short time from now, this corridor, the cave will close."

Rodgers paused to let his words sink in. Then he began again. "We have come to look on it as a great horse shoe, turning in on itself through the strength of some incredible power. Where it crosses, you have a corridor. We think that we can prove; if anyone could be persuaded to even listen to a theory such as this, it has touched in the valley of the wind cave on at least three occasions in the life of this planet. When it disappears, however, it is gone for a period of hundreds, perhaps thousands of years. The ancients were aware of this *corridor,* as we call it today, appearing and disappearing in various parts of the world.

"The actual working of the mechanism is a very difficult scenario to contemplate. You see, a man can go from here to the future and live in a time line, and he can always return to where he began, or to any point along the line. However if he returns to a point in his original life, which is earlier than his time of departure, his memory of events that transpire after is gone. Simply put, they haven't happened yet, so there is nothing to remember. So if a person seeks to retain this knowledge, he must return to a point roughly the same as where he left the past, within a few days, to be exact. This being the case, he can use the cave to give him almost perpetual youth. However in any one line he must continue to age and finally return to the past or die. If he is killed in the future, his body can be brought back to the Cave and he will live again, but if old age takes him, then his life is over.

"Oh," Rodgers stopped as if to re-gather a point, "there is one more concern in this which I will take care of by our leaving."

"What is that?" asked Banyon.

"If a man returns to a future from the past, he will never find that future that he left. It may be different in ways that, to him, are imperceptible, but still it will be different. These changes, however, may very well be major, depending on things that have changed in the past. Or worse yet, a man may return to a future where he himself never existed."

"Like me?" the former agent stared.

"Yes, just exactly! The professor paused for a moment to let the man absorb his words. "You see, you have a great deal of personal stake in the way this comes out, Dan. If we don't do this right, you, like the tens of thousands in your time who disappeared in your investigation, were possibly never born."

Chapter 6

I did not know then, how much was ended.
Black Elk 1930

The Cantonment
January 1877
Omega Line

The afternoon of the day they arrived at the cantonment, Rodgers and He Dog prepared to leave. The scholar came to Banyon's lodge, ostensibly to see how he was coming with his studies.

After answering a few historical questions that were unclear, he sat and pondered the former agent for a long moment before speaking. "I was wondering if you would come with me for a little bit. I have something very important to do that deals with an item not in your book, but still, in all probability, something that will help you, if you will let it. It has not been done before, but it is a direction that we have contemplated for a long while."

The former convict, long tired of his enforced study in the lodge, readily agreed to accompany the scholar, and the two walked together toward the center of the Indian camp. Neither was surprised to find Crazy Horse close at hand and joining them before they had gotten very far.

"What is it you seek?" asked the Oglala headman.

"We seek a boy, the son of your cousin Black Elk. The boy also has, or will have the same name and will be in his fifteenth winter."

Crazy Horse stared for a long moment at the historian and

then, without comment, led them to a lodge at the northern end of the camp. Without directions or introduction, Rodgers walked into a group of five or six young bucks and placed himself in front of the *young* Black Elk.

"Would you join us for a moment, Nephew? We have words to share with you."

The former agent turned to Sharpfish who was standing close at hand and asked, "Who is he? I recognize the name, but I can't quite place it beyond that."

The young Lakota responded in English. "He is to become a great spiritual leader of the people. He received a great vision that he believed would show the people a correct path. In it he would become the keeper of the sacred tree, the heart of the nation."

"So what happened?" queried Banyon.

"It didn't happen," responded. Sharpfish. "In the end of his autobiography[1], dictated as an old person, he lamented that the vision had been given to such a weak man, for as such he saw himself. It has always been a mystery to the Lakota that with such instruction from the powers, he never found the way to 'The Good Red Road.'"

The young man was obviously confused, but came quickly at a signal from Crazy Horse.

When they had walked a short distance, the scholar turned suddenly to face the young man. "I have a need of you, Nephew. You were given a vision at an early age. *What have you done with it?*

The young man fell back as if struck, a look of fear clearly in his eyes.

---

1 *Black Elk Speaks, John G. Neihardt. Omicron Manuscript.*

"It was a great vision, and was given to help the people. What have you done with it?" Rodgers demanded again.

The young man looked as if he was about to flee, when Rodgers suddenly gestured to the rapidly growing Oglala camp and said, *"Behold a good nation walking in a sacred manner in a good land."*

There was nothing in the appearance of the Lakota camp that would make it fit the description that Rodgers had just given, but still the boy appeared to understand a deeper meaning and was shocked to the core.

Rodgers gave every indication of being pleased with the result, and quickly followed up with equally disquieting verbiage directed at the young man. "And then the voice said, *'Behold your nation . . . for thenceforth your people walk in difficulties.'* 1 And then you saw the people breaking camp again, and saw the Black Road before them . . .. and black clouds, and they did not want to go, but could not stay. "2

The expression of the young Lakota could not have been more stunned if Rodgers had struck him with a war club.

"I need you to help this man, this Wasichu. If you do, and if you are true to the vision, you will see it fulfilled."

With that, Rodgers began to sing, to chant really, the words to a haunting song. Banyon failed at first to understand, then felt, more than heard, the pronunciation of the joy and the promise.

"A good nation we will make live
This the nation above has said
They have given us the power to make over."[7]

---

1 *Ibid*
2 *Ibid*

Then, turning as if to leave, he began another chant as his hand made a circular movement that seemed to encompass the quiet camp; the song drew in the young man and all who watched.

"My horses, prancing they are coming,
My horses neighing they are coming,
Prancing they are coming.
All over the universe they come.
They will dance, may you behold them
They will dance, may you behold them
A horse nation they will dance,
May you behold them
All over the universe they have finished a day of happiness"

Rodgers turned sharply back to the boy, now standing side by side with Crazy Horse. His eyes were like stone as he chanted.

"Behold for it is yours to make!" [1]

From that moment on, the white man was never entirely alone. The young Black Elk was always at his side if he were about the camp or sitting in or near the lodge.

As he read and reread the book, he realized that the time line he had known, before the disappearances, had certainly been broken!

Before him he could see the village of the Oglala camped along the frozen shores of the Yellowstone within sight of the soldiers' cantonment, a place and circumstance changed from the fabric of time, as he knew it. The book in his hands had spoken of a Cheyenne warrior with the band who had been killed in the fight on the Hanging Woman.

---

1 *Ibid*

The young man's name was *Big Crow*.1 He had met him in his first days on the Yellowstone and now watched him warming himself at the fire outside his own lodge.

He wondered aloud, "How does this work in reverse? In my world, are there suddenly people alive that were never there before?"

The former agent remembered that Crazy Horse had told him that the old men had said this was the worst winter since the Lakota had crossed the Missouri in their migration west. The young interpreter found himself agreeing. This indeed is a very bad winter, he thought. One that now offered a spring beyond the pages of the history that he had known.

The white interpreter put the book away as he heard scratching on the entrance of the lodge. It was the Lakota way of asking permission to enter a closed lodge. He looked to make certain the book was out of sight and asked the visitor to enter.

It was Crazy Horse. Rodgers had told him that Crazy Horse would become a great friend, and he had been right. Something in the great warrior had a need to hear, and the former agent, for his part, had an equal need to tell. Rodgers had given the former agent specific instructions to not tell the Oglala too much about the future that he had lived, or of what might happen if that line were used as a reference.

The former agent had grown to appreciate the formalities of Lakota hospitality. Crazy Horse brought with him a short pipe, filled with a form of bark that was smoked in place of tobacco.

"The people are poor," he smiled.

After both had smoked, the Strange One of the Lakota seemed to struggle a moment with his thoughts. Finding his

---

1 . *Correct as per Omicron line. Black Elk said that the man was angry over the killing of relatives by white troops and had no interest in living further.*

place, he asked, "On this other road, you say I will be killed by a bayonet or knife, while my hands are held by others at Fort Robinson. You said that both arms would be held, one by a white soldier. The other then . . . by whom…?"

Banyon recalled again the emphatic Rodgers, as he counseled that he should not share information about the time line he referred to as *Omicron* with those of the past.

Then again, he remembered the sound of a gun and his own pain as he writhed on snow before the same man.

"One of your own, a man by the name of Little Big Man.!"[1]

*

Toward the Valley of the Wind Cave
January 1877
Omega Line

The snows had been relentless as Hergin Rodgers and He Dog made their way slowly back toward the Paha Sapa. Rodgers, for his part, thoroughly enjoyed the company of the young chieftain. The Indian himself was quite surprised at the attitude of the Wasichu toward him and, at first, was hesitant to talk much

---

1 *Historically correct in Omicron. Many historians paint Little Big Man as a traitor to his friend Crazy Horse. Others however claim that he was only trying to keep him out of trouble as he was totally surrounded by armed troops. Little Big Man on one occasion said that he killed Crazy Horse accidentally while fighting for the knife that he wielded.*

at all. The unrelenting enthusiasm and happiness of the white man, however, gradually won him over and, after the first day, the warrior was participating in the ongoing conversation as if Rodgers were his oldest friend.

It was uncanny; in the way the warrior saw things that such a man could even exist among the whites, a people who had always been so odd to the Lakota. Maybe it was because of his ability to speak Lakota with such ease, which made communication so much easier and made the white man seem so much more like a human being.

But then, there was so much that the white man knew, not just about the Lakota, but also about He Dog himself.

After the first day, when He Dog began, in his turn, to ask questions of the white man about the past, the white man was able to respond specifically.

"Yes!" he had responded, "the whites did get the chiefs at Fort Robinson to sign the paper selling the Black Hills.

"No! It had not been any one of the chiefs trying for honor among the whites. The chiefs had been forced on threat of imprisonment and, indeed, worse. The fort commander had threatened them with the possibility of withholding food from the helpless ones.*1*

"Yes, it is true that the Fort Laramie treaty prohibited such a sale without three of every four Lakotas signing the paper."

"Why then could they do it?"

"That is a good question, argued for years. In the end, it is because the victor may do as he sees fit."

The victor...?" He Dog stared thoughtfully at the white man. "You know a lot, Wasichu, but you do not know my people. The Lakota will never allow the white man to win. Battles, yes, they may win. But in the end, they must lose. Wakan -Tanka will not let the people be destroyed!"

---

1 *This was one of the reasons given by the chiefs in Omicron*

At his last word, He Dog brought himself up short. This was not something new, this talk with this white man in the snow. It was something old, something Wakan.

Rodgers smiled back at the young warrior. "Do you remember this, my old friend? Do you remember this conversation? Do you remember this event?"

He Dog stared incredulously at the white man in front of him. He did remember this dream, or was it a dream? This white man, yes…as a young man, not here, but in a different place, this white man as a young man, and himself . . . himself, when he was old!

Seven days later, they stood before the Wakan Cave. Whatever would be his fate, the Lakota warrior was now prepared to face it.

As Rodgers walked toward the cave, he turned to face He Dog once again. "Remember, my friend, I will be returning to an earlier point in the future than when I left. When you find me, I may not remember you at first, even as you did not remember me, but you must remind me. You must lead me back to this knowledge or there is no hope for your people or for mine, there will be no hope for *our* family!"

He Dog waited for a time after the white man had left and then turned to look again at the valley of the Wakan Cave. He had always loved this place. He had always loved the stories of the old men as they talked about the workings of the powers as they, from this beautiful valley, worked for the good of the people. It was said they used men to do their jobs in the world of the living; that it was through brave men that all good would come to the Lakota.

The snows were gaining in ferocity as He Dog tied his exhausted pony to a young sapling pine, growing almost at the entrance of the cave. Without another thought, *for fear stalks the thoughts of the brave*, he walked into the cave that had so recently received the white man.

The fire was warm inside, as his friend had foretold. The Lakota wondered that there was no sign of firewood, as whoever had built the fire would need fuel against the great storm that raged outside. If this was the fire of them that are Wakan, then he would bring fuel for them, he thought, and he turned and walked back out from whence he came.

Shocked, the warrior fell back, almost to the entrance. Before him he saw the moon, shining its sacred light on the valley of the cave. Across the valley, grass in its summer splendor waved at the moonlit night in adoration of all that was peace. Trees in their full summer foliage moaned with the passing of the warm summer breeze. Coming toward him, the warrior could see two lights, moving with great speed. The warrior felt to run, then to reach for his weapons, as the voice he had heard so many times since the days of his first reckoning came again.

Yes, it was true, he *had* been here before, and there was much to do.

Again came the voice:

"A good nation we will make live.
This, the nation above has said.
We have given you the power to make over."

**

_____

Lakota Camp outside of cantonment, confluence of the Tongue
and Yellowstone
February 1877
Omega Line

_____

Every day, as the long high country winter worked itself angrily toward spring, Crazy Horse met with the Wasichu[1] and the returned Lakota that had come with them from the cave. The names of these men in the white tongue would not form in the

_____

1 *The word used for "White people" also translated as,"they are many!"*

mouths of the people. The young Lakota they had begun to call *Smiles at the People.*

Neither Banyon, nor anyone else in the camp of the Strange One, was too surprised at the name. Leonard Sharpfish had one of those infectious smiles that drew all that was living into its spell. It made everyone want to be close to him and it was seldom he was ever seen alone. The children especially found him to be a source of constant delight, and it was obvious that the feeling was mutual. He had a particular affinity for the game of "*Wasichu the Bear.*"

The young boys of the band stood careful watch at all hours of the day and, some believed, into the night, for they knew that the "Wasichu Bear," Smiles at the People, might be anywhere. In this they were seldom disappointed. As one would sit down to eat at the evening meal or as the first step was taken out of the lodge of his mother in the morning, the Wasichu Bear would be upon him, seemingly from nowhere, growling and grabbing... Of course, at that signal, all of the young warriors of the band would come running from all sides of the camp, and the mighty Wasichu Bear would be surrounded and *killed* by the skills of the great hunters to be. How the great Bear would roar and thrash as one warrior boy after another would rush in to count coup on this great enemy. Never had there been, in the history of the people, such a great bear as this, never were there such great hearts as these who ran forward to face the great smiling *enemy*. The helpless ones fled behind the boy warriors and shouted praise to give courage to the fighting Lakota. In the end, it was always the same. After so great a battle, the great Wasichu Bear would fall into the mud or snow, only to be buried beneath the bodies of the boy warriors of the people.

To the rear, safe at last, the mothers and sisters of the great warriors sounded the tremolo of praise, to think that among the people there were still such great hearts.

Even Crazy Horse had a hard time not getting wrapped up in the battles with the great bear, and the Silent One found himself, with the rest, shouting encouragement to the boy warriors and to the great bear who would teach them to be men.

A name for the white man however, was difficult for the people until a hunt up the Tongue, where a great bull elk had heard the hunters coming and made his escape far beyond the range of the guns.

The white man had run to a place along the river where the stump of a fallen tree flanked the beginning thaw of late winter.

The Wasichu had placed his rifle on the broken stump and followed the fleeing bull.

But this could not be, thought the men of the Lakota. The bull now was twice the range of a good gun.

As the white appeared ready to fire, Crazy Horse leaned from his saddle. "Ammunition is short and the people depend on us; Shoot straight!" The roar of the rifle filled the little canyon as the elk bound for an upper ledge above the riverbank and fell.

Shoots Straight and Smiles at the People met with Crazy Horse daily. In the lodge of first one, then the other, the questions would go on into the night.

"What is left to ask?" pondered the warrior one day, as the three companions hunted on the upper reaches of the Tongue south of the cantonment.

"There is only one question left for us," Shoots Straight had answered. "When will we know?"

Rodgers had said before he left that the only surety he could offer was that the changes would be in time.

"In time for what…?" Banyon had asked.

"In time to act, if it is required," the scholar had responded. "in time to not act, if that is required. It all depends on the outcome. What may seem terrible in the short run may be for the good of all in the long. What seems good in the short may lead to disaster. Only the book and maybe something else, if we are lucky, can tell us which it will be. Only after you have gained knowledge should you act to effect a change.

"The other thing you must know," added the departing Rodgers as an afterthought, "...is that it may be just in time, at the very last minute."

Shoots Straight looked off at the ridges, not so very distant physically from where the Oglala had stood to await the troops, some two months past now. "Yet so very far in other ways," he mumbled, as he turned his horse north toward the cantonment.

***

Since the surrender, there had been a constant communication from government bureaucrats and army men in Washington. What had been said to the leaders of the Lakota and the intent of the war department were two very different things, and it was time to bring in men who could mold one into the other. On the morning of the 27th of February, a delegation from the war department entered the snowy camp, Shoots Straight, as everyone, even the whites, now called him, was asked to be the translator for the Lakota at the evening meeting.

It did not go well at best! At every front, the government men had pressed the leaders of the band to remove to Fort Robinson, where the remainder of the Lakota were located. Even more persistent were the constant references to the new reservations back in the old land along the Missouri.

"There is no game in that land," the chiefs had consistently responded. "The people will soon be like those at Fort Robinson, who must count on the white man to eat."

The white commissioners had done their best to assure the leaders that there was no need to worry about food in these places. The United States government had purchased the Black Hills from the Lakota and, in return, the people would be fed and given clothing and even farm implements, along with those to teach them how to use them. In a matter of time, the Sioux would be farmers, walking down the good road of the white man.

Banyon, in his translating duties, could not miss the blankets being raised to cover the faces of the chiefs at this talk, the blankets futilely shielding the headmen from these bad words.

"The Paha Sapa is the sacred land of the people," Big Road had responded. "It cannot be sold by the bad-faces for a white man's promise. We hear from the people at Fort Robinson and we know that they starve! Will you stand here and say such lies in council, and then ask us to consider more promises?"

"Hou, Hou," came the response from the council lodge.

Crazy Horse stood to speak, and quiet was restored. Shoots Straight translated his words as he spoke.

"When we surrendered to Bear Coat, we agreed that we would come here to live. We said this because Three Stars Crook, who is the big chief over the soldiers in this country, had made the promise to us. It is good then, we have come here and we have put fighting behind us. We are here to keep our promises, and we ask you to keep yours."

Without another word, the warrior turned and walked out of the lodge with Shoots Straight and the headmen at his heels.

Leaving the council lodge at the cantonment, Shoots Straight was very aware that there were a great number of Crow scouts, posted at various intervals along the pathway to the gate. There were over two hundred Crow and Shoshone scouts employed by the regiment, but never in his recollection had he seen so many in one place.

Crazy Horse seemed indifferent to their presence and continued on toward the gate. Considering the tremendous hatred that had always existed between Crazy Horse and the Crow, Banyon wondered at his indifference. According to anyone's estimation, the Crow were a formidable foe at any range.[1] Given their sudden, premeditated killing of the peace chiefs the previous December, it seemed folly to ignore them.

---

1 *Considered by many as the best fighting men of the northern plains!*

As the chiefs turned and mounted their ponies, Crazy Horse leaned next to Shoots Straight as he settled on his tall bay.

"How much longer do we wait?"

"The waiting is over," the interpreter responded. "As I studied today, I came to the surrender on the Hanging Woman, written just as it happened *here!*"

A sudden look of anxiousness came to the face of the Strange One of the Oglala. Beyond him however, the Lakota's interpreter, Shoots Straight, could not miss the beaming face of Smiles at the People.

As quickly as propriety would permit, the three detached themselves from the other headmen and headed directly to the lodge of the former agent. It had been a favorite gathering place, as it was devoid of listening ears. Devoid, that is; save for the young Black Elk who, uninvited, had repeatedly found his way to the entrance of the lodge. It was doubtful that he had heard much that he could understand in the innumerable conferences that had been held inside. He did, however, make it clear that he felt he had a part there and would wait for the day when he was invited to meet with the men inside.

The three men sat down beside the dying fire and waited through the smoking of the pipe as each pondered what the news of the evening would bring to them and the people.

Shoots Straight brought the book from his pocket and turned to one of the middle chapters.

Reading to himself, the interpreter seemed troubled and, turning the pages quickly before him, studied them again for a moment. Then, looking each of his friends in the eye in turn; began to explain.

"The text reads correctly as to what we have seen in the last month and a half. "The surrender on the Hanging Woman is especially accurate, as if the author were there himself.

"The text flows perfectly after the surrender, even noting that the Lakota . . . *'had been aided by an interpreter, thought by historians to be a squaw man by the name of Shoots Straight.*

The squaw man interpreter had enabled the people to communicate on a higher level with the military and government officials relative to the final move to the reservations."

Crazy Horse pulled back slightly at the mention of the reservations as Banyon continued.

"On February 28th, Crazy Horse, his interpreter, and another unknown Lakota were killed by vengeful Crow scouts while eating in the lodge of the white interpreter. The attack came within the hour of what was deemed a very productive meeting with government officials, in which it was affirmed that Crazy Horse had agreed to the removal of his people to the reservations in Dakota Territory."

In a heartbeat Shoots Straight was on his feet heading for the door of the lodge.

"No," came the voice of Crazy Horse, in frantic opposition. "Read the rest!"

"The rest you've heard. They are going to kill us tonight, maybe as we speak."

"We are dead already!" barked back the Lakota fighter. "It is the end that matters. What is the end, my friend?"

Banyon grabbed the book from his pocket as he looked frantically through the tent flap and began to read. "After the death of their leader, the unarmed Oglala were taken prisoner by the troops of the garrison who had been set in position during the council."

Shoots Straight skipped contemptuously to the last chapter of the book and read again. *"The fate of the Lakota Sioux was to fade from existence by the middle of the 20th century, leaving only the memory of a savage people destined by fate to be destroyed before the merciless wheels of progress."*

In another heartbeat, all were on their feet and slipping from the entrance of the tent.

The people had no guns after the surrender. Only those issued by the fort for a specific hunt were allowed. Without it being said, the three knew that if there were a fight, the innocent ones in camp would be the real losers.

Even if they had guns, the presence of the troops outside the camp, foretold by the book, would make short work of the unprepared Lakota.

"We have one option," whispered the interpreter desperately. "We have to get by the troops and into the trees before the Crow attack the lodge."

The other two acknowledged his decision as correct, and in moments they were approaching the camp perimeter. Just as the book had warned, the running companions could sense the mounted men in the trees.

As they reached the edge of the outermost lodge, the bark of rifles exploded behind them as the camp, so recently asleep, roared to life.

"In here, quickly!" came a strong female voice from the lodge beside them. The words were Lakota but accented strongly. The three men, as one, broke for the lodge entrance. To their rear, they could hear the troops moving past them, toward the now empty lodge of Shoots Straight the interpreter.

"Quiet," demanded the voice, "they are many!"

Outside, riders were moving silently toward the center of the camp where the commotion indicated that, although unarmed, the fighting men of the Sioux were making it hot for the Crow warriors. Frustrated in finding the empty lodge, the Crow scouts sought to extend their search to the outlying areas.

Lying flat on his stomach, facing out under the slightly raised flap of the lodge, Banyon saw the main line of troops pass, followed momentarily by their officers, mounted and awaiting the outcome of the increasingly furious fight at the center of the camp. Nelson Miles was obviously in command and set his tall bay horse not twenty feet from them.

Chapter 7

...if the enemy is numerous, disciplined, and about to advance,
how should we respond to them?
...first seize something that they love!
Sun Tzu
The Art of War

South Dakota
Present Day
Omega Line

Hergin Rodgers sat staring dumbly into what seemed to be a living computer screen. He had been up all night since his return, and as sleep had fled from his being, hope had filled him.

He had always known that this moment could happen, knew that it had been attempted endless times without success. In the nights of ten thousand days, he had pondered what would happen when the process had begun, and now he could see it before him.

As his mind reeled, the computer screen in front of him continued to change almost magically. Historical information, previously unknown to the world before this moment, continued to unfold on his roiling computer screen. And even as he watched, Hergin Rodgers could feel the ranting of the spirits in his own brain, those that had driven him for thirty years and two thousand years to where he sat today. Amid their ranting, he knew that the information on the computer was true. He also knew that by the time the world awakened in the now looming morning, things would appear as if they had always been.

Historically, this was a totally new line, unseen before in the annals of man. It would be defined by what the information on the screen now revealed, what the old men, although at times seemingly confused at the specifics, remembered. It would be *the* history, and everyone would remember that it was so. But still, there would be a haunting, an uncertainty, where those who thought they remembered one thing would sit and ponder the written word. Searching deep inside themselves, they would say, "That's not the way I remember it!"

The cursor ran slower now, as the historian knew that it would. It began to crawl, methodically, to a point in the Lakota wars where the great warrior chieftains were slowly surrendering to the combined power of the United States cavalry. It was there that the axial point had been established by their insertion. It was there that what *would be* had the possibility of being redefined.

The cursor suddenly stopped in the Lakota camp of hostile Oglala and Cheyenne camped outside the future Fort Keogh under the command of Col. Nelson Miles, U.S. Cavalry.

When the cursor began again, it was moving slowly, as if anticipating, waiting on the past. The greatest historian of his time, or maybe any time, looked deeply into what was and what yet could be . . .

. . .in a bungled attempt to capture the warrior chief Crazy Horse and to force an end to the Lakota resistance to the government reservations, Crow scouts, backed up by the cavalry divisions of the future Fort Keogh, found only an empty lodge. In their failure to capture the illusive chief, the scouts and supporting troops were drawn into a fierce hand-to-hand fight with Crazy Horse warriors, thinking that they, themselves, were protecting their chief.

In the midst of the ensuing fight, Crazy Horse and his interpreter were hidden in a Cheyenne lodge at the outskirts of the camp. The lodge was owned by Buffalo Calf Road, the same Cheyenne girl who had charged the lines of Gen. George Crook the previous June, amid a hail of bullets, to rescue her unhorsed brother. In her honor, the victorious warriors would always remember the fight as the "Fight Where the Girl Saved Her

Brother.[1]

Rodgers let out a sigh of relief. "We have him back to her," he said out loud.

The cursor stuttered and stopped for what seemed an eternity.

It was determined that during the fight Col. Nelson Miles, the same officer who, the following fall, was to defeat Chief Joseph and the Nez Perce in their flight to Canada, located himself unknowingly within a short distance from the very lodge that held the illusive warrior chief . . .

The cursor did not move. Rodgers attempted to advance it only to find that it remained.

A smile crept ever so slowly onto the worried features of the great scholar; after all these years, had they done it; after a thousand tries and as many failures were they now to have it right?

The historian moved slowly, never taking his eyes off the blinking cursor. Picking up the phone beside the desk, he hit a preprogrammed button and waited impatiently as the phone rang again and again. Finally on the other end, the voice of an old man rang clear in response.

Rodgers almost shouted into the phone, "We have it! We have equilibrium, and with it, the possibility of synergism!"

On the other end the voice was strong in response, "I will be right there, what does it say now?"

"It says they are in the lodge of Buffalo Calf Road and that Nelson is outside."

There was a protracted silence. "Do you remember, Old Friend, what we were told could happen when we gained a link?"

Rodgers swallowed hard. He did remember. Yes, it would be a mixed blessing, they had always thought. But still they had,

---

1 *The girl was at the battle to hold horses when her brother was unhorsed close to the soldier's lines. Both sides claimed that the fight paused momentarily as the fighters watched to see how the man would die. Just at that moment the girl swept in front of the troops and rescued him amid a hail of gunfire and cheering!! Omicron and Omega.*

in their pondering of this salient possibility, believed that it would be worth the price that must be paid. They had been told that when that day came, the cave *would* begin to close.

"This may be our last chance, my friend. I am going to tell them to take Nelson Miles."

Hergin Rodgers placed the phone at his side and began to type, knowing that what he would type would one day be printed in a book that he would, one day in the future, hand to Dan Banyon at the cave. That in the doing, they would begin the very line in which he now lived, *the last line*, he thought to himself. "Well named, *Omega*," he mused aloud. The cursor was moving freely now under his dancing hands . . .

Hidden in the lodge of Buffalo Calf Road, Crazy Horse and his companions were able to ambush Col. Nelson Miles and, holding a knife to the throat of the fort commander, escape into the surrounding trees . . .

Rodgers picked up the phone again and waited.

"What's happening?" started the voice on the other end.

"It's moving. I don't know where, but it is moving." Rodgers looked back to the previous paragraph that had referred to Nelson Miles defeating the Nez Perce.

The reference was gone!

*

Lakota Camp
1877
Omega Line

In the lodge of Buffalo Calf Road, Banyon spoke quickly. Crazy Horse pulled a knife from a hidden sheath and moved silently, catlike, toward the entrance. His companions were on their feet and at his hip as the three sprang from the lodge toward the mounted officer. In a single movement, Crazy Horse was on the back of the horse of Nelson Miles with his knife at the officer's throat as chaos was unleashed by his two companions when they unhorsed the two closest subordinate officers.

Before any resistance could be mounted or help summoned, the combined officers' corp saw their commander disappear into the trees with the knife of Crazy Horse at his throat. The voice they had all come to recognize as that of Shoots Straight the interpreter roared back at the startled and confused officers.

"Follow us and he dies instantly!"

Beneath his leg, the former agent could feel the shape of a rifle in a scabbard. The moonlight allowed the faintest of views of his fast riding companions, but he could see that the army officers, whose mounts they rode, had all carried rifles, tucked carefully into well-formed scabbards.

What was it that he had read about the officers of the cavalry?

Yes, he remembered now. The enlisted men had been provided with weapons, while the officers were given the option to provide their own. Most chose the Winchester lever action repeater, the west's most accurate and fastest weapon.

"*If we are lucky,*" gasped the former agent as his leg rubbed repeatedly against the covered bulge in the scabbard, the contents of which could bring endless possibilities in the hands of one called, Shoots Straight!

As the horses raced frantically into the ever-thickening trees along the river, Crazy Horse held the knife firmly at the throat of Nelson Miles. With every leap of the fleeing horse, Shoots Straight expected to see blood coming from the throat of the officer. Yet the hand of the Lakota was steady, and as the din of the fighting in the camp faded behind them, the knife moved to the officer's side. The horses were pulled to a stop on a small knoll overlooking the swollen banks of the Yellowstone.

Shoots Straight stared malevolently at the captive officer. "So, you would kill us just like that, would you Col. Miles? Not so much as an hour since you sat in council with us and pledged your good faith?"

Nelson Miles returned the interpreter's glare with haughty disdain. "I have my orders, Squaw Man. I don't have to explain them to you. Nor do I have to give an accounting of why they were given."

Crazy Horse could not understand the conversation between the two men, as they conversed in English; however, the tone of the army officers' remark made the gist of it clear to him. Without an additional word, he threw the man from the horse onto the ragged ice.

Miles was immediately on his feet as Crazy Horse dismounted to face him. Shoots Straight was faster, however, and before the officer could adjust to the unsteady footing of the river bank, the former agent caught him with a solid right, sending him crashing to the ground. The interpreter stood before the fallen army man and waited, but there was no movement and neither would there be any for a time yet. His temper boiling inside him still, he turned to look in the direction of the Lakota camp, now over a mile to their rear.

Banyon had felt, more than seen, the riders following them in the mad dash from the camp. He knew that they were friendly by the fact that, at any point, they could have killed the escaping men without effort. Now he saw the boy, Black Elk, and *the woman,* who had helped them in the camp, dismounting a short distance into the trees – dismounting and watching back along the path that had brought them.

Shoots Straight fixed his eyes on the woman, realizing at that moment how much they owed her. Another thought came clearly to his mind. From where, he couldn't begin to understand.

"You are Buffalo Calf Road, aren't you?"

The woman nodded, imploringly, thought shoots straight. When he did not respond in kind, she turned with questioning eyes toward Crazy Horse.

Banyon followed her gaze to see the Oglala Strange Man assessing him carefully while holding the reins of the horses. His eyes went repeatedly to Shoots Straight, then to Nelson Miles, and again to the woman and the boy.

"You have met this Cheyenne woman before, my brother?"

The former agent was caught unexpectedly by the question. No, now that he thought of it, he had never met the woman before the fight in the camp. Neither, as he probed further, could he remember seeing her about camp. His gaze turned back to the Cheyenne girl, searching now. No, he thought, definitely not. The girl was probably the most beautiful woman he had seen since coming through the cave. Tall and well formed, she carried herself with an almost regal bearing. The bearing of a warrior, thought Shoots Straight. And yet, there was something about her that did seem familiar that pulled at something inside him and left him with an unexplainable need to go to her, to be near her. As he stared purposefully at the girl, searching for recognition, he realized that she was staring back at him. The eyes were dark and fixed, and filled with . . . filled with what?

No, there could be no room for doubt. This one, he, or any other man, would have remembered.

Crazy Horse had moved the horses close to Shoots Straight, and stood at their heads soothing them.

"What else do you remember, my friend?"

Banyon was confused now. He did have memories that seemed fresh to him. But could something he had read tell him how to recognize someone he had never met?

Still, there they were, and not alone, but with friends. Specific, interrelating, substantive, but still totally new memories of the past!

"The book said that a woman would help us to escape and to take Col. Miles. It said that her name would be Buffalo Calf Road. By this I know her . . . I think." remaining fixed on the girl as he spoke.

114

The Oglala headman stared hard at the struggling Shoots Straight. "What else did it say?"

"It said that the future of the Lakota would mix with that of the Pierced Noses, of the Nez Perce."

Crazy Horse had handed the reins to the boy, and now stood quietly beside the unconscious army officer. "And this one?" kicking Miles lightly with his moccasin.

"It says that his life may soon be traded for victory," responded Banyon.

Nelson Miles was coming around now, and Crazy Horse helped the dazed man roughly to a sitting position in the snow, much the way that a man would handle a pile of old rags.

"What *more* than victory is his life worth? I have seen many victories, and inside them there is always the shadow of future defeat."

Shoots Straight suddenly "*remembered*" what more the book had said. The new words seemed to race to his mind, substituting themselves aggressively for those they would replace.

In the next moment, the eyes of the two friends locked substantively, found understanding, and the conversation halted abruptly as the warrior realized that *whatever* had made its way into the mind of his friend should not, even by mistake, find its way into the ears of the Wasichu Colonel.

Crazy Horse turned and looked at the waters of the frozen Yellowstone at their backs. He could hear them again, yes, the voices were returning from the bowels of the Wakan cave. They had come to him many times since that first night as he slept by the warm fire. Yet the voices were still strange to him, strange and foreign! Now a single voice seemed to resonate above the rest, a single, familiar voice.

"Prancing, they are coming
a horse nation . . .
May you behold them!"

The voice of the Strange Man of the Oglala was quiet now as he spoke, seemingly to the river at his front. "The land of the

Pierced Noses is far."*1*

"No," responded Shoots Straight, "it is for them to come to the land of the Lakota."

"The Nez Perce also will fight the cavalry and will head toward us, by the summer, followed by the pursuing army."

"To where will they hope to escape?" asked the warrior resolutely.

"To Sitting Bull," answered the former agent.

At this Crazy Horse's gaze went beyond the river, searching the treetops to the North. "Sitting Bull is not a friend of the Pierced Noses. In this path, my friend, will the Lakota help these friends of the Crow?"

Shoots Straight responded without hesitation, "Not by themselves. Not without help."*2*

**

South Dakota
Present Day
Omega Line

As Rodgers stopped typing, the cursor began to move again on its own. The scholar leaned back in his chair and watched, as the running cursor seemed to suddenly pick up speed until the pace seemed frenzied.

Fifty miles away on the Pine Ridge reservation, an old man got into an equally ancient pickup truck and headed it toward the city. Rain had been falling lightly for the last hour, and thunder

---

1. *The Nez Perce homeland was the Walla Walla valley, western Idaho*
2. *The Nez Perce had been a friend with the Crow for many generations Joseph, Looking Glass and many others believed that the Crow would help them in their flight to Canada. In Omicron, they refused!*

was rolling in the distant west. The spirits of the Paha Sapa were anxious, the old warrior thought to himself. This is good. This is very good!

The old man drove with the careful deliberateness native to those who daily do with their hands things their minds tell them cannot be done.

"With the left foot, push on the flat headed stick, while letting off with the right. Left hand, stay on the path. Right, change the upper stick from the top to the bottom and then to the top again." Everyone who had ever been in his presence had been blessed with his gracious smile and the calming sense of peace that so permeated his relationship with others. So much, in fact, that no one would have recognized the intense, stress-crippled driver of the old pick-up.

"How should the people not fear, when the minds of the whites bring such machines to us?"

Inwardly he knew and appreciated the value of the automobile and the swiftness with which it made possible his not too frequent forays into the city. It was not uncommon, however, for him to ask one of the younger Lakota to drive and save him the days of unsteadiness that always followed a driving experience.

This time that was not possible, and the old man was grateful, even in his fear of the driving machine. There would be no questioning eyes as he did what had to be done. How would he explain such a thing anyway? Would he tell the young people that he sought a way to erase all they knew of life? Or, if it was one of his own family, could he possibly explain to them that he had dedicated his life to finding a way that would allow them to never exist here. Such things could not be explained and so were left for the powers to make right.

The important thing was that they were successful and, if they were, then everything was possible. If they failed, then everything would fail with them. The powers had foretold it, and it had been written in the books. A long life and endless days in the swirls of broken paths had taught him not to doubt that their cause was desperate and that, in the face of great odds, they must somehow succeed.

Many times they had taken the trails to the end to see if the words of the books were true, the words the powers had caused to be written by his friend brother. At the end of every trail, it was the same. The crooked paths of the white man always ended in disaster for the Lakota, *and then for the whites themselves.*

Even now they cannot see the foolishness of their path, he thought, as the old truck slowed at the beginning outreaches of the city.

"Their young men they coddle and protect," he spoke out loud as if to a quietly listening companion. "They live their lives in their large buildings and, except for play, they know nothing of the earth which is their mother. They sleep at night beneath the protection of their wooden homes and know nothing of their father, the sky, except that which they learn in their books. How foolish they are to believe that such young men will defend the people when the enemy comes in the night. How deceived are the parents of the young to believe that the enemy will not come again. It is the way of human beings that there will always be another enemy at the edge of the camp. Those who believe they are safe are those who are always the first to die."

Yes, thought the old warrior, *I have seen it with these old eyes many, many, times, and if we cannot find the Red Road again, then at the end of this road also we will find ourselves destroyed, creatures unable to protect even our young. We will change ourselves into men unable to bear the cold, or hunger, or pain in the defense of the helpless ones who must die with us.*

The old truck came to a stop in front of the old brick building.

Inside the entrance, the old man could see the face of his brother friend smiling out at him through the pouring rain. Lightning struck close and, for a moment, the entire building was lit by its blinding brilliance.

The old man mused softly, as if speaking to the rain. "The building, like men of learning; so filled with knowledge of things as they are or seem to be. Lightning; like wisdom, bringing enlightenment to those dark halls."

Rodgers greeted his old friend with unreserved excitement. "I think we have it this time. We seem to be able to elicit response by altering the manuscript."

Rodgers hurried along the long hallway, with the old man striding easily at his side. Rodgers watched carefully out the side of his eye, observing the response of his old friend as he recounted what he had been able to adjust so far.

"They survived the attack at the camp and have taken Nelson Miles captive. I have instructed them to cross the Yellowstone immediately to escape the soldiers. There can be no question that somehow this path is interwoven with the Nez Perce retreat. The beginnings of Joseph's eastward movements have written themselves into the pattern of the weave.

"Assuming there is some benefit in meeting with Joseph and his group, I have written in the stop to leave the wounded warrior at the pass. If they plan correctly and are not overly confused by the terrain, they will be there within a day's ride, one way or the other, of the main body of the Nez Perce. The problem before us is that I cannot tell if they must all go, or just Leonard – or if none of them should go. The road is too new, and the responses to the changes they will make are too unpredictable this early."

The old warrior seemed doubtful, yet anxious, as he stared at the moving cursor. "What do we know about the path of others?"

Rodgers hit an upper key on his computer keyboard and a list under the title of *Ancillary Events* appeared instantly. The scholar moved the cursor systematically over the list, highlighting four as he went. Four screens, each smaller than the first, appeared, one moving, the others still. The old warrior noted the titles above the smaller screens.

Lt. Frank D. Baldwin Leads 2nd in Pursuit . . .
News of Miles' Capture Reaches the Eastern Press . . .
Nez Perce Defeat Army in the Battle of . . .

The eyes of both men looked toward the one moving screen and began to read.

Sitting Bull and the Miniconjous Under Lame Deer Reported in Canada.

The two old friends stared at each other. Rodgers was the first to speak. "Sitting Bull is supposed to arrive in Canada by the middle of May, but Lame Deer and his Miniconjous were destroyed by . . ."[1]

The old warrior looked grim. "By Bear Coat Miles, who now is too busy with Crazy Horse's band to be out searching for the Miniconjous."

Rodgers seemed deep in thought. "When they are needed, Sitting Bull and his warriors will be too far away to help the Nez Perce. What if they were closer?"

"How much closer?" asked the aged warrior, eyeing his friend cautiously. "And would being closer make a difference against the troops coming for the Pierced Noses?"

Rodgers had opened a book containing a series of old maps and was reviewing carefully the lay of the soldier forts.

"What if the soldiers couldn't be re-supplied and the Lakota had sufficient arms to hold the Missouri?"

The old warrior looked at the map in front of the scholar.

The historian was pointing directly at the location of the old Fort Peck, on the convergence of the Missouri and the Milk rivers.

"Didn't Sitting Bull cross near Fort Peck on his way north?"

"Yes," replied the old warrior, "many of the Hunkpapas stayed at the Fort Peck agency after the treaty of 1871. Some

---

1 *Lame Deer and his village were destroyed by the troops of Nelson Miles May 7,1877, Omicron line.*

married with the Yanktonais, and so the people of the Fort Peck agency were relatives of the Sitting Bull Band."

Rodgers watched as the cursor stopped moving on the main screen and began its monotonous blinking, waiting on events at the axial point.

The scholar sat at the terminal and began to type.

"Part of the escaping Crazy Horse warriors fled to the west and were later reported to have joined with the retreating Nez Perce warriors under Chief Joseph. Others, including Crazy Horse and his interpreter, escaped to the north and were reported to have joined with Sitting Bull in his camp upstream from Fort Peck on or before the 16th of March 1877."

***

Yellowstone River
1877
Omega Line

Banyon turned to the girl and the young Black Elk. There could be no question that the girl looked at him strangely. At the same moment, he thought, she seemed familiar beyond chance. Every word that he spoke she followed with a singular attention. At one point, she had reached toward him, almost touching before retreating to the boy.

"Go back into camp," said Shoots Straight to the girl and the young Black Elk. "Tell Big Road that we head north, and the soldiers will follow. Tell him to bring many warriors and meet us at Fort Peck."

Shoots Straight could feel the gaze of the Strange Man of the Oglala as he finished his orders to the girl and the boy. In an instant they were gone through the snow in the direction of the camp, with only a backward glance from the girl. Again her eyes were filled with an emotion he could not name. He watched them for a moment, fascinated and then turned back to the task at hand.

Crazy Horse stood beside Smiles at the People and the now fully conscious Nelson Miles and watched as the Wasichu interpreter walked back toward them. Banyon motioned toward the Lakota warrior, and they walked a short distance off to escape any hearing by the Bear Coat.

Shoots Straight looked deeply into the eyes of the warrior chieftain and tried to find the words to explain what was happening.

"I don't know how to explain it, my friend, but somehow the words of the book have changed inside me. What I have read of what was to come has somehow changed and in it's changing, the memories of it are also different.

"It seems that somehow I can see what will happen by what I have read in the book, even though it changes. I have told you we are from a path that *can* come in the future. It is there that the white man, Rodgers, is writing what we do here many years from now. Later he gives the book to me in the cave and I read it as it is written in the future. In that, I know what will be and I must ask you to believe me and believe that I will never tell a lie to you. Your friend Sitting Bull asked once at a council at Fort Peck to find him one white man who tells the truth. There was no such man, but I tell you from the heart that I will never lie to you."

The Oglala chieftain looked toward the ground uncertainly. Banyon knew, from all he had read and all he had observed that before him was a man who had no reason to trust the words of any white man. A man who owed every ounce of grief in his life to the lies that had come from the white race.

The words came slowly, deliberately. "So tell me, then. Tell me a truth that you are willing to gamble your life on. Tell me something that will show me, and the others, that what you say is true – that there *is* one white man who can speak the truth."

The former agent searched through his memories as a man flips through the pages of a book. There must be something that would give him a point to build on, something that was concrete.

Then it was there!

"We must go north, as I told you, toward the camp of Sitting Bull and arrive in sixteen days or less. When we arrive, we will find Sitting Bull's band camped on the river bottom upstream from the fort. We will find only fifteen lodges of Hunkpapa with Sitting Bull, but now will also find the Miniconjous of Lame Deer with them. The next day we must change camp, and you must help me to convince the others because in eighteen days from today the river will rush suddenly from upstream and destroy all around it. Fort Peck, and everything and everyone in it, will be destroyed."[1]

Crazy Horse seemed perplexed by the specifics of the interpreter's prediction. A sense of uncertainty accented his voice as he turned toward the army officer seated in the snow behind them. "And this one…?"

"Bear Coat goes with us. He may be something we can use. Smiles at the People must go west and try to find the Pierced Noses. He will need some men to go with him that can help him to find them – and one thing else."

Banyon looked deeply into the eyes of the man he had thought was his friend. He realized that he was asking him to trust the future of his whole people to him. He knew that it was a hard jump to take, mentally. But, somehow, he just had to do it.

"He must know we have taken Fort Peck."

The Oglala chieftain seemed shocked to the very core. "Fort Peck has many soldiers with many guns. We have few guns and almost no ammunition!"

---

1 Ft. Peck was destroyed by a massive flood, all lines!

"He must know that we have taken Fort Peck when he talks to Joseph or he will have nothing to offer."

"How is it, friend of my dreams, that we capture a white man's fort that is destroyed by the flood of the Missouri?"

"We do it before it happens, if we can convince the chiefs to fight."

Crazy Horse turned and looked at Nelson Miles, shivering now in the snow.

Chapter 8

Men having often abandoned what was visible for the sake of what was uncertain, have not got what they expected and have lost what they had, being unfortunate by an enigmatical sort of calamity.

Athenaeaus   (Circa 200 A.D.)

South Dakota
Present Day
Omega Line

The cursor on the computer terminal had ceased to move, and the two friends studied carefully what was on the screen, but to no avail. Rodgers tried to move it forward. Nothing! He tried to type in something to the text. Nothing moved.

He called up the ancillary events file and watched carefully as the numbered files were reviewed. The moving cursor was something strange and significant to the old warrior. It was not for Rodgers. He understood very well who had preprogrammed the cursor to move. It was he himself, in an earlier day, editing and searching, finding history and recording it, subsequently re-recording facts upon receiving better information. It was the source of this information that he had never told the world of Academia. He did know however, that the information was correct as to the time line it recorded. When the cursor halted, it was because there was a branching in the time continuum and a pause, if it could be called that, in the fabric of the pattern of what was. This was something that happened seldom, if ever, under normal circumstances where there was no actual link. What was; simply was! There was no decision to be made. With an active link, however, the future was fluid and dependent on decisions not yet made over one hundred and twenty-five years before.

They reviewed some of the subtitles available on the screen:

Yellowstone National Park

Rodgers clicked on the file and it came immediately to the screen.

In the summer of 1877, the new Yellowstone National Park saw its first visitors. One of the groups of distinguished tourists was none other than William Tecumseh Sherman, Commanding General of the Army and long time close friend and comrade in arms to former President Grant...[1]

The two men stared uncomprehendingly at the screen. Was it the Yellowstone or Sherman that was the hold up?

"Wait a minute!" started Rodgers. "The Nez Perce go right through the Yellowstone while Sherman is there. It seems like I remember something about him hearing about them coming through and issued some orders to bring in more troops to head them off.

The gaze of the old warrior was unblinking. He knew that his brother friend would discern what there was to discern. They had been here too many times for him to doubt him now. Yet there was a certain amount of nonsense in the approach, as he saw it.

Capturing or killing one Wasichu general, even if he was the big chief, did not seem that important when the future of the people hung in the balance. He had made it a point not to question his friend in this, as he had shown his loyalty before in so many ways over so many years. Yet now, maybe, there had been too many failures, and with the cave possibly closing, he must speak.

"Hergin, do you believe that the path we are following will save the people?"

---

1 *Correct as per Omicron*

The historian looked pensively at the floor. "It is too early for me to know, my friend. So many times we have thought we had found the right road, only to have it turn against us at the end. This looks promising."

The old warrior looked deeply into the dark grey eyes of the historian. "I feel the strength of this path. There is something here that has its own spirit. At the same time, there is something else that seems unattended. If we do not find that one thing, all will be for nothing. We have gone off looking for the one thing that would change our path many times. I believe now that it is not one *thing* that we're looking for it is something of the spirit. It is something in the hearts of the people. I believe that when *that* is found, then the path will be before our feet, whatever the specific events."

The historian nodded at what his old friend was saying, yet there was something more that had to be asked. He felt that now was the right moment.

"Maybe you are right, yet we do not have the time now to be wrong. Whatever we must do must be done soon. There will be little time for testing specifics."

He Dog stared resolutely into the eyes of his old friend. There had always been a special bond between them, something more than the hundred battles that they had fought together. More than the thousands of nights they had ridden, side by side, toward different futures. Now, however, there was silence of an uncommon depth, a silence born of uncertainty, of fear.

"Do we know as a fact the cave is closing, my friend?" the old warrior asked.

Hergin Rodgers stared into space for a moment, gathering his thoughts before speaking. "Closing is one way to see it, my friend. I believe that it is preparing to move, as it has many times before. To those here it will be closed, but to others, *like my own* people, it will be opening. I cannot know for certain, but I believe that we will see that event soon. Still, there is time to act if we do so with diligence and forethought. If we are wise, we will yet win, and the figure of the man with the flute may be carved on the wall outside of the cave."

The old man then turned away from the piercing gaze and went back toward the small leather case he had brought in from the truck. With infinite care, he untied the strings and reached inside.

Rodgers knew what he carried in the case, and he was not surprised when the weathered fingers extracted a finely carved cedar flute, about nineteen inches in length. The historian gazed at the flute with great appreciation for what it represented.

The old hands caressed the grain of the instrument, as one would touch something of ageless antiquity. At the mouth end of the old flute hung several leather strings and, on each string, a myriad of multicolored beads of varying sizes.

Rodgers noted, as he had so many times before, that the flute had six holes in its body, rather than the traditional five holes of the Lakota Love Flute. He had always pondered that this instrument would be called a Love Flute, as he had never seen it used so. Only the rumors of its magical qualities in the attraction of a Lakota maiden to the attentions of a suitor gave the name any pretense of credibility. The only use that the historian had ever seen that particular flute utilized in was in another major phase of a man's life. He had seen it used only by a friend brother as he played a death song for a departed one or *for a more significant event*.

Still, this flute was more than that. Over what now were more than two thousand years, it, in the hands of the man before him, had meant a great deal more. To endless generations it had been a signal of hope. To those who had worked for the future it had been inanimate applause. Carved into rocks from Central America to the depths of the Canadian woodlands, it had told those who knew of its meaning that there had been a success. That a new and better direction had been found!

The old warrior held the flute toward the blank stare of the historian. "You may need this soon, my brother."

The scholar stared blankly at his old friend, knowing what was being said and why. "Then we must take you back and soon. If you stay here, you are a dead man, and all our dreams are illusion."

The flash of the changing computer screen forced the eyes of both men reluctantly to the computer terminal. The cursor had begun to move at a frenzied rate. Hergin Rodgers saw the end of a fleeing sentence as fear gripped his insides.

. . . cavalry, under Capt. Owen Hale, caught the fleeing Crazy Horse with his back to the Yellowstone River and destroyed the escaping party before they could effect a crossing. Col. Nelson Miles, commander, was killed in the attempted rescue . . .

"I told them to go quickly!" the historian yelled at the computer terminal.

Hergin Rodgers pulled the keyboard into his lap and deftly moved the cursor back to the previous paragraph. *. . .the fleeing hostiles hesitated for a time at the river. The doomed men were unaware that the troops of the 7th had been kept in reserve, in case any of the hostiles escaped the attack in the camp.*

The cursor hesitated a moment, then began to move again as the historian and the old warrior stared at the emerging past.

*

The interpreter Shoots Straight grabbed Crazy Horse and shoved him to the ground. Both could feel the rush of bullets crashing into the trees not five feet beyond them.

"Sometimes barely in time," thought the former agent.

Both men were scrambling now as Smiles at the People fought to control the terrified horses. Shoots Straight and Crazy Horse reached the chaos around the former inmate at the same moment, each grabbing for a horse; Banyon found his horse to be almost beyond control as he reached for the rifle butt facing toward him. The horse suddenly bolted to the left as another roar of rifles poured into the chaos of horses and would-be riders. As he fell, he could feel the rifle come loose in his hands as he hit hard on the frozen ground. To his left, he could see Smiles at the People as he fell awkwardly under the feet of the horse he was trying to control. The horse had been hit, and its screams pierced the night as it went to its knees, fought again to rise, and then shuddered as it collapsed suddenly onto the frozen earth.

Banyon let go the reins of the horse he was holding and leapt to the far side of the fallen horse, landing on the inert form of Smiles at the People. He did not like the lack of movement he felt in his friend as he tumbled behind the still quivering horse.

The former agent was unprepared for the fury of rifle fire that now bore frantically into the downed cavalry mount. Pieces of flesh ripped from the carcass flew at the two men, stopping all attempts at return fire. To his right, he could feel, rather than see, Crazy Horse. He had escaped into the trees, dragging Nelson Miles, who seemed to be injured. In doing so, he had found at least temporary respite from the fusillade of bullets that bore relentlessly at his companions behind the dead animal.

In the darkness, the troops could not be certain of their targets, but the screams of the dying horse and the rush of bodies around it as it fell had provided a focus. Throwing themselves haphazardly into the trees before the river, the oncoming 7th, directed by Captain Hale himself, poured in a withering fire.

The former agent knew that in a moment they would be dead if no advantage could be found. With the unrelenting eruption of rifles to his front, there was no opportunity to mount a defense.

He tried to roll to the side, hoping to get to the trees, only to have the ground shredded in front of him by the devastating fire.

He had seen men pinned down like this before in antiterrorist campaigns in *Omicron*, and he knew that their chances were very slim if something didn't change. The carcass of the horse was now moving from the sheer accumulated force of the deadly lead wall that now encompassed them.

Banyon yelled in pain as a bullet struck him in the shoulder. Grasping for the injured appendage, he felt the spot where it had struck and knew the shell had passed right through the body of the horse and struck him with its dying momentum, bruising but not entering the skin. He realized that the total time since the horse had fallen could not have been more than a minute or two, but in that time the sheer savagery of the force thrown at them had brought their hopes of survival to nothing.

For reasons unknown to the fallen fighter, there seemed to be a slight lull in the firing; allowing him time to desperately lever a shell into the Winchester and fire over the top of the prostrate horse.

The return fire was beyond belief. It seemed that every gun had fired at once at the flash of his rifle. Then, for a moment, there was silence as Banyon levered another shell and prepared for what he believed would be his last shot before death took him again . . . again?

"Yes, again," came the thought back to him, over a vast darkness.

One hundred and ten years into the future, practiced hands reached for the keyboard and began to type one letter at a time.

. . .*the troops of the 7th cavalry were armed with Springfield breach-loading rifles. This weapon was a single shot rifle known for its accuracy but also for jamming after the fourth or fifth shot in rapid succession. In battle situations it was estimated that the Springfield, with the copper cartridge standard issue, stood a seventy percent chance of jamming by the fourth shot if firing was rapid.*[1]

The besieged interpreter did not have the time to be surprised at the sudden memory that came to his mind. There was only time to act and act quickly. Firing over the top of the fallen animal, he again was staggered by the pure volume of the returning fire. Rolling to his left as he levered another shell, he fired again almost before the sound of his first shot had left his

---

[1] *Looked on by many experts as a major reason for Custer's defeat eight months previous. Modern studies show that the single shot, prone to jam rifles, were no match for the repeaters in the hands of the Indians.*

ringing ears. Silence was the only response.

"That was it then," he thought as he rolled back to his right and levered another shell. They were firing as a group, probably by order from an officer. That was standard practice in an organized attack. Fire on order, reload, and fire again on command. Only ability to reload determined the speed of return fire. To the rear of the troops, he could hear the unmistakable drum of running horses coming from the camp. He had no question these were additional troops following the code of the cavalry of the day and rushing to the sound of firing. The former agent knew from the sound of the advancing hooves that his life would last only minutes if he could not escape immediately.

Banyon ripped off his jacket and looked quickly to his right, where he was able to make out the fallen form of Nelson Miles covered by Crazy Horse about thirty yards from his position and pinned down by secondary fire. The Oglala fighter had seen something in the life of the arrogant colonel of the army that he valued more than his own safety, and now protected the army officer with his own body.

Shoots Straight rolled catlike to his left and threw the jacket into the trees. There was a deafening roar as the directed fire of the troops ripped into the jacket and the trees that now held its shredded remnants. Rolling instantly to the right, the desperate man secured a hold on the jacket of the unconscious form of Smiles at the People. If he was wrong about this plan, he knew he would die before his second step and that, even if he was right, the officers' guns would not be single shots but repeaters, which would be just as effective as a whole army if they caught him in the open.

The roar of the previous fusillade ebbed, and he knew that his information was right. His lungs roared with exploding rage as he ripped Smiles at the People from the ground in the direction of the trees, only to be jerked backward to the ground, landing hard on the packed ice. As he hit, he could feel hot lead enter his skin at the bottom of his arm as he rolled backward in a single movement to the cover of the horse barricade. His eyes immediately took in the previously unnoticed view of the leg of Smiles at the People, lodged firmly beneath the dead horse. Lead was coming at them like hail as the former agent reached for the leg of his friend and pulled with everything he had. Nothing!

Banyon could hear hard-ridden horses pulling to a stop in the trees behind the hidden troops. Looking back to his right, he could discern no sign of Crazy Horse or Miles.

"Run!" screamed a voice from inside the trees, "run now or we are lost!" There could be no question that the voice was a woman's and further; there could be no question that she was right. Looking desperately back to the lifeless form of Smiles at the People, he decided.

Levering another shell into the chamber he rolled again to the left, firing as he went, while the roar of answering fire ripped into the foliage. He rolled to the right and sprinted for the cover of the trees. There were still the rifles of the officers, but he also knew his time was up.

His lungs near to bursting, he fought for the remaining space to cover. Just as he reached the trees, a terrible blow spun him to the right as he fought to keep his balance. Out of the brush he felt a hand reach toward him, jerking him backward. Landing hard on his back, he could feel his momentum take him over onto the twisting form of whoever had pulled him into the trees.

Then he was rolling, thrashing, fighting for his feet and, finding them, faced the unmistakable reality of the fact that the troops had charged and were upon them. To his right, he could see Crazy Horse locked in deadly struggle with a blue coat soldier. Like an explosion, a wall of soldiers hit him, driving him to the ground. Somehow he had found his knife and, swinging it under hand, found flesh as an agonized scream filled his ears. There was a sudden break around him as the wounded officer fell into his comrade's arms and others fell back before the flashing blade.

Almost on a signal, the blue clad men drew side arms, pointing them frantically toward him. Out of the trees came a rush of movement, accompanied by the soul-wrenching yell of Lakota warriors. The men around Shoots Straight turned to meet them. The tempo of fighting was furious, beyond anything that Banyon had ever known. Side arms fired at point blank range, only to be silenced by a massive onslaught of war clubs and knives. At such close range, the war clubs had the advantage, but others instantly reinforced the troops from the rear. Fear and confusion turned now to rage. Neither side gave quarter nor sought it, and men fell, irrespective of side, as fast as a man can clap his hands. If there was organization, it was not apparent, and each side sought to kill without thought of tactics or retreat.

Shoots Straight could feel his arms tiring as he slashed over and over at his immediate adversary. The man had a sidearm in his hand, but he had been wounded somewhere in the fight and was staggering, apparently unable to focus enough to fire the weapon. Banyon moved toward him, but stopped as he saw Crazy Horse to his right, on the ground and hurt. A smallish warrior had come to his side and was fighting a losing battle against the three troopers who ringed him, trying to finish the Lakota headman.

Leaping in the direction of the struggling men, he slashed at the man closest to him and kicked viciously in the direction of a man with a gun pointed toward the head of Crazy Horse. The gun went off as the Lakota head man jerked violently on the ground. Shoots Straight felt rage become him as he kicked again at a stunned cavalryman, sending him hard to the packed ground. Behind him, he could hear the thunderous sound of oncoming horses and turned toward them as the lead horse smashed into him, throwing him heavily to the ground. Spinning to rise, he saw the barrel of a rifle directly at his front and then . . .

Wakan Cave, Valley of the Wind,
Center of Time

...he awoke, as he had before, to the comforting feel of the fire. It had always been an amazement to him that the fire itself could be so warm and yet so small. He was not surprised to see Hergin Rodgers sitting across from him. The historian was sitting on a buffalo robe and warming his hands as recognition and memory came slowly back.

"Where are they?"

"Where are who?" responded the scholar.

"Crazy Horse and Leonard, where are they now?"

Leonard is out with the horses, but there is someone else here that I thought you would have asked for first.

"Who," queried the former agent?

"The girl, of course, who do think pulled you into the bushes? She died trying to save Crazy Horse, close to where you fell."

He could remember the scene vaguely.

"Yes, the smallish warrior who was fighting with the troopers. Girl...? Wait a minute, what girl? You're saying that was Buffalo Calf Road?"

"Yes," responded Rodgers. "It was her. It has always been her, this time and many others."

Banyon blinked back his surprise, yet the words penetrated his foggy consciousness.

It has always been her!

The former agent thought of the deep loneliness he had felt after his grandmother left and how he had searched the eyes of every woman he met, only to find a world of strangers. He had often felt that the woman he sought was already there, in his memories, but always out of reach. Rodgers' words penetrated to his very center. *It has always been her!*

"They are sleeping. I brought you back sooner so that we could talk uninterrupted."

The former interpreter fought to rise to a sitting position, his head pounding with the realization that for all their efforts they had failed and were back where they started.

"No, no, just lie there for a bit longer. We can talk while you rest. There is a lot that must be said, and although time is very short in the real sense, in another sense, there is all the time in the world."

The former agent found that he too was lying on a buffalo skin, and the drawing comfort pulled him again onto his back. "What happened?" he asked as he fought sleep.

"You were killed in the fight. So was Crazy Horse. The girl went down trying to drag you both to cover."

Banyon's hands reached slowly over his naked torso. There were no wounds. *He knew that there would not be.* "Who brought us here?"

"Leonard."

"Leonard? I thought that he . . . "

"Was dead? No, just unconscious. Gratefully, the troops thought he was dead also. Covered from head to foot with horse blood, you can understand their thinking."

The former interpreter felt sleep taking him, but Rodgers would not allow it, shaking him from across the fire. "There will be time to sleep. Right now we must talk."

He felt almost drugged, but he fought to listen. "Go ahead, talk. Don't mind me, I'm just dead!"

The subtle chuckle from the historian wafted across the fire. "Okay then, dead man. I'll talk, you listen."

The scholar was silent for a moment. "We almost won you know," he said finally.

Now it was Banyon's turn to chuckle. "If that is your idea of almost winning, you must consider yourself to be a very successful man. To me, that's not called winning. That is called getting your head handed to you on a plate."

The chuckle of the former agent now had raised an octave or two, to that pitch often credited to the intoxicated. "Yes, I played in a football game like that once. Their score seventy-nine, ours thirteen, but, like you say, we almost won."

"I thought you said that I was doing the talking and you were going to listen," smiled the historian.

Banyon muffled his almost convulsive giggling and tried to pay attention. The professor, however, had turned serious, and the more serious the scholar became, the more frantically the former agent wanted to laugh. "Hey Professor, just one minute, you see, I've got a question."

Rodgers sat motionless now, the look on his face much like that of a kindergarten teacher with a headstrong five-year-old.

"I mean; I know I have asked you this before, but I'll try again. My question is this. Who, just exactly, and we must be exact about these things you know, for history sake, who exactly, again, do we think that we are?"

"What do you mean?" responded the scholar.

"I mean, *who exactly do we think that we are?* You say that I have been in on this from the beginning, and I do have some memories that would tend to confirm that. So I guess I can't exactly put all the responsibility on you, but who *do* we think we are, that we can just deal whatever cards seem right to us. Then we wake up in the cave with a bit of a buzz on. What about those who don't?

"As an example, just before the lights went out I killed a man. Well, he was still alive when I went out, but he was dead, as sure as I can be. He will suffer terribly for hours or, if he has no luck, a few days, and then he will die. We on the other hand, will walk out of the cave as if nothing ever happened. When does he walk out of the cave? To me, his lights go out and they stay out, while you and I play God. Who, I repeat, *exactly* do we think that we are?

"Then again, I don't know why I asked that, when I already know the answer. You are going to tell me that in a generation or five in one time line or another that *a family* has or will disappear. Now I know you will tell me that they, in truth, never existed and thus felt no pain. Well I can tell you that their would-be ancestor felt pain. He felt a lot of pain."

Rodgers sat looking into the fire, but the former agent had said his piece, and silence filled the cave of the Paha Sapa. Behind the two at the fire, there was a small movement, and the historian looked off in the direction of the sleeping man and woman. After a moment, his eyes drifted back to stare into the fire.

"The man that you killed was Capt. Owen Hale of the 7th Cavalry. In the time line of your current memories, *Omicron*, he was back east on recruiting duty when his outfit, under George Custer, marched to the Little Big Horn.

"Those closest to him said he mourned not being with his regiment in that final battle. From that time forward, he sought a place with his fallen friends.

"At the battle with the Nez Perce at the Bear Paw, Hale led a charge at the Nez Perce entrenchments. As the 7th began to move their horses forward, he was heard to say, 'My God, do I really have to go out and get killed in such cold weather?'"

The historian had not looked up from the fire.

"What happened to him?" asked Banyon.

"He was shot from his horse at the beginning of the charge. He was the first man to die."

"Then what you're saying is that the only *additional* suffering involved here is my own."

The bare statement of fact was not posed as a question, but its effect left both men silent for several minutes.

"Actually," started the historian, "you are the one who will suffer the least if you can see it from a correct perspective."

Banyon's return stare was not blank now, neither was there a sense of comedy in his undisguised contempt for the scholar's last statement.

"I felt the knife in him, Rodgers, this is not new to me. Even with today's technology he would not survive for more than a few days. How can you say that to me? Is it okay that I killed the man just because he was going to die anyway? That type of logic would give us license to kill the world."

Rodgers held up a hand to settle the grieving younger man. "I am not telling you that it is okay. I'm just telling you that you need not suffer for something that did, but may not happen."

"What do you mean?" queried Banyon.

"Simply because you have the option of seeing that it doesn't happen that way next time."

"Next time?"

"Well, this time, really," responded Rodgers.

The younger man was up on his elbow and staring at the historian. "Are you saying that we are trying again?"

"That's exactly what I'm saying."

"But why? It didn't work! We got ourselves killed and there was no progress whatsoever! I mean, you said that we 'almost won,' but that wasn't very close in my book . . ."

Rodgers interrupted him mid-sentence and though, the recovering man reflected, the historian did not express the contempt for the agent's objections that he had in his previous journey through the cave, he did see a deep weariness that was not there before.

"We did almost win, regardless of your perspective. In fact, we came so close that we could almost touch it. Just things changed too fast, too unexpectedly, and the outcome could not have been predicted."

Now it was Banyon's turn to interrupt. "By outcome you mean my death?"

"No, not at all, in fact, your death was the very least consequence of all that happened there."

Banyon was angry now and, strength failing him, he lashed out with words as his weapons. "Maybe to you my death means nothing, but to me it's pretty important. In fact, since the very beginning it has seemed to me that I was the expendable one!"

The scholar was silent for a moment after this outburst. Then he rose and walked to the shelf of books in the wall of the cave.

"Do you remember the end of the time line that we read here before?"

The former agent could feel a cold dread beginning to cover him.

"Yes, yes, I remember. I agree that something must be done, but I refuse to believe that going back and getting ourselves killed again on the Yellowstone River is going to solve that problem."

Rodgers was back, sitting on the buffalo robe. "Then that would make you wrong. We have indeed already solved that problem."

The younger man's chin rose again at the remark. "What do you mean? You said that we almost won. Is that what you were talking about? That we made things better? That we somehow changed the future by what we've done and saved ourselves in doing so?"

Rodgers stared back intensely. "No, I did not mean that we saved ourselves. I did mean that what we have done has changed the future. We are no longer under threat of a nuclear war started by terrorists. That world was forever changed by what we did. But in doing so, we most certainly did not save ourselves. In fact, if I knew how to get back to where we were without changing the good that we have accomplished, I would do so."

Banyon felt a cold chill run up his back as the scholar opened to the middle section of the volume and began to read.

"On the twenty fourth of February 1877, Col. Nelson Miles, commander of the 2nd Cavalry at the confluence of the Tongue and Yellowstone rivers, was taken by force by the hostiles under Chief Crazy Horse, camped under the pretense of surrender at the future Fort Keogh. In the flight following his capture, Miles was killed by the hostiles."

Rodgers paused for effect, looking at the now fully alert Banyon. The news of Nelson Miles' death was new, but not totally surprising to the former agent.

"The pure volume of lead pouring at us during the fight was un-survivable. It's not that big a surprise."

As he continued his review of the fight and the probable events after his own death, Rodgers was skipping forward in the volume in his hands.

Interrupting the former agent, he began to read again. "National outrage over the treacherous death of Col. Nelson Miles galvanized the resolve of the United States Congress against the Western tribes. Leading the war advocates was General William Tecumseh Sherman, commanding General of the Army and uncle to the widow of the gallant Miles.

"The general's outrage over the death of this officer was quoted in every major newspaper in the nation. 'We have tried every friendly overture to appease and make peace with these people, and to no avail. To have so treacherously taken and killed Nelson, right after a council of peace, constitutes the vilest betrayal. I would not ask any American to accept an appointment to a peace council with these animals. Neither would I believe, on the firmest assurances from their leaders, that any such council would be safe from their depredation even under a flag of truce' . . ."

Banyon was sitting upright, straight as a post as the scholar finished the last of the paragraph.

"But that's not at all what happened! It was they who were treacherous with us, it was the army with their scouts, all under the command of Nelson Miles who attempted . . ." the younger man's tirade paused for just a moment, "and then succeeded in killing us. If Miles was killed in the fight, there was no one to blame but themselves!"

The outrage slowed and then stopped as he met the eyes of the historian who was looking at him with a look of utmost sympathy.

"Do you remember what I said before you left *Omicron*? The victors write history and in this case, there was absolutely no one on our side of the fence who lived to tell the story. They wrote what they chose to write, knowing that there was no one to contradict."

"But wait just a minute, there were survivors. You said that Leonard survived. Why didn't he? . . ."

"First of all, Leonard was unconscious almost from the first of the fight. Second, Leonard, for all his English skill, was still a part of the hostile faction. One of the kidnappers, we would say. He would be the last one listened to if there were anyone listening, which I assure you there was not."

Rodgers began to read again. "Responding to the immense public outcry over the treacherous murder of Col. Nelson Miles, the secretary of war, under direct authorization from the President and the support of Congress, ordered General Sherman to take whatever steps necessary to bring the Sioux to heel.

"Forces under the command of the best and most experienced officers in the country were immediately transferred to the department of the Platte under the immediate command of General George Crook.

"Troops formerly stationed in the east or the south were brought in large numbers up the Missouri to the Yellowstone to garrison and strengthen the new Fort Peck (formerly destroyed by spring flooding), Fort Abraham Lincoln, Fort Bernhold, and the newly funded Forts Keogh and Custer.

"The United States Congress unilaterally declared the Sioux in a state of war against the United States, in direct violation of the Fort Laramie treaty, and declared that treaty null and void. The absolution of the Fort Laramie treaty nullified all legal relations between the Lakota and the United States and all former treaty lands and reserves forfeit.

"Chiefs Red Cloud and Spotted Tail, titular head of the reservation Sioux, were imprisoned, along with all principal leaders of the reservation Indians. Stripped of their leaders, the reservation Sioux began to attempt escape toward the North Country, where they hoped to find help from the bands still eluding the troops in the Powder River range.

"With stunning effectiveness, the troops of the combined cavalry and infantry of the west hunted these groups like animals and destroyed them summarily. Before the end of June 1877, over half of the Lakota people had escaped to Canada. The remainder were destroyed or taken by the United States Army as prisoners of war.

"By September 1877, over eight thousand Lakota refugees were reported to be on the Canadian side of the Milk River. On the opposite bank waited over twenty thousand heavily armed U.S. troops under the direct command of William Tecumseh Sherman.

"On September 18, a lone assailant, reported to be a Lakota sharpshooter under direct orders from the combined Lakota leadership in exile, assassinated General Sherman while he was inspecting the troops.

"The President of the United States, on receipt of the news of the death of America's most famous general, ordered the United States armies under General Philip Sheridan to attack the hostile Sioux forces over the Canadian border.

"As per their long-standing promises to the Lakota refugees, the combined forces of the Canadian Mounted Police opposed the initial invasion as a direct assault on the borders of Canada. In the ensuing battle the vastly outnumbered Canadian troops and their Sioux allies were decimated by the United States army.

"On October 1, 1877, Britain declared war on the United States and began landing troops in large numbers on the east coast of Canada. The war itself was short lived, but bloody, leaving lasting bitterness on both sides.*2*"During the ensuing thirty years, relations between the former combatants were cold. During the First World War, the United States retreated stoically into isolationism. Britain and her allies in Europe, without supplies and equipment from America, fought Germany and her allies to an unsteady armistice. After over ten years of bloody slaughter, Great Britain and her allies stood exhausted against the growing power of the Nazis in postwar Germany.

"On April 17, 1942, Great Britain, under the onslaught of the combined axis powers and without material aid from the United States, surrendered as all resistance across Europe ceased . . ."*3*

Rodgers laid the book across his lap and looked at Banyon. "How much further do you want me to read?"

The former agent stared disconsolately at the fire. "We shouldn't have gone back."

Rodgers was quick to respond, "There was no choice, it had to be tried. Now we must try again."

Banyon searched the unflinching features of the historian. There was something different in the face, something that he hadn't noticed before. It was a look that he remembered from someplace else, a place that hung on the edge of memory, on the edge of reality. It was the look of despair!!!

---

2 Omega Line aborted
3 Ibid

Chapter 9

Cast them into hopeless situations and they will be preserved; have them penetrate fatal terrain and they will live. Only after the masses have penetrated dangerous terrain will they be able to craft victory out of defeat.

Sun Tzu
The Art of War

The Hanging Woman, subsequent penetration
January 1877
Omega Line

Nine days later, they entered the camp on the Tongue.

Banyon could see that as before the people were preparing to move. In the distance, a column of soldiers was approaching a lower camp, and the sound of gunfire began to fill the primordial wilderness as the warriors formed a line against the whites to give the innocents a chance to move toward Crazy Horse.

The sound of gunfire continued throughout the day as the terrified squaws herded their animals and children up the river toward the looming bluffs. The talk in camp was hushed, and centered on the future of the people and the strange white men that had been brought into camp by their Strange One.

After the surrender, as the initial meeting of the army officers and the Lakota head men began to lose some of its stiffness, Banyon saw Capt. Hale standing behind Nelson Miles, talking with a Lieutenant Baldwin. The former agent got up and moved himself to within a couple yards of the officer and waited for a lull in the conversation.

The three men felt the press of the squaw man watching them and soon turned to appraise him.

The former agent offered his hand in introduction. "You are Capt. Owen Hale?" he asked.

He had expected the perplexed look on the face of the officer. What he did not expect, however, was the look of concern on the face of Hergin Rodgers, who now stood beside them, his hand on the former agent's shoulder.

During the following month, the interpreter was seen frequently in the company of the young officer and his friend, Lt. Baldwin.

Through their association, Hale and Baldwin came to know Crazy Horse, and friendship among the group became the talk of the camp.

Nelson Miles, aware of the budding friendship, encouraged his junior officers, stating flatly, "There needs to be a better understanding between us and the hostiles and, if possible, the beginning of trust."

*

Back at his office, Hergin Rodgers sat at his computer and went online:

United States Army personnel 1870-1880.

"Search: Capt. Owen Hale, 7th Cavalry," he muttered as he typed.

The screen went blank for a moment, then blossomed with information.

Capt. Owen Hale

Born July 23, 1843, in Troy, NY

Father: Zenas Hanmer Perley Hale

Mother: Maria Van Vorhis

Died: Feb 25,1877 (killed in action, confluence of Yellowstone and Tongue Rivers Sioux Wars)

Rodgers looked curiously at the maiden name of Hale's mother. It seemed he remembered a Van Vorhis family that was prominent in the history of New York.

If so, we're in luck, thought Rodgers.

The majority of the politically or socially well placed was literate and above that, seemed quite prolific in the keeping of journals to chronicle their lives.

State Historical Archives New York
      Search . . . Maria Van Vorhis
      Searching . . . Journal: <u>1838-1842</u>, <u>1843-1885</u>

Rodgers clicked on the 1843-1885.

As the computer was pulling up the text, the historian pondered his findings. The time period of the last journal was very long, over forty years, to be exact. It would have big gaps in the time line, but there would hopefully be something they could use, something unknowable that could be made known.

Rodgers scrolled through the text of the early adolescence of the future mother of the young Captain. Nothing of note caught his attention.

Marriage: 1830

Birth of fifth son: Owen, 1843.

The storms of the black South Dakota night rolled and broke against the old brick building as time moved through the middle 1800's, paused in a little hamlet in up state New York, and stopped...

When it moved again... there was hope!

**

Hale and his friend, Lt. Baldwin, sat one especially cold evening in the lodge of the interpreter, along with Crazy Horse and Smiles at the People.

There had been a lull in the conversation, and Hale poked at the embers at the edge of the smoky fire.

"I still don't understand how you know all that you know. I mean it's interesting, but I still think you are just guessing at some of it."

Banyon, now called Shoots Straight by everyone in camp, feigned a chuckle. His relationship with the officer was begun with intent. The intent had to do with a plan that had been forming since his last visit to the cave. Yet it had become more. Capt. Hale was described historically as a favorite of the regiment, and Shoots Straight was not long in discovering why. The young officer was taller than the average, standing just over six feet tall and powerfully built. It was his personality, however, that endeared him to his fellow officers and the men. Although very serious in his demeanor while involved in official functions, and known in the regiment for his extreme courage under fire, off duty or on patrol with his own men, the Captain kept everyone around him in a state of extreme good humor. The man had a strong baritone voice that he was not hesitant to use in the performance of any tune that came to mind. The lyrics, however, were often strictly his own and given toward the ridiculous and irreverent.

On a scouting patrol north of the Yellowstone, Shoots Straight had been invited to join Hale and his immediate command on a cold February morning.

As they pulled out of earshot of the cantonment, Hale, as if on cue, broke into his finest voice.

> *I left my girl, my girl I left*
> *Turned on my heel to flee*
> *I thought that I would find*
> *Escape in the U.S. Cavalry*

His command, to the man, joined with him in the chorus as husky male voices filled and echoed throughout the deserted plains of the northern Yellowstone.

> *Cavalry! Cavalry!*
> *I thought that I would find*
> *Escape in the U.S. Cavalry.*
> *I left the bank, the bank I left*
> *Before they cornered me-e.*
> *The judge said*

I could find my death,
in the U.S. Cavalry.
Cavalry! Cavalry!
He said I'd go to hell and back
In the U.S. Cavalry.

It was no surprise to the interpreter that Hale was a favorite to all who knew him and, in spite of his plans; he found it very hard not to feel the same.

Hale poked at the embers again and reached behind him to grab another couple sticks of wood and place them on the fire.

"In fact," he grinned, "I think that you old boys are just pullin' my leg with what you've learned from the other men."

Banyon whistled quietly the little cavalry ditty they had enjoyed on patrol.

"Well," he said, "what if I could tell you something that only you or your closest family could know, then would you start to believe me?"

Hales, obviously enjoying the ongoing joke, chuckled the affirmative and turned to smile at Lt. Baldwin to his left. Turning back, his eyes glittered with amusement and good humor.

"What did you have in mind?"

"Oh," the interpreter said, as he drew in a deep breath, "how about if I told you that at age ten, you fell out of a tree and broke that leg," pointing to the left leg of the officer.

Hales looked startled, but not for long.

"No, that won't do. I think I've told that story to the boys on patrol a time or two. You'd have to do better than that."

Shoots Straight was warming to his task and even had a moment to reflect that, for the first time in a great long while, he was genuinely enjoying himself.

"Well," drawled the former agent, "What if I told you that the leg was set by Dr. O.B. Jenkins, whose office was on 2nd Avenue, just above the city building."

Hales was still smiling, but a bit of the fluff had come out of his demeanor.

149

"That's pretty good," mumbled the officer as he turned again to smile at Lt. Baldwin, who sat staring at the scene before him.

"Yeah, that's real good, but I might have said somethin' like that on a night that I was dippin' a little too much into the punch. Yeah, I could have said that."

The interpreter's face was a bit serious for the taste of the officer now, but he was intrigued and waited anxiously for the interpreter to up the ante.

Banyon was indeed giving the appearance of being a lot more serious now, but inside he was delighted at the course of events. "Well," started the agent, "then I guess you wouldn't be impressed if I told you I also know that your father was the one who was first on the scene to help you, or that he called you a little fool as he knelt beside you."

Hale was not smiling now, but he was shaking his head. He was still not buying what the agent and his group were selling.

"Or that your mother, unbeknownst to you, was watching from the house, and she saw you fall from the tree while you were trying to find a place to balance a pie you had just stolen from the neighbor lady's window sill. The pie stayed stuck in the crotch of the branch after you fell while trying to save it from falling. Only you and your mother, *who never told you* of her knowledge of the accident, ever knew."

The officer stared without expression at the interpreter.

"Or, that your song is not just irreverent lyrics. That on July 3, 1859, you and two of your friends, on a prank, but nevertheless in fact, stuck up the Troy Commerce Bank at gunpoint, removing $136.45 from the premises.

"Neither your father, nor anyone else in your neighborhood or family ever knew about that hold up. Only your mother knew, and she brought you by night to the local judge who was her cousin, Orrin J. Van Vorhis, to return the money and look for a way to save you and the family name.

"The solution was simple. The money was returned, and the next day you and your erstwhile companions in crime left to enlist in the army."

The interpreter began to sing in a low, untrained, but mirth-filled voice.

> *I left my home, my home I left*
> *Before they cornered me-e,*
> *The judge said I could find my*
> *Death in the U.S. Cavalry.*

Hale jumped into the chorus with his usual lusty baritone.

> *It looks like I'll be*
> *found at last,*
> *In the U.S. Cavalry.*

Banyon slapped the officer on the knee in a manner that firmly communicated this information was not to be used against him, and he could be certain of the friendship, and silence, of the interpreter, Shoots Straight.

The officer seemed almost eager now as he returned the slap on the knee and looked firmly into the eyes of the former agent. "We're not going to go into the subject of the girl now, are we?"

The interpreter began to sing again.

> *I left my girl my girl I left*
> *Her name was Carrie Lee*
> *I left her so to find a life,*
> *In the U.S. Cavalry . . .*

The former agent stopped amid the rolling laughter and turned purposefully toward the other officer.

"Now, Lt. Baldwin, lets talk about you."

The conversations went well into the night and many nights that followed.

As the junior officers were leaving the first night, the somewhat confused Baldwin expressed concern that they were out past military curfew.

"It's all right, Lieutenant, there is time, but just barely. *Turn to your left and you will be O.K.!*" It became a tradition between them each night as the young officers took their leave.

"It's all right, Lieutenant . . . *turn to your left . . .*"

***

Early one afternoon, Banyon saw a group of women passing by his lodge and recognized among them the girl, Buffalo Calf Road. She stood out among the other women as one who held her head high and carried herself as one with a purpose.

Later that afternoon, he turned in time to see Buffalo Calf Road disappearing into the trees. As soon as he could, he followed her path toward the river. He found her sitting on a fallen log staring out at the half-frozen water. She looked up quickly, obviously startled by his presence there. Shoots Straight stood awkwardly for a moment, not sure what to say.

"I thought you might need some help," he said lamely.

She smiled at his attempt, and motioned for him to sit next to her. He hesitantly sat on the fallen tree as far as possible away from Buffalo Calf Road.

Her presence made him *confused*, and he fought to push back the thoughts that seemed to flood in and smother his mind whenever he was near her. He focused hard on this reality, this moment, and tried to block out all others. He looked up and realized she was studying him, a look of concern in her beautiful eyes as she spoke. "You must learn to control your thoughts, to focus. *That is the only thing that will save you!*"

Banyon was shocked at the words. How could she know of the terrible confusion that threatened to overtake him? As his thoughts began to swirl again, he felt her hands on his shoulders. "*Look at me, Dan. Focus on my eyes.*"

The agent's eyes found hers and locked. The world swirled away from him, but her eyes were an anchor in the confusion, the one thing that remained steady. Through the storm of confusion, he heard snatches of her voice, and he clung to them. They were words of comfort, of reassurance, and they were somehow already familiar to him. The swirling cloud in his mind slowed and then dissipated. He was again aware of the river beside them and the trees standing over them. He realized he was cold and that her hands were no longer upon his shoulders. He looked into her eyes and saw relief within their depths.

"Thank you," he said uncertainly, embarrassed now at losing his control. Her smile was reassuring as she stood, looking at him with tear filled eyes. Eyes that he knew had brought him to this place; had made him who he was.

"You are not ready yet she said looking questioningly into the very depths of his soul. The time is soon here!

The young woman turned on her heel and walked purposefully away from the interpreter. "You must prepare yourself ", he heard her say as she disappeared into the trees.

Banyon was left alone to wonder at what had just happened. He held to the feeling now in his heart that he remembered from long ago. It was the feeling of coming home.

****

On the night of The 25th of February, after the meeting with the government negotiators, over two hundred Crow scouts backed by the mounted troops of the 2nd cavalry attacked the empty lodge of the interpreter...

After taking Nelson Miles captive, the escaping Shoots Straight, Crazy Horse, and Smiles at the People fled to the trees at the confluence of the Tongue and the Yellowstone.

. . . Suddenly the interpreter Shoots Straight grabbed Crazy Horse and shoved him to the ground. Both could feel the rush of bullets crashing into the trees not five feet beyond them. Both men were scrambling now as Smiles at the People fought to control the terrified horses.

Shoots Straight and Crazy Horse reached the chaos around

153

Smiles at the People at the same moment, each grabbing for a horse. Banyon finding his horse almost beyond control reached for the rifle butt facing toward him. The horse suddenly bolted to the left as another roar of rifles poured into the tangle of horses and riders. The former agent, *as he expected,* could feel the rifle come loose in his hands as he fell hard to the ground. To his left, he could see Smiles at the People as he fell awkwardly under the feet of the horse he was trying to control. The horse had been hit, and its screams pierced the night as it went to its knees, fought again to rise, and then shuddered as it collapsed suddenly onto the frozen earth.

Banyon let go the reins of the horse he was holding and scrambled to the far side of the fallen horse, landing on the inert form of Smiles at the People. He *understood* the lack of movement he felt in his friend as he tumbled behind the still quivering horse and took comfort in it.

He was prepared then for the fury of the rifle fire that now bore frantically into the downed cavalry mount. Pieces of flesh ripped from the carcass flew at the two men, stopping all attempts at return fire. To his right, he could feel, rather than see, Crazy Horse. He had escaped into the trees, dragging Nelson Miles, and had found at least temporary respite from the fusillade of bullets that bore relentlessly into his companions behind the dead animal.

In the darkness, the troops could not be certain of their targets, but the scream of the dying horse and the rush of bodies around it as it fell had provided a focus. Throwing themselves haphazardly into the trees before the river, the 7th, directed by Captain Hale, poured in a withering fire.

Shoots Straight *knew* they would not die then, if they only kept their wits and *did not change* a *thing*. With the unrelenting eruption of rifles to his front, there was no opportunity, *he knew*, to mount a defense.

He tried to roll to the side, following the exact pattern that gave him control. The ground instantly shredded in front of him by the devastating fire.

Banyon had seen men pinned down like this before, in war, and knew their chances were very slim if something didn't change. Yet *he knew* that he would survive, if even for just a moment more. The carcass of the horse was now moving from the sheer accumulated force of the deadly lead wall that now encompassed them.

He yelled in pain as a bullet struck him in the shoulder. Grasping for the injured appendage, he felt the form of the bullet where it had struck *and knew* that the shell had passed right through the body of the horse and struck him with its dying momentum. He remembered that the total time since the horse had fallen was not more than a minute or two, but in that time the sheer savagery of the force thrown at them had made him hope that his memories were correct.

For reasons *well understood* to the fallen fighter, there was a slight lull in the firing, allowing him to calmly lever a shell into the Winchester and fire over the top of the prostrate horse.

The return fire was as expected. Every gun had fired at once at the flash of his rifle. Then for the briefest moment, there was silence as he levered another shell and prepared for his next move . . .

He was not surprised at a thought being brought to the forefront in his mind. Once again, the memory of the jamming rifles was written into his mind. Just hedging their bets, thought the former agent. But it was not necessary.

There was time to act and act correctly firing over the top of the fallen animal he again was staggered by the pure volume of the returning fire. Rolling to his left as he levered another shell, he fired again, almost before the sound of his first shot had left his ringing ears. Silence, as expected, was the only response.

That was it then, he thought as he rolled back to his right and levered another shell. They were firing, as expected, as a group on signal from an officer. The specifics of the situation were all too familiar to the former agent. To the rear of the troops, he could hear the unmistakable drum of running horses coming from the camp. He *knew* whom these would be, and wasn't at all surprised by the arrival of the reinforcements. He knew from the sound of the advancing hooves that his life would last only minutes if his plan did not work.

The former agent ripped off his jacket and looked quickly to his right, where he saw the fallen form of Nelson Miles covered by Crazy Horse. The Oglala fighter was once again trying to protect whatever he had seen of value in the bellicose colonel. The former agent hoped fervently that the warriors' timing would fit the scene he had previously described to Capt. Hale.

Banyon rolled catlike to his right and threw the jacket into the trees. There was a deafening roar as the directed fire of the troops ripped into the jacket and the trees that now held its shredded remnants as he again found the refuge of the fallen horse. He rolled again to the right, grabbing the unconscious form of Smiles at the People and was on his feet running. *Everything had to be the same, right to the fraction of a second or the plan would fail.* He knew the officers' guns would not be single shots, but repeaters, and would be just as effective as a whole army if they caught him in the open.

His lungs roared with exploding rage as he ripped Smiles at the People from the ground in the direction of the trees only to be jerked backward to the ground, landing hard on the packed ice. It still hurt just as badly the second time around! He lifted his free arm just slightly and felt a bullet pass by into the frozen ground.

As he rolled backward in a single movement to the cover of the horse barricade, he looked at the leg of Smiles at the People, lodged firmly beneath the horse. The lead was coming at them like hail as he reached for the leg of his friend and pulled with everything he had. It did not move, as he had known it wouldn't.

Banyon could hear hard ridden horses pulling to an abrupt stop in the trees behind the hidden troops. Looking back to his left, he could discern no sign of Crazy Horse or Miles.

"Run!" screamed the voice of the girl in the trees, "Run now or we are lost!"

There could be no question that the voice was Buffalo Calf Road and further he knew she was right! Looking back to the prone form of Smiles at the People, he noted that the book he had jammed hurriedly into his friend's shirt was still there.

Levering another shell into the chamber, he rolled again to the left, firing as he went, while the roar of answering fire ripped into the foliage. He rolled to the right and sprinted for the cover of the trees. There was still the rifle of the officer, but he also knew where it would come.

His lungs near to bursting, he fought for another step, and turned sharply to the right. The roar of the officer's gun and the feel of the passing bullet were instantaneous, as he fought to keep his balance and gain the third step. Suddenly he felt the hand of Buffalo Calf Road jerk him backwards into the trees, and then he was rolling, thrashing, fighting for his feet and, finding them, turned to face the troops that had charged and were upon them. Then the wall of soldiers was all around him, driving him to the ground. He found his knife and, swinging it under hand . . .

Struck only air…!

There was a sudden break around him as the troopers fell back before the flashing blade.

On a signal from their officer, the blue clad men stepped back two steps toward the trees as their officer, Cap. Owen Hale, stared past the desperate interpreter at the scene of Crazy Horse, with his knife at the throat of Nelson Miles.

"The next move, he dies!" exploded Shoots Straight.

Hale and his troops froze as the interpreter backed slowly away from them toward Crazy Horse.

"I told you that we would be the victims, Captain, and you can see that clearly if you will. I told you that you could save Miles if you could control your men."

Out of the trees came a rush of movement, accompanied by the soul-wrenching yell of Lakota warriors. The men around Hale turned to meet them as a unit. Side arms still holstered, the troops met the oncoming Lakota with their bare hands and were driven back into the trees by a massive onslaught of war clubs and knives. At such close range, the war clubs had effect, and others instantly reinforced the troops from the rear. The advantage was to the charging warriors as fear and confusion turned now to retreat. If there was organization, it was not apparent. Neither side sought to break off the conflict, or retreat.

Banyon could feel that Nelson Miles was unconscious still, and as he helped Crazy Horse to drag him away from the fight, he saw that the Colonel had a bullet hole through his left arm and was bleeding profusely. To his right he could hear the approach of rushing horses and, throwing himself heavily to the ground, he covered the inert body of the officer.

Looking up from that position, he saw directly before him the barrel of a rifle pointing at him, and then . . .

. . .a shot rang out from the left, driving the rifle in a flash of pain from the soldier's hand.

Shoots Straight had only a fraction of a second to turn and see the smoke rising from the rifle of Capt. Owen Hale, and behind it, *a very irreverent smile!*

Lakota fighters were dismounting and handing reins or jaw ropes to Shoots Straight and Crazy Horse. The still unconscious body of Nelson Miles was loaded onto still another horse, and a brave jumped on with him to keep him from falling.

"Stop the bleeding!" Banyon yelled at the brave, "He's no good to us dead."

As the sounds of fighting continued behind them, the small group of warriors and their wounded prisoner crossed the Yellowstone and pointed themselves north.

*****

In the old brick building, the scholar typed again into the text:

. . .*the trip by horseback from the cantonment on the Yellowstone to Fort Peck in inclement weather was twelve days*

158

forced march . . . The original Fort Peck was washed away in spring flooding on the 16th of March 1877. 4

Shoots Straight made a mental note that if the weather did not become more of a factor, they should arrive on the Missouri on or around the ninth of March, a full week before the flood would take out the fort.

Hergin Rodgers knew better than to look at the end of the line before action in the past had ceased. He knew all too well that with almost every action at the point of change, what they had come to call the axial point, the end of the line would change at an exponential rate. Every minuscule difference would send forward ripples into the future. These ripples would be small at first, almost unnoticeable. Yet as they made their way through years and decades beyond, they would have incredible impact. At the end of the line, events would be changing at a rate so fast as to be incomprehensible to the reader, the words becoming more a river of developing knowledge than fixed events and records.

Still, this was not the first time they had gotten past the fight on the Yellowstone. This was the first time, however, that they had done so with Banyon as the lead man. The future was still very dependent on what would happen at almost every footstep at the axial point, but he could not stop himself from looking to the end to discern, if he could, if this path might find them an acceptable future.

The flow would be slower, he knew, as the Crazy Horse group found its way toward Fort Peck. Every action would not necessarily create reaction, and with that there was time to reevaluate.

Rodgers forced the cursor forward to the last chapter. He could see that the ripples were still working themselves through the fabric of time.

---

4 *Lt. Alex Baldwin in command of the 2nd. Made the trip in 10 days after his campaign against Sitting Bull near Ft. Peck Dec. 1876*

The individual lines, as he suspected, were a blur, unreadable. But the chapter subtitles remained stable, sometimes for minutes, and allowed the scholar to ponder their meanings.

German Rule over Europe Comes to a Violent End

Mexico's Fascist Government under Ramona De La Vega Threatens the United States with War Over Border Disputes

Modern Europe Averts War, Unites Under a Common Flag

President Declares that U.S. Constitution Hangs by a Thread

U.S. Courts Declare New Constitution Legal

United Liberation Forces Declare Themselves Free and Independent Nation

Civil War between East and West Drags to a Standstill

U.S. Guerrilla Movement Declares Western United States Secured

United States Reaffirms Original Constitution as the Law of the Land

Invading Forces Driven from Continental North America

Nuclear Holocaust Destroys Modern Europe

World War Three Ends the Rule of Man as a Species

The change stopped at the last entry and seemed to waver. Hergin Rodgers turned the text hesitantly.

As he moved backward, the print seemed to take on substance and grow more stable...

North of the Yellowstone
February 1877
Omega Line

On the morning of the first day after the escape from the cantonment, Banyon was amazed at what had transpired. Literally the entire band had broken camp during the night and had reformed, in motion, as the group pointed inexorably toward the north.

The ground was covered with snow and ice to a degree that the former agent would have said travel off modern paved roads was impossible. Yet there they were, moving with what was incredible speed across the snowy plains.

The former agent had been through the area in another time and had always thought of it as a wasteland, inhabited by only the smallest population of die-hard ranchers and thousands, maybe millions, of cattle. It had always been his impression that the whole of it was not worth fighting for and wondered that the Indians had valued it so highly as to risk certain defeat to attempt to save it.

The Black Hills; now he had always understood the attraction there. The endless beauty of the tree filled mountains and the luxurious grasslands caught and held the imagination of most who visited there. Neither had he ever thought, despite the views of the romantics and skeptics in the world of history, that the Lakota had not understood the value of the hills. As they saw the approaching bad road of the whites, which for a hundred years had haunted their dreams and forced changes in the lives of the people, they had seen that the hills would have tremendous value, or at least bargaining power. He had read once that twenty-two percent of all the gold on reserve in Fort Knox had come from the

Black Hills, over 32 billion dollars in *Omicron* 20th century value. Yes, they had to have known, or at least suspected, that the hills, to quote Red Cloud, were their bank, their savings against an uncertain future.

This northern country, however, he had never understood. After the second day, he began to understand *very clearly*! Since he had come through the cave, he had several times been involved in small buffalo hunts. The numbers had been few, and the net effect seemingly unimportant.

As they moved north, however, he began to see first a few, then a great number, of the shaggy herds. Twenty merged into hundreds, hundreds into thousands, and thousands into a solid mass of moving, breathing bedlam.

In the beginning, the small herds had fled before the Lakota band as it threw itself into the North Country. As they grew in numbers, and as the snows of the great storm raged around them, they no longer ran. The band soon found it impossible unable to continue in a straight path because of the great number of buffalo amassed before them. In all his travels, Banyon could not remember a single sight to compare with the enormity of the mighty herd.

Then came the memories once again, seeping at first from that great well of knowledge that gave him direction. The words then rushed in a flood, finally settling to a smooth, understandable path.

The year 1877; to the best guess of those who afterwards studied the extermination; was the last year that sufficient buffalo existed on the northern plains to allow the future survival of the western tribes.

With the surrender of the hostile Oglala to the south, and the retreat of the Hunkpapa to the north, the entire northern range was left open to the teams of white hunters.

Although a remnant of the herd still existed at the end of 1878, there were insufficient numbers to feed the future needs of the northern tribes. Even if the killing by the whites had been stopped after that fateful year, the number remaining, were inadequate. Given the historical reality of the 1877-78 slaughter, there would be fewer buffalo every succeeding year, effectively sealing the fate of the hunter nations.[5]

That was it then, thought the former agent that was the reason the cave had opened where it did. It wasn't the fight on the Hanging Woman so much as it was the fight to save the buffalo that would determine a viable future. The agent thought back to the hunger that stalked the homes of the Lakota in his youth. Totally dependent on the good will or welfare of the whites, the modern remnants of the fighting Lakota were helpless without the buffalo. They were helpless to save themselves, and powerless to save their culture.

As the procession of travois-laden horses headed north through the snowy hills, Banyon estimated that there must be over fifteen hundred people in movement. Taking into account the Cheyenne, that number could be off by over five hundred souls, he had guessed. Still, the band moved with a singular fluidity beside the northern-moving herd.

The temperature was just below freezing, but the children over toddler stage raced back and forth between their mothers' horse-drawn travois as if they were neighborhood children in a modern suburb visiting next door. Next door, however, was moving – moving at a pace that required the children afoot to have to run to keep up. Most of the older children and the toddler-age infants sat mounted on family horses and exhibited the greatest sense of satisfaction and even pleasure that he had ever seen in children of their age.

When he had first been made aware that the women and children had escaped from the camp across from the cantonment, he had questioned Crazy Horse about the wisdom of bringing along the helpless ones on so dangerous a path.

---

5 *This was also the timing of the first introduction of the first Texas cattle herds to the northern plains bringing Brucillosis or contagious abortion that was spread to the buffalo herds, in Omicron!*

The Lakota headman seemed perplexed by the question and immediately responded, "If we left the defenseless ones in the hands of our enemies to save ourselves, we would not be warriors."

"Yes," Banyon had responded, "but do you doubt that the army will be after us in the very moment they can get organized and break camp?"

Crazy Horse shook his head. Only a fool would doubt the probability of that action and the Lakota headman was not a fool.

"They will not be hindered by women and children and household goods when they take the trail. They will move faster, and in a twelve-day march they will catch us long before we reach Fort Peck."

The Lakota fighter nodded his head in the affirmative.

The interpreter Shoots Straight was still confused. "Why, then, are we doing this difficult thing?"

Crazy Horse turned on his pony and looked steadily at the interpreter. "The future, you have said, is changing. At the end of this, there may be the black road of the white man still before us. But there also may be that which we seek, the Good Red Road of our fathers. Should we find it, our families will be with us."

Banyon could see that the warrior was growing weary of his questions but tried one last time to make his point. "And if the army finds us before the helpless ones can escape, what then?"

"Then many will die."

"Yes, I know that what you say is true," Shoots Straight started.

Crazy Horse interrupted, "They are all already dead, as you have shown me. I have seen them dead on the field at the Hanging Woman with these two eyes. I will not be without them again. What path we will take, we will go down together."

There was silence for a minute; then the famous fighter finished his thought. "You whites, you fight for many things, for power over other men, for land, and for the things that the land can give you. We fight for only one thing. We fight for our families and for the right to prove ourselves men. Nothing else is more important to us.

"If we do these things, then we are true human beings. If we run and hide to save our lives, then those lives are not worth living. A man without his family is not a man, only the illusion of manhood can be found in him. His life is without purpose and, when he returns home from this dream, he will see those who wait will turn their heads from him in shame. Shoots Straight, my friend," mumbled the warrior, "tell me, when you can, about your family."

Never in his life had the former agent felt as unimportant as he felt at that moment.

The Lakota headman did not press him for an answer, and the former agent knew that somehow, he already knew there could be none.

Off to the west, however, he could not help noticing the girl, Buffalo Calf Road, riding a somewhat spirited dun mare. One more thing he noticed, she was watching him.

When camp was made that night, Banyon was surprised to see that a lodge had been set up for him next to that of Crazy Horse and his wife, Black Shawl.

As he entered that evening, he thought the furnishings looked familiar. It seemed, at least on preliminary inspection, that the interior strongly resembled the lodge of Buffalo Calf Road that they had hidden in the evening before. In fact, as the former agent examined the interior more closely, he became certain that was the case.

"Why would the girl abandon her lodge for me?" asked the interpreter out loud. Still, that wasn't the main question he had about the girl. There was something about her that nagged at him incessantly. "She is beautiful," he heard himself say out loud.

Yea, sure, there is that, his thoughts redirected, but it was something more. Something he thought had to do with the changing of lines. Of that he felt certain. But still there was more

165

yet. She reminded him of someone. Someone back in *Omicron*, but with his most thorough review, he could not place her there.

As the camp quieted in the oncoming night, Banyon sat thinking about the girl and the feelings that she brought to him. What was it Rodgers had said in the cave, that he was surprised he didn't remember her? Did he really say that, or was it just a product of his newly rewritten mind?

When she had revived in the cave, she had sat by the fire with them for a long time. He had tried to talk to her but had experienced a strange physical reaction every time he addressed her. The only way to describe it, he had thought later, was deep profound confusion, followed by a lapse in the ability to deal with his surroundings.

Rodgers had noticed the reaction and seemed genuinely concerned. Still, he did not ask the girl to leave, although when she went to speak, he cautioned her with a hand signal. "He may not be ready yet," he had said to the girl.

Ready for what...? The former agent pondered in the lodge.

At the time, he believed that the historian was referring to his difficulties in regaining his thought process after his "death." Now he was not so sure. She always seemed to trigger the confusion. But still, by the river it was she who was able to bring him out of that lapse, to bring him back to reality. Banyon pondered the phenomena that she was both the cause and the solution to his lapses into confusion, which filled his mind with darkness.

Shoots Straight believed that the camp was asleep now, and so was surprised when he heard a scratching at the door.

It was Crazy Horse, with the girl. It was obvious she had been crying, and the former agent immediately moved to make her comfortable in the hopes of soothing her problem, whatever it was.

Crazy Horse refused to sit, seeming agitated at the events that had preceded their coming to the lodge. "This woman," the warrior paused, trying to gather his own thoughts. "This woman, who I have known for all her life, who has never had a man to my knowledge or to the knowledge of the people, this woman says that she is, and always has been, your wife!"

Chapter 10

Fortune may have yet a better success in reserve for you,
and they who lose today may win tomorrow.
Miguel De Cervantes,
Don Quixote (1547-1616)

The confluence of the Tongue and Yellowstone
1877
Omega line

When Smiles at the People came to, he was lying in freshly fallen snow. There was a wicked pain in his right shoulder and a pervasive fog that hounded his pounding head. He could see that his leg was held fast under the body of the dead horse. He felt crusty all over and was not surprised to come to the understanding that he was covered with blood. Trying to look at the whole scene, he did not have to ponder long on the why's of him being there alone. The scene was one of ghastly horror, looking from the outside in. The horse was not only dead, but was shot, literally, to pieces. It was hard to recognize any feature of the animal without focus. Smiles at the People could not guess why such an awesome quantity of lead had been poured into the dead animal, but he had no question that it had to have been for a very important reason. He began working his leg under the carcass and found that he could, by pushing on the horse with his good arm, gain a little here and there. Finally, he felt the leg slip from underneath the grisly remnants. The former inmate scooted a few yards away while he got oriented.

There was a bullet wound in his right shoulder that appeared to have entered from below, and passed out the top of his

168

shoulder. He had to assume that the bullet had struck him as he was lying on the ground. He could not judge which of the blood at the site was his and what was of the horse, or perhaps some other entity not known to him. He did know that he would be correct in saying he had lost a great deal of blood. His leg, however, seemed to be serviceable, and on his second attempt he was able to get to his feet.

From where he stood, he could see where the signs of the camp should have been. It was morning, and there should have been smoke in the air from over two hundred campfires. There should also have been the sounds of children playing. He had noticed, on other mornings that even at a distance the cumulative sounds of happiness carried as the people prepared for a new day.

But there was nothing. Not a human sound met the ear. Looking across the Tongue to the soldier's cantonment, Smiles at the People could not make out any movement whatsoever.

Only the pounding in his head gave him any indication of what had caused his unconsciousness. He found himself fantasizing of Tylenol for a moment. Other than dizziness, however, and the shoulder wound, he seemed to be all right.

Feeling beneath his shirt, he discovered the book that he immediately recognized from the many nights in the lodge of Shoots Straight. He found, in addition to the book, a short note in Banyon's distinctly rigid handwriting.

He studied it for a moment. The first part made sense, telling him to pursue the original plan. That meant he would have to start toward the Nez Perce before very long. If only his head would stop pounding. The second part did not make sense, however, and he studied it over and over, wondering at its implications.

"Do not kill the general. No matter what the circumstances may seem to warrant, do not kill him!"

Smiles at the People looked at the fallen horse for anything he might be able to use. There were saddlebags and tack that might be useful but, on closer examination, there was nothing left of value. Sharpfish stared at the saddle on the former cavalry mount and guessed there were not less than thirty holes in the seat.

In the saddlebags were many items that could have been of value, but they also were chewed, as if in a giant machine. Nothing here would serve him, he concluded, and started walking slowly toward the camp.

The camp itself showed signs of being left in a hurry. Several lodges were still standing. Smiles at the People stood for a few minutes in front of the lodge they had been in when they first learned of the impending attack. The buffalo skin covering reminded him of the riddled horse back at the river.

He walked back to the lodge that had been his own for the past month and a half and looked inside.

Nothing had been disturbed. It was in that moment he realized that whatever had happened while he had been unconscious, the groups involved had moved from the area quickly with no intent to return. The families of the Lakota and their Cheyenne allies had gathered up their every belonging and had left, taking no notice in the night of their neighbor, or the absence of any one individual.

The army also seemed to have not returned to the camp after the initial attack or, Smiles at the People had no doubt, all of his possessions would have been forfeit to the Crow scouts and souvenir hunters from among the troops.

He entered the lodge and sat on the buffalo robe situated next to the dead fire. From beneath an adjacent robe he pulled a sack of dried meat and began to feed his weakened body.

"*Don't kill the general . . . no matter what happens,*" he repeated to himself. Why would that message be so important that it would be stuffed in the book? Thinking about the note also led him to the realization that the book had come into his possession with intent. It had not been placed there out of desperation or in an attempt to hide it. It was, with the note, given to him with forethought, for purposes that he could not comprehend. Perhaps it would be needed in his search for the Nez Perce. The lodge began to roll slightly, he thought, and even seemed as if it was spinning slowly. As a sense of nausea gripped his innards, he knew that he could not remain conscious for long if he did not get out of the lodge and get some air. Pampering his injured shoulder, he tried to rise to his feet and, failing, tried again, forcing himself toward the opening. He felt himself falling face first toward the ground but was unable to stop his fall.

His thoughts were a whirl, and as he hit the frozen surface they seemed to turn with the surrounding lodge.

He had no intention to kill a general. Neither did he know a general that he could kill if he was so inclined. And those horses outside, where did they come from? And men, Crow, he thought, yes, maybe Crow . . . the edges folded together and there was darkness – troubled, restless, unyielding darkness!

*

Smiles at the People awoke again to see the familiar sides of the lodge and breathed a sigh of relief. It had been a dream then, he thought. A dream that, gratefully, had no substance in fact and *a good thing, too*, he thought to himself as he felt the pain of the wounded shoulder begin to come back through the fog.

In the dream there had been mounted warriors, Crow warriors, and he remembered being helpless in some way before their coming. The Crow were the mortal enemy of the Sioux. To find oneself in the presence of the Crow fighting men was to face death.

In spite of the many other views that surrounded the telling of history, Smiles at the People had always thought of the Crow or the Absarokee people, as the best fighting men of the northern plains tribes. Compared to their enemies, they were a very small group. Their enemies, simply stated, were everyone else! In fact, except for the Shoshone with whom there had been a tenuous peace, thanks only to the white father's insistence, the only real allies the Crows had were the... yes, that was it, he did remember. The only friends the Crows claimed, and who claimed them, were the Nez Perce in the faraway Walla Walla Valley.

In his years in prison, he had had time to study the history of the Indian peoples and had always wondered at the friendship between the two groups. Separated by mutually unintelligible languages, and blood, the Nez Perce warriors had still, for generations, made the pilgrimage across the Lolo Trail to hunt buffalo with their Crow friends.

The point was also not lost on him that having a friend as far away as the Nez Perce, in the days before modern travel, was as helpful as having a friend in France when you are in a fist fight in California.

Still, history was replete with examples of visiting Nez Perce joining in the defense of their host's village when attacked by hostile Lakota, Blackfeet or any other of the legion of Crow enemies.

He also well remembered the Crow friendship with the whites and the disgrace, in his view, of the fleeing Nez Perce plea for help being rejected by their "friends" the Crow when pursued by the white troops.

Yes, the dream had placed him helpless before Crow warriors. He remembered falling and, as he fell, he remembered one of the first of the Crow warriors leaping from his pony and walking slowly toward him, scalping knife in hand.

In the dream he had also heard a command from behind the approaching warrior. A command, he had perceived by its tone and inflection as the Crow language, which had a Lakota feel. It was not, however, readily understandable to his Lakota ears, those two groups having separated so distantly in the forgotten past that neither remembered the day when the language was either the same or similar.

Smiles at the People's senses were returning rapidly, and soon he was able to discern what sounded like burning wood on a campfire. Yes, he thought, he could feel the warmth of it behind him. But a fire; he did not remember starting any fire when he had come to the lodge.

Slowly, ever so slowly, since he rested on his left shoulder and was loath to move the injured right, he pushed himself up to a sitting position and turned toward the fire. On the other side of the flames sat a Crow warrior.

"Then it wasn't a dream," Smiles at the People murmured out loud.

He sensed immediately that his guest had heard his words, and in them had found an answer that he was seeking.

Yes, he thought, to be a Lakota when at the mercy of the Crow was a fatal error. Better to be a white man now, in whatever way suited his captors.

His eyes, now out of necessity, focusing on this single individual sitting calmly at the edge of the fire, noticed several things. Number one, he noticed that whoever this man was, he had the look of someone who would not be trifled with. In spite of the bitter cold outside the lodge, this one was stripped to the waist and showed every sign of a man who knew and was at home in the fight for life. Yes, thought Smiles at the People, this one was a warrior indeed, and not to be treated lightly.

The second point, however, was the one that drew his eyes to focus, and his every sense to the alert. In the hand of this man, opened to a section near the end, was *the book*.

A thousand thoughts flooded to the head of the former inmate. Somehow, he must have an answer for the questions he was sure would soon be asked.

But suddenly, just as it seemed that the thousand explanations would desert him in a heap of confusion and attempted lies, he noticed that the man had raised the book, as if to read, studying the contents intensely. As he raised it, Smiles at the People realized that the book was upside down.

Just as he could feel his stomach and its tenuous hold on its contents begin to settle, the door of the lodge opened, and in stepped Captain Hale. Sharpfish knew Hale and indeed called him friend after the many nights in his company in the lodge of Banyon.

Still, as he saw the Indian hand the book to Hale, the former Washicu Bear knew that the time for escape or reprieve was gone. Hale turned the book right side up and, turning to a pre-marked place, began to read out loud. "At the beginning of 1943 . . ."

**

The girl Buffalo Calf Road sat across from Shoots Straight inside the lodge and looked determinedly at the confused former agent. There was no question she had been crying and, given the look of frustration on the face of Crazy Horse as he left, he had to assume there had been a very significant confrontation between them before the Strange Man of the Oglala had finally agreed to bring her to him.

Banyon remembered how Rodgers had made every effort to keep her away from him in the trip from the cave back to the Hanging Woman. It was also apparent, as time had gone on that the woman was not happy about the arrangement. He, for his part, felt better when he stayed away from the girl, and although he was uncertain why, he made it his business to avoid her after he had followed her to the river. They would meet again on the night of the attack on the camp and again at the fight along the river. There was time then, he had told himself, time to figure it all out.

Well, he thought as he tried to avoid the piercing eyes across from him, I guess this is the time.

The girl had said little after she had entered with Crazy Horse, but as he began to speak, that all changed. Her first words however caught him completely unprepared . . .

"You are not the boy I raised, Grandson"

Suddenly it came again, the rush of confusion, the tearing at reality that had caused him so much pain in the past. The past...? The former agent felt the black begin to take him, then equally unexpected, the black began to separate, to divide into colors and the colors into scenes.

The scenes began to move. First one and then the other as they created a place, then a situation; always seen by him as a participant and beside him he could always see or sometimes feel . . . her!

They were riding . . . no walking . . . again riding once toward the sun, next away . . . they were being attacked and then they were attacking. He was dying and she was holding him. Then it was reversed. She was dying, and he was taking her south, then north. Always he knew that they were headed toward . . . toward where? *The cave*! Yes, he remembered now, they had always headed toward the cave. In the end there was always a reason to go.

They were not always alone, but they were always together. Then there were scenes that told of an earlier time than most, a time that they had *won*; yes they had not always failed. There was not always death before they returned to the cave. In each of these Rodgers was there and, was it? . . . Yes there was also He Dog. Sometimes he was older, others not, but always there was the flute. Yes, he could see it clearly. In the hand of the great warrior He Dog there would, without exception, be *the flute*.

Beyond that, there would be another memory, the memory of the flute player carved into a rock face. Carved to tell any who would come that way again to have hope. To say *at that point, at least, the road was straight.*

He could see the figure repeatedly, on sandstone and limestone. He was aware of it on black lava rock and carved carefully into the white stone of the desert, and more than where he could sense the when. He could see future time where the carving was given names and histories that aligned it to people in a certain culture. Always there was that carving, that petroglyph, and with it came direction for those who sought it.

He could feel the girl beside him now, shaking him, talking to him in soothing tones. Telling him he had to fight against it;

that he had to come back to where she waited for him. As he slipped tentatively toward the reality of the lodge, she watched him gravely, looking at him with concern, but still in it all he could feel, as well as hear, the words that came out of her mouth.

"It is time to bring it all together in this place. It is time to bring the flute player to where we will raise our children!"

Out of the mist he pondered that to all men, their individual history had to have a purpose, a life must have a center. As he gazed back into the eyes of the girl, he knew he had reclaimed his. Whatever happened in this time line, or any other, he now had something worth living for. His vision cleared, and he reached for her hand. His hand knew hers, and they fit together as if they had never been apart. He held on tightly and felt all the loneliness and ache in his heart melt away. Yes, it was time to bring it all together and make this the only reality,

…the reality in which they were together…

***

On the fourth day of the Crazy Horse band's flight from the cantonment on the Yellowstone, slowed by the women, children, and the wounded from the fight in camp, the army under Lt. Baldwin could be seen closing from the south.

With the exception of just a few rifles taken from the soldiers and scouts in the fight, the warriors were largely unarmed and unprepared for a fight.

Flight was the only answer, and it was flight that was chosen.

While the warriors delayed the oncoming troops as they could, the children were taken on the backs of the surplus horses. Superfluous baggage was discarded, and the band, against hope, continued its headlong flight northward. With all they could do, however, the army continued to close the gap between them.

From the warriors' initial attempts to delay their pursuers, Lt. Baldwin had confirmed his belief that there was precious little weaponry of any kind in the hostile band and had redoubled his troops' speed in pursuit. An armed warrior, firing in a delaying action, would find himself charged immediately by numbers of soldiers and Crow scouts, heedless of their own safety, owing to the knowledge that the Lakota ability to respond or to ambush them was very small. The retreat of the Lakota fighting men behind the fleeing helpless ones turned very quickly into a rout.

By the end of that day, the soldiers were within firing range of the camp and showed no signs of slowing. Crazy Horse and his chiefs had been running against daylight and had hoped that the coming night would drive the soldiers into camp, giving them the chance to widen the gap between them by night travel.

This, however, was not to be. Before they could escape into the oncoming darkness, the Lakota could see that Lt. Baldwin had divided his regiment. One half, by forced march, had pulled up to the east, thereby flanking the fleeing people and was preparing to attack.

Banyon and the girl, riding in the rear guard with Crazy Horse, could see that the Indians had no chance whatsoever of surviving what was upon them. The former agent made his belief clear to Crazy Horse.

The latter did not respond, but rather continued to push stragglers ahead, even as the bullets of the troops began to take their toll on the slower elements of the band.

"We have to give him up!" yelled Shoots Straight to the Lakota fighter. "They will never stop until they have him. Dead or alive, they will take him back rather than leave him in our hands. I have no question, given the way they are pursuing, that they received orders by telegraph before they even left the Yellowstone."

Crazy Horse, all the more desperate now, responded immediately, "There is no talking wire at the soldier camp. They could have not heard from their chief so quickly."

Shoots Straight was taken aback, only for a moment, and then he had the answer, responding amid the growing hail of bullets.

"There is a knoll west of the soldier camp. On this knoll, they have found they can send messages to the soldier chiefs, now in the Black Hills. If it is daylight, they can send and receive messages up to a hundred miles from the camp. That is why they were delayed in following us. That is why they act so bravely. These orders must be that they should take him back. In reality, their whole campaign depends on it. If they allow us to take Miles successfully, every commander in the west will be a potential hostage."

The thing that Banyon did not share with his leader friend, were the memories that had flooded his mind since the morning. The text had rolled into his mind with the crashing effect of the knell of funeral bells. He could almost see the words as he had "read" them in the lodge on the Tongue.

...caught on the open plains countries north of the Yellowstone, the treacherous Sioux were forced to turn and fight. Although heavily armed, the Indians were no match for the fine troops of the U.S. Cavalry. In one of the fiercest battles in the history of Indian warfare, they were destroyed to the man ... in retaliation for the killing of the regiment's commanding officer...

The former agent could almost hear the words of the historian as he taught him in the cave. "The victors write the history. They can tell the story as they choose. There is no one to contradict the telling if there are no witnesses."

Forcing his winded horse to the side of Crazy Horse, he grabbed the single jaw rein and pulled the yellow pinto to a stop. Almost immediately, he felt the horse take a round from the oncoming troops, quiver, and begin to fall.

The girl moved suddenly between the wounded horse and rider acting as a moving shield between them and death.

The look on the face of the warrior chieftain was not passive now. This was the very horse he had ridden from the camp to turn back the initial attack of Custer's men under Marcus Reno at the battle of the Little Big Horn.

The horse was finished now, and it was clear that it was Banyon's fault.

"Get on back," he yelled at the Lakota. As the words left his mouth, the pinto fell head over heels, throwing Crazy Horse violently to the ground.

Shoots Straight was off his horse and beside the fallen man almost in the same instant, pulling him free from the dying animal.

Buffalo Calf Road was forcing her horse back and forth between the oncoming troops and the fallen fighters, distracting them, giving them a target to focus on.

"You cannot help them if you are dead!" the interpreter yelled at the shaken chieftain. "At the end of this there will be no survivors, no one to bring us back to the cave. If we do not surrender him, there is no future. It all dies here in the blood and snow."

They were scrambling now, bullets pounding into the earth beside them. He knew from the angle of the bullets that those who were firing at them must be very close indeed. In a single move, he was back on the frightened horse, feeling Crazy Horse land on behind him.

Shoots Straight knew that Miles was in the front of the band being held by a small, specially chosen guard. He also knew that the distance from their position in the rear guard to his location was too far. Much too far!

"Call for a white flag," he yelled at his passenger. Crazy Horse hesitated just a moment.

"Call for a white flag or it's over," yelled the former agent.

Crazy Horse yelled the order to the nearest warrior, who disappeared instantly into the huddling mass of women and children, and returned momentarily with a white cloth tied to a broken branch. Shoots Straight sprinted the horse to the man and grabbed the flag from his hand.

Without another word, he turned the brown cavalry mount and raced toward the oncoming troops.

He could see the vanguard riders slow slightly as he raced toward them. Even from a distance, he could see that Lt. Baldwin was among them.

He had a great number of "memories" about the junior officer and was not surprised at all to find him at the front of his regiment. As they rode closer, Baldwin, with an honor guard of four men, left the halted vanguard behind and rode out to meet them.

Banyon turned to Buffalo Calf Road at his rear and demanded that she return to the women and children. The look he received in return left no question that she would do no such thing!

As the two groups met, they stopped about ten yards from each other. Baldwin waited with a calmness that belied the extreme explosiveness of the situation.

Baldwin spoke first. "I demand your immediate and unconditional surrender. I will not hold my men further, allowing you to gain preferential position. Your surrender must be immediate or we will destroy you without further negotiation."

The Lakota leader had slid down from the interpreter's horse and was now standing facing the Lieutenant, rifle in hand.

Shoots Straight interpreted immediately the demand of the officer and waited for a reply.

Crazy Horse looked quickly around before speaking. He could see that the people had stopped retreating and were gathering toward the center, with the troops fanning to the west and east to complete their encirclement.

By the lack of firing he had heard in the last few minutes, Banyon knew, as did the chief, that the warriors were out of ammunition or close to it.

Crazy Horse turned back to the officer and began to speak. "Left to myself, my warriors and I would fight you to the last man. You have taken everything from us but our lives and we would give those also if the helpless ones could live. To save them we will surrender as you say."

Banyon turned back to the officer and translated.
"Crazy Horse says you can go to hell!"

****

Smiles at the People slept fitfully in the lodge on the Tongue. He had tried to offer an explanation and had found that the captain refused to listen.

All he had said was, "So, this is how your friend knew so much about things."

The former inmate attempted several times to introduce direction, or at least perspective, to what was being read. His every attempt was met by the upraised hand of the army officer, who sat almost motionless, poring over the contents of the book.

The Crow, who Hale had introduced as Plenty Coups, one of their head chiefs, had stayed watching for a while. Not having more than rudimentary English skills, he had soon left, returning again in the late afternoon. With him was a young woman in her late twenties, the former inmate guessed. Her English skills were sufficient and enabled the Crow chieftain to join in what Smiles at the People guessed would be the conversation of a lifetime; or, better said, many lifetimes, thought Sharpfish.

The officer seemed oblivious to the newcomers and continued to read the book.

Plenty Coups, however, directed questions at the young Lakota through the girl.

"Why are you still in camp?"

"I was wounded in the fight and was left for dead," responded Smiles at the People.

"Are you Lakota?" translated the girl.

"I am a friend," he responded, as his mind fought for an appropriate answer. To say that he was Lakota, to a man who had spent a lifetime killing every Lakota that he could, would be a blunder!

The girl translated, and Smiles at the People could see the muscles in the well-defined arms of the Crow chieftain tighten. He spoke again.

The girl translated. "Plenty Coups says he will not listen to lies. If you lie to him again, he will kill you, even in spite of the soldier chief."

Hale looked up momentarily from the book and grinned roguishly at Smiles at the People. Then, looking down, he started to read again as the girl asked another question from the chieftain.

"You speak and dress like a white man, how is it that you are with the Lakota?"

Smiles at the People could not see any other way out and finally responded, prompted by another grin from the army officer. He was right, thought the young man, there is nothing to lose now.

Gathering his sense of humor around him, he began. "Well, I was captured by the white man's government after two white men were killed. These men were chiefs in the White Father's police. I was there when they were killed, but I did not kill them. The white men took me and put me in their stone house for three years. After that time, they told me they would never let me go, so I escaped to try and return to my people. As I escaped, I was shot and killed."

The girl, who had been translating as he talked, stopped suddenly and smiled sympathetically at Smiles at the People, throwing him off balance with her strange reaction to the bizarre news. "Please say that again."

"I said, that as I escaped, I was shot dead," continued the young Lakota. "A friend was there to help me with the escape. When I was killed, he shot and killed the white man who killed me, and then he took his hair."

The girl translated as the warrior stared malevolently at the wounded man.

Smiles at the People could see clearly the man reach for his knife and pull it into his lap.

The girl began to speak again, "Plenty Coups says to tell you he can see very clearly that you are not Lakota. Even the Lakota have more honor than to lie such. He also asks me to tell you that with your very next lie, he will cut out your tongue and then take your heart and feed it to the dogs in camp."

The young Lakota was suddenly not so amused by his little joke, as he was certain that the man meant exactly what he said. Just as it seemed that bad was going to worse, Hale dropped the book and jumped into the fray.

"No, no, wait a minute. What he is saying is true."

The girl translated quickly and Plenty Coups turned his gaze on the Captain. Neither the Captain nor the injured Sharpfish could mistake the look of disgust on the face of the Crow fighter.

The grin on the face of the Captain was somewhat disarming, but the officer still needed to pull heavily on his many months of friendship with the Crow leader to gain control of the conversation.

"Look, look right here, this man's name is Leonard Sharpfish. It says that he escaped from a place called Marion Penitentiary in the year 1999; that during the escape, it was reported that Sharpfish was shot and killed by a guard. The body was never found but the quantity of blood on the scene made it clear that the wound was mortal. It was assumed that the body was retrieved by friends who were assisting in the escape."

The chieftain looked bewildered as the final words fell from the lips of the soldier. The girl, looking not at all confused, translated to Plenty Coups. The chief looked from the officer to the injured Smiles at the People, then back again.

The former convict had little question in his mind that the Crow could kill both of them before either could put up a defense. This was a fighting man in every sense of the word, and not given to flights of fantasy. From the way he was looking, Leonard discerned that he was also a man of great intelligence and profound understanding. Nothing, however, in his experience had prepared him to accept the reality of the story that was being handed to him now.

The chief spoke again and the girl, who remained unaffected, translated in short, quick sentences. "When is the year of which you speak? The year in which this one was killed..."

The officer did a quick calculation and responded, "One hundred and twenty-four years from this time."

Plenty Coups stared unbelievingly at the officer's response and began to rise.

"Wait, wait," said Hale, as he put his hand on the warrior's leg and bade him sit. "I think there is a way to prove what we are saying is true. Let me try."

Smiles at the People felt he would like to join the conversation, but also realized that the army officer had the only shred of credibility left with the Crow chieftain. He himself had none whatsoever. That being the case, he allowed him to carry the weight of the conversation, leaning heavily, as he believed, on the old boast of the Crow that never had their people shed the blood of a white man.

Hale was fumbling through the book now and soon came to a spot where he studied for a minute and then, turning to the chief, said, "This book talks about you also, Plenty Coups."

The warrior stared blankly at the man, uncertain what to make of this new turn.

"It says that you live to be a very old man and that, in your old age, you tell your story to a white man who writes it down for the benefit of your people."

Hale was reading aloud now, skipping a line here and there, reading the next, realizing that his opportunity to win was very short. Then suddenly he arrived at the point he was looking for and began to read very slowly, allowing the girl time to be as exact as possible.

"The book says that when you were a young boy, you went on a vision quest. That it was a great vision and you told parts of it to the elders of the tribe on your return. You did not tell all, though, and in your old age, you told everything for the first time to the white man who wrote down your words.

"It says that you will say in your old age that you heard a voice from behind you and the voice called you by name. You responded without moving and the voice, still behind you, said, 'They want you, Plenty Coups. I have been sent to fetch you.'"

The eyes of the warrior were very large now. It was obvious that Hale was right about the story. The story would not be told to anyone in this time line for another fifty years, and Plenty Coups knew what they said was the truth.

Hale was still not certain he had won the day, so he continued. "When you were in the lodge, you found yourself in the presence of many old warriors. You said that you knew they were warriors by their faces and bearing. You said they had been counting coup; you knew this because before each, sticking in the ground, was a white coup stick bearing the breath feathers of a war eagle."[6]

The voice of the captain held a sense of wonder as the roguish grin that had made him the favorite of the regiment broke across his face.

The Crow chieftain, at the most difficult moments in his life, by his training, had been able to keep his face expressionless and stoic. This was not one of those times.

Hale, on the other hand, appeared delighted. Knowing that the chief would probably be more comfortable if he were to quit, he put in one more nail to gain further credibility.

"In the end, the chief of the dwarves gave you not a medicine bundle, which he declared to be a burdensome thing and often in a warrior's way, but advice. He said, 'In you, as in all men; are natural powers. You have will...! Learn to use it. Make it work for you!'"[7]

---

6 <u>Plenty Coups, Chief of the Crows</u>, Frank Linderman. Omicron manuscript
7 Ibid

Hale lowered the book in the face of the astounded chief. "You have a will, Plenty Coups. Now it is time for you, and us, to use it."

The chief was looking at the fire now. The girl sat quietly at his side. The spirit of the lodge left little doubt of the truth of what had been said there.

Smiles at the People had heard that the chief of the Crows had been a great statesman and he had led his people down the Black Road of the whites because he felt they did not have another choice.

"Not for the love of the white man," he had once said. "They are liars who deceive only themselves." But because the powers had told him that, for the Crow, there was no other choice.

As the warrior sat and stared at the book now in the lap of Captain Hale, a connection seemed to form in his mind, *if this is true, then* . . . Purpose replaced doubt, direction supplanted confusion. The girl instantly translated the words that the chief spoke.

"What happens to my people?"

Captain Hale stared at the next page in the book and shook his head. Without comment, he handed the book to Smiles at the People, pointing to a section and indicating that he should read it.

The wounded man held the book in his left hand and began. "By the end of 1889, all buffalo on the plains were believed to be dead, and the breed extinct. The final herd was slaughtered by a group of army officers and Arrikara scouts who killed them to the last animal. For the next twenty years, it was believed that not a single animal had survived, and the American Bison was gone forever.

"The surviving Indians of the plains refused to believe that the buffalo would forsake them and continued year after year to look for their return. But as year succeeded year, the facts became clear to them all. The buffalo was gone for good, and so was the life that it had allowed.

186

"Now confined to reservations, often under the supervision of unsympathetic agents, his camps became foul, and he could not move them. Twice in earlier days, white men had brought scourges of smallpox to the Indians of the Northwest Plains, and each time many thousands died. Now, with the buffalo gone and freedom denied him, two equally hideous strangers, famine and tuberculosis visited the Indian. He could cope with neither. His pride was broken. He felt himself an outcast, a stranger in his own country."[8]

The young Lakota looked up from reading, expecting to see a look of grief or hopelessness on the face of the Crow fighting man. He was shocked to see a slight smile beneath the beaked nose of the man who would some day be chosen to represent all tribes in laying a wreath at the Grave of the Unknown Soldier.[9]

Plenty Coups seemed to relax from that moment, and even though he often would find himself staring thoughtfully at the young prisoner, he did not hesitate in having women come in and dress his wound, and the provide Lakota with food.

Late that evening, as he was obviously preparing to leave, he seemed almost haunted by something. After he posed the question, the girl turned to Smiles at the People and translated.

"After you were dead . . ." the girl hesitated for a minute, trying to translate the meaning. "You came alive again. I know of the place where men go after death. We call it the Beyond Country. Yet you did not go there, you came here. How was this done?"

Smiles at the People felt that, in all there had been between them in the day, it would dishonor them all if he were to lie now. Such being the truth, he proceeded. "I awoke in a cave in the bowels of the Black Hills. There was a man there who told me we had a chance to make a change . . ."

---

8 *Plenty- Coups, Chief of the Crows, Frank B. Linderman, Omicron line manuscript*
9 *In Omicron Line*

The warrior was focused now, the eyes keen, all senses alert. "I know this cave," translated the girl. "Before the Lakota took it from us, the hills were ours and so was this cave. This man who was with you, was his name Hergin?"

Now it was the young Lakota's turn to have his mouth agape. "Yes, yes it was."

The Crow started again, translated by the young girl. "Did he tell you that the first six human beings came through that cave into this world?"

Sharpfish nodded that he had.

"And did he also tell you that he was the man who called to me in that first vision and led me to the warriors in the lodge?"

Plenty Coups waited patiently for an answer.

"No," answered Smiles at the People, "No, that he did not say."

Chapter 11

I am glad to learn that (Sitting) Bull is relieved of his miseries, even if it took the bullet to do it. A man who wields such power as he once did, that of a King, over a wild spirited people cannot endure abject poverty and beggary without suffering great mental pain, and death is a relief . . . Bull's confidence and belief in the Great Spirit was stronger than I ever saw in any other man. He trusted to him implicitly . . . History does not tell us that a greater Indian than Bull ever lived. He was the Mohammad of his people, the law and kingmaker of the Sioux.

James M. Walsh
North West Mounted Police
(On hearing of the killing of Sitting Bull)
December 15, 1890, *Omicron line*

North of the Yellowstone
March 1877
Omega Line

Lt. Baldwin blinked like he had been struck. "He said what?" the Lieutenant responded.

"Crazy Horse said that he did not come here to surrender, but rather to set things right and give you a chance."

"Give me a chance, huh?" the Lieutenant smiled.

"Yes," responded the interpreter. "Give you a chance to follow your orders and avoid a court martial, if possible."

Baldwin looked back and forth at his honor guard to both sides and to the rear of him. The look made the men sit up straighter in the saddle, ready, the former agent thought, to handle whatever kind of a trick the Lakota chieftain was playing.

Crazy Horse looked curious at what was being said. The girl sat calmly on the dun, her face impassive against what was before them.

Banyon turned to Crazy Horse abruptly and said, "The Lieutenant does not want your surrender, but rather his chief, Miles, whom we have captured. He does not trust interpreters like me so he says that if you mean to turn over the Colonel and leave peaceably, to hold your rifle in the air and continue holding it there as a sign to both sides that there is to be no more fighting."

Crazy Horse was staring deeply into the eyes of the smiling interpreter. Something, he was sure, was not right. But still, trusting in the friendship that had developed between them, he slowly raised his rifle over his head and looked first at the troops lined up on the plains before them and then turning to his own people, who watched nervously from behind.

Now it was Baldwin's turn to be curious. "What is he doing?" queried the Lieutenant.

Shoots Straight responded immediately. "Crazy Horse has given orders to those who are guarding Bear Coat Miles that he will raise his arm with his rifle as a signal to them that you will not let them leave without a fight. When he lowers his arm, they are to kill Miles immediately."

Baldwin stared malevolently at the Oglala chieftain as Crazy Horse, seeing that all had seen his gesture, began slowly to lower his arm.

"No!" yelled Lt. Baldwin.

Crazy Horse, understanding the word "No" in the white man's talk, raised the rifle back up, thinking the officer didn't think he had done it sufficiently.

"Tell Crazy Horse that my orders are to bring them and Col. Miles back to the cantonment safely."

Banyon turned back to Crazy Horse and interpreted immediately. "Lt. Baldwin says that if you will surrender the officer, you may go in peace."

Crazy Horse, very confused by now, nodded his assent and began to lower his arm.

"Okay, Okay," yelled Baldwin.

Baldwin signaled to Crazy Horse, in a lifting movement, to raise his arm again, which he immediately did.

"The Lieutenant says he has told his troops that if you lower your arm while the meeting is still in progress, they are to attack."

Crazy Horse, thoroughly confused now, raised his rifle even higher and stared disconcertingly at the stupid army officer who would place the lives of the innocent ones in harm's way for such a thoughtless reason.

Baldwin began again. "I have my orders. Is there some compromise that can be struck to save the Colonel's life?"

"Actually," replied Banyon, "There is. You can stop lying to a holy man of the Lakota," indicating Crazy Horse.

Baldwin looked nervous but determined. "What do you perceive that I am lying about, Interpreter?"

"Your orders were to rescue Miles and return to base. There is nothing in your orders that refers to slaughtering these people if they do not surrender."

Baldwin stared blankly at the interpreter. "How do you know my orders, squaw man?"

"I not only know your orders, but I also know that last week before the orders were given to attack an innocent village at night, you wrote your wife a letter."

Baldwin gave no appearance of being amused, but allowed the interpreter to continue.

"In that letter, you said that you hoped the Crazy Horse band would break out and you would be given the chance to go after them."[10]

Baldwin sat silently, stunned at what he was hearing.

---

10 *Baldwin did right this letter in Omicron as well as Omega, the texts were the same*

"Then you said, 'Wouldn't it be something if your old man whipped these Redskins after Crook and Custer and Miles all failed?'"

Shoots Straight was quiet, waiting for the impact of what he had said to sink in.

"I expect that the letter will be found. In fact, I can tell you that it will be found, and used to cite motive at your court martial."

Baldwin stared deeply into the eyes of the interpreter, seeking something that would, for now, elude him. After a moment, he looked at the tiring Crazy Horse, with the rifle held only tenuously over his head.

"What are you suggesting?" asked the junior officer.

"We are saying that we only took Miles to escape being murdered by your people. You can have him back if you will allow us to leave unmolested."

Baldwin looked quickly at his regiment, now firmly surrounding the unarmed and helpless Lakota. "I don't have to give such generous terms considering your present situation."

"Then I will tell you something more about your future," said Banyon. "On June 24, of this year, at Fort Abraham Lincoln, a court martial will be convened to consider your case. You will be charged with willingly and knowingly causing the death of a fellow officer and one hundred thirty-seven unarmed Lakota. The court will, after reviewing your case, be urged to leniency, owing to the death of your wife by her own hand after the breaking of the story of this massacre, and your arrest. The court, however, will not heed that recommendation."

The officer sat wordlessly in the saddle, but by the way his eyes were moving back and forth between himself and Crazy Horse, the interpreter knew he was struggling for direction.

He decided to make his decision for him.

He began to speak in a moderate tone, clearly trying to make the Lieutenant understand that he was not translating now, but rather the words were his own.

"If you do as we are suggesting here, you will have Miles back and will be considered the hero of this action. There is a greater victory to be had, and it will be yours if you can see the vision."

Baldwin was sitting just a little straighter in the saddle now, thought the former agent. He was listening, and that was all he needed. "On the 16th of March, a combined force of Lakota and Cheyenne under Crazy Horse and Sitting Bull, the exact same group who defeated Custer last summer, will attack Fort Peck. Miles is wounded and will not be able to command this regiment. The plan is that this will be a surprise attack, and I promise you that it will be a success if the garrison at Fort Peck is not reinforced.

"If it is reinforced, in one fell swoop some officer will be the one to gain a permanent place in history as the one who dealt with Sitting Bull and Crazy Horse and brought to an end the Sioux war."

Baldwin sat, staring blankly at the former agent. "Why would you tell me this?" he whispered.

Banyon responded in a firm, certain voice. "Two reasons: One, because it is time for all this to end! There is no future in this war, only grief. Two:" a look of disgust creeping onto his features, "because I am a man of long term loyalties, unlike you, apparently, *my friend!!*"

Moments later, Shoots Straight and Crazy Horse turned slowly, and, with Crazy Horse on the rear keeping his arm and rifle high for all to see, returned to the waiting camp. A decision had been reached.

As they rode, the white interpreter thought irreverently that he had learned a great deal in this encounter. *He had learned that you only had to start out with the truth!*

As they approached the waiting Lakota, Little Big Man headed toward them with the bay gelding belonging to Crazy Horse.

As they loped toward each other, it seemed to the former agent that Crazy Horse was being very quiet indeed. Before the warrior could reach them, Crazy Horse finally asked the question that the interpreter had been waiting for.

"What did you tell the officer at the end of your conversation?"

Banyon responded immediately. "I told him we would make a small camp and leave Miles and four warriors to guard him. That we would leave at our fastest pace and tomorrow morning, if they, or we, were not attacked, that the four warriors would ride off, leaving the commander in his hands. I also told him that if they were approached before tomorrow morning, or if any of the troops got so much as within rifle range, that they would kill Bear Coat instantly."

He paused for a moment as he began to slow the big horse before the oncoming Little Big Man. "I also told him that we will attack Fort Peck in the *Moon of Snow Blindness*, (March) and that he should reinforce the garrison against that attack as soon as possible."

Crazy Horse instantly knew what his white friend had done. He also realized that if the young Lieutenant did what Shoots Straight had suggested, the Lakota would win their greatest military victory in the history of the plains . . .

. . . without firing a shot!

*

The Lodge of Smiles at the People, Tongue River
March 1877
Omega Line

When Plenty Coups left the lodge on the Tongue, both Smiles at the People and Hale were surprised that the girl had stayed. Both men stared anxiously at the girl, hardly believing that she had been left behind. To say that there were many things they wanted to discuss was an understatement. Both men knew, however, that the girl's English was plenty sufficient to assure that everything they discussed would be shared with Plenty Coups.

Sharpfish smiled congenially at the girl and then turned purposefully to the army officer whose blessing, and curse it seemed, was that his face immediately showed his every feeling. At that moment the face showed deep concern. Would letting the girl, and subsequently the Crow, in on what he had discovered somehow threaten the ability to control the situation?

Before his thoughts could carry him any further, the former inmate offered the solution.

"Just understanding the words does not necessarily give a common frame of reference. Without that reference, they are just words."

A light of understanding dawned in the eyes of the Captain.

Hale began with the subject that hung closest on his mind. "There is an army captain killed in an early charge against the Nez Perce. Is this something that will happen, or something that may happen?"[11]

"Everything you read is something that from here may happen. From where we came from, it did certainly happen."

Captain Hale took a moment to digest the information and then, seeming reassured, continued. "This fight with the Nez Perce, is it also something that may happen?"

"It is something that will happen if there is no change from here," responded Smiles at the People.

"This Joseph, I think that the history refers to him continually as Chief Joseph. He seems like a very good man as I read it. Still, why did he end up looking so very good and we, the cavalry I mean, be remembered so poorly?"

---

11 *Hale himself was the Captain in the reference. He was the first man killed in the final battle with the Nez Perce. Omicron Line*

"Simply because the Nez Perce were only trying to escape to Canada, fighting only for a chance to remain free. In the other time that we refer to, it is seen that they, the Nez Perce, *were* very good men, simply trying to first preserve their home land, and then, when that was lost, to preserve their liberty by leaving the country."

"So why were they not allowed to simply leave?" questioned the Captain.

"That is the question that has haunted all of those who have studied the campaign. The answer most believe is in the concept that men, and especially governments of men, seem to have an innate drive to exert their authority over other men. In that, they perceive themselves as powerful. When that power is threatened, they will fight to maintain it."

The girl sat watching the fire, obviously listening, but, as both men believed, probably not understanding a great deal . . .

"What would have happened if the Nez Perce would have just been let go?" asked the army captain.

"No one ever knows for certain what would happen if a particular facet of history is changed. That is why we are so meticulous in our planning and carrying out of what we do here. The one thing that I would say, however, is that a certain segment of the Nez Perce under Chief White Bird did escape to Canada and there lived out their lives as model citizens in an area to become known as the Crows Nest Pass.*12* Some eventually returned to the United States and were positive additions to their communities."

"What you're saying then, is that those who died in that campaign died for nothing?"

"Yes," answered the young Lakota, "relative to any conceivable good that history, in hindsight, can perceive, *everyone*," Sharpfish stared forcefully into the eyes of Captain Hale, "who died in that campaign, died without purpose!

---

12 Near Coleman, Crow's Nest Pass Alberta.

Furthermore, I can tell you that those who died on the side of the cavalry were not remembered honorably by their nation. Most historians considered them in retrospect to be power hungry tyrants in command of mindless fools, inflicting death and destruction of property on a good, freedom-loving tribe. Most of the common people of the nation just choose to ignore that part of our history as unfortunate and beyond comprehension to a freedom-loving nation. A nation that would eventually set itself up as the example to the world of a people dedicated to human rights and liberties. A nation that would send armies thousands of miles from its shores to insure the rights and freedom of people not unlike the Nez Perce; in the broad sense of history,

...we are seen as hypocrites!"

If Smiles at the People had expected this information to humble or humiliate Owen Hale, he soon found himself to be in error. The Captain, unless he read it wrong, was angry. Not angry, as he would have expected, at the history, but at him.

"If this nation, whose values you think so highly of, turns out so well", exploded Hale, "and is such a blessing to the world, then I have to ask why you are here. Further, I have to ask why I should not shoot you where you sit, then get on my horse, find your companion, and settle with him the same?"

To say that Sharpfish was astounded by the response of the Captain barely told the tale.

"You think in your perspective of hindsight," threateningly continued the Captain, "that we are mindless fools. You, however, fail to understand that we see ourselves as the builders of that great nation you refer to. You fail to realize that the majority of us are here fighting and knowing that we may give our lives, to quote Mr. Lincoln, that this very nation might live.

"What you tell me, is, whether it seems right or wrong to you, what we did here accomplished in the end just what we dreamed of. That you are here in your arrogance to change everything we did and try to create something new that even you cannot be certain of."

The captain had his sidearm out now and was waving it, first to one side of the lodge then another. Pointing it at one point at Sharpfish, then at the mildly terrified girl, the former convict believed now that he was dealing with a madman, very possibly a madman who would take his life without further thought. The forty-five sidearm of the Captain returned now to point directly at the former inmate and there it stayed!

The young Lakota's mind searched frantically for the words that would somehow stand between him and the pull of the trigger he knew was at hand. In his fear for life, there came a certain cleansing of thought that is reserved for those who face death, a cleansing and a repositioning. Suddenly he realized that the view of what had happened to the country that he had shared with the Captain was badly flawed.

In his perspective, as well as those of his day, he had always seen the United States as a powerful and good nation, a world power representing the cause of liberty and freedom to a benighted but hopeful mankind. In his reorientation, he realized that in the time he was now in, no such perspectives existed except in the minds of the most optimistic and visionary of its leaders. Most of the nations of the world still looked on the United States as a struggling agricultural experiment and looked on the concept of a nation founded on such principles as ridiculous.

The man pointing the revolver at his face was one of those millions who believed they were fighting for the very existence of their homeland and would give all they had to ensure that very same future that the former convict so disdainfully dismissed as flawed and changeable.

"It wasn't enough," retorted Sharpfish in between breaths. "It didn't last, and in the end, it went down in failure. This is the reason we are here."

Hale was still angry and determined, but the young brave Smiles at the People believed he saw his features soften slightly before he spoke.

"So you believe that if we save these Indians it *will* last?"

Sharpfish responded immediately, hoping to keep the momentum going. "We can't know that, as we can't know the effects of anything we do here. What we do know, is that there were some errors made, and we know they were made at this point in the time line."

"What were these *errors*, as you call them?" asked Hale.

"In the end, we learned that the country was a living, breathing body made up of many distinct, but important parts. Each of these parts had something to give to the health and future of the whole." He was talking too fast! He knew that, and the impression it gave was not favorable. But he did feel that he had, at least for the moment, gained a reprieve from the end that was facing him just minutes before.

"As with any body, however, we learned that the removal of any one part would affect the health and survivability of the whole. With the destruction of the culture of the native peoples, history found that a very valuable something belonging to the body of the nation had been destroyed, amputated from our being by our own hand. Not just this very valuable corporal entity but, in a larger reckoning, a part of our very soul and maybe that very part we would need in a difficult future to ultimately save the us all."

"My People for our part; because of what happened or didn't happen here could never really establish themselves as a part of a bigger picture, without that vision, they never could find themselves in the fabric of the whole. They were never able to do that which they were pre-destined to accomplish for the good of everyone."

Smiles at the People tried very hard to keep the sigh escaping from him at a reasonable level as the Captain lowered the forty-five back to his lap and then replaced it in its holster.

The smile had returned to his features and the former convict thought he could also detect a sigh escaping from the army Captain.

Hale picked up the book again and began to read for a moment. Looking up repeatedly at the still shaken Sharpfish, he browsed the open section of the book, his lips moving silently with the words. Seemingly coming to an understanding, he asked the question. "Tell me about this German and the bomb he made to destroy our cities?"

"What?" shot back the former convict, grabbing the book.

Hale looked on thoughtfully as the former convict read the text in what seemed to be mounting concern.

The girl waited for him to read a few pages and, judging that he was at a point of departure, interrupted his reading and spoke the first words of the day that were truly her own.

"If you are through trying to get us killed, I have a message for you." Both men looked at the girl visibly confused.

"Hergin says to tell you that it is time to tell Hale and Plenty Coups the *whole* truth."

**

Approaching Fort Peck area, on the Missouri River
March 1877
Omega Line

On the eleventh day after their flight from the cantonment, the Crazy Horse band met scouts sent from the camp of Sitting Bull. The following day they rode into that camp amid the trilling of the women of the Hunkpapa and the Miniconjous under Lame Deer. The dancing went on into the night as Crazy Horse and Shoots Straight met with the leaders of the combined bands.

Banyon found himself sitting directly across the fire from Sitting Bull and found the actual presence of the great Lakota holy man to be compelling. For reasons unknown to him, the Sioux chieftain had always held a place in his mind as a small square man with a slightly overlarge head. The Sioux considered him a holy man and so the former agent had also envisioned him as a somewhat anemic type of a serious bent.

What he actually saw was quite different. Sitting Bull, in reality, was almost six feet tall by Banyon's estimation. The former agent had been trained to note the approximate dimensions of a man for future identification. His best guess was that the chief was not less than 230 pounds, and if there was any fat in the mixture, the former agent could not identify it. In this meeting, the holy man wore a single feather in his hair as opposed to the other chiefs present who in welcoming the Crazy Horse people, had dressed in their finery. Banyon noticed that Crazy Horse and Sitting Bull were the only two chiefs not wearing a full headdress.

The Hunkpapa head man also seemed genial in the extreme, taking every opportunity to see that his guests were comfortable and well entertained.

His attitude toward the white man initially had been the reverse.

The former agent remembered that it was said that Sitting Bull hated all white men and had made very few exceptions to that rule in his life. Two times, to be exact, he had befriended and even saved white men from certain death and taken them to his lodge as friends. In each of these occasions, the men had partaken of his hospitality over a period of time and then, given the opportunity, had betrayed him and put him and his people in peril in the doing.

One of these incidents was the previous year, and the interpreter noted that the former friend of the Hunkpapa chief was now an interpreter for the oncoming army.

On being introduced, Banyon had proffered his hand to the Lakota headman, only to have it refused. He could feel the hand of Crazy Horse on his arm pulling him back a step, warning him.

Shoots Straight, despite his personal affront by the man whom he had always admired so greatly, was a man with a purpose, and that purpose was also tied to a schedule.

That schedule had everything to do with the approaching army of the wounded Nelson Miles, which was not more than three days behind them. If what he had in mind was to succeed, he knew he had to break down the wall between himself and the Sioux leader immediately.

Pulling away from the imploring Crazy Horse, Banyon yelled at the famous Lakota leader.

"You claim that you care only for the future of your people, but you lie!"

The sound of rifles being brought to bear was not lost on the former soldier. This was a gamble he must win, yet he was prepared and he knew if he were to die, that it would be in a very good attempt.

Sitting Bull, who had turned away from the proffered hand, was now shaking hands with Big Road, one of the other chiefs of the Crazy Horse band.

Banyon could detect nothing in the comportment of the Chief to tell him what reaction his words had affected, if any.

Sitting Bull continued greeting Big Road, seemingly oblivious to the fact that thirty to forty rifles were pointing at the white man just an arm's length from him.

Crazy Horse was too stunned to speak.

Sitting Bull finished the amenities with Big Road who, not unlike the others, glared fiercely at the white man. It was true he had been a help to the people in their escape from the whites, but such manners were not to be tolerated among the Lakota and especially not to a man as thoroughly proven as Sitting Bull.

Turning back to Banyon, the man recognized as the chief of all the Lakota had a look of extreme distaste as he appraised the white man.

The Hunkpapa reached out and took the smaller white man by the chin like a child and, pinching the flesh between powerful fingers, he shook the agent's head back and forth.

"You will die in a moment, but before you do, I will show the Lakota that I am not a liar like the white man. I will tell you, and all of these, that I will drop your innards on the ground like those of a butchered buffalo."

Only in those words did the interpreter feel the point of the knife, now pressed against his stomach.

Crazy Horse was now beside them talking rapidly and Shoots Straight could see that the friendship between them would be served in this encounter. The Oglala spoke rapidly and with a sense of the urgent.

"He is sent from the powers, my friend. He has saved us from the soldiers with the knowledge given him by the powers to help us."

Sitting Bull did not flinch or in any way indicate that he had lost his resolve relative to the former agent. The old warrior looked deeply into the eyes of the interpreter searching for fear. There was none!

"Tell me something, white man that you know from the powers. Tell me something that will stop my blade."

The former agent did not hesitate but, searching deeply in his new thoughts, leapt toward the opportunity with steely resolve.

"Once, when you were out alone after antelope, you had a strange experience."

Shoots Straight thought that he could see a flicker of recognition in the eyes of the headman, but not being certain, continued forcefully.

"You heard someone singing over a ridge and looked over to see. It was a wolf and he ended his song with a long howl. Hiu! Hiu! The wolf was telling you how you must live and what you must do."

There was no question that he had the effect he imagined. He could no longer feel the prick of the knifepoint against his stomach.

"That is not enough white man, I have told this story over many a fire. In the devious ways of the whites, you may have also heard it."

Banyon was unflinching before the words from Sitting Bull.

"Yes, yes you are right my friend, but the song the wolf was singing, you have never shared over a fire or even with those closest to you. This song you sing only to yourself, the song is this:

I am a lonely wolf, wandering
Pretty much all over the world.
He, he, he! What is the matter?
I am having a hard time friend.
This that I tell you,
You will have to do also.
Whatever I want, I always get it.
Your name will be big,
As mine is big. Hiu! Hiu![13]

Nothing had changed. The former agent began to feel the beginnings of uncertainty. He decided to take a chance. "You were singing this song to yourself on the day you heard from your scouts that the people of Crazy Horse were coming!"

Sitting Bull let go of Banyon's chin and stepped back two steps. "Then I would ask you a question. If you are really from the powers, you will know the answer. Soon after I was made chief, I belonged to a society of men who had been organized to help the people. All of these men were proven, and their council had a strange name. In their meetings there was no singing or joking, only serious talk about the future of the people. All of these meetings were secret and held at night. No one but the members knew when they would be held. One night, although it was forbidden, I sang a song in this council. Two of these men survived and are here right now, pointing rifles at your head. Tell me, white man, if you would live, what was this council and sing me this song."

Shoots Straight was in trouble and he knew it. Most of his memories had been given on his own field, as it were. The request from Sitting Bull was altogether different and he raced to

---

13 *Sitting Bull, Champion of the Sioux* StanleyVestal. *Omicron manuscript*

try to answer. He had been told that electrical impulses in the brain could race at a speed relegating the fastest computers to shame.

Yes, thought the former agent, but the real trick is if such impulses could find something if that something wasn't there. He knew he was entirely dependent on information that these men would give at some point in their lives to white authors. What if Sitting Bull had never given that song to anyone to be written?

***

Over a hundred years into the future, old hands typed words into a box. Rodgers watched, fascinated, as the words emerged.

"How did you know that, my friend?" he queried.

"I was a member of the Silent Eaters society. I remember this song."

Hergin gazed at his old friend and thought again how grateful he was for this man's amazing mind. He Dog's ability to remember even the smallest details of everything he had ever seen had been an invaluable resource to him. This was one of the reasons it had always been so important to keep him here in the present, away from the danger at the axial point. That reason and also another; here in Omicron, He Dog had a family. His children now had children of their own, and those genes had produced another asset vital to their mission. That asset was Dan Banyon.

He Dog reached to the shelf behind him and took hold of the flute. "There is no more that we can do here; it is only there that we can seal the line. It is time to go!"

****

Shoots Straight began to sing as Sitting Bull and two others dropped their weapons and wondered at what Wakan Tanka had wrought.

"Young men, help me, do help me!

I love my country so
that is why I am fighting . . . "

As the former agent now sat in the lodge listening to the council of chiefs, he was gratified that Sitting Bull was every bit as gracious to him as he was to his other guests.

He sat quietly as Sitting Bull questioned the chiefs of the Crazy Horse band about their experiences after the surrender. As the events in which Banyon was involved were related, Sitting Bull would turn during their telling and look intently at the former agent.

When he was told of special knowledge that he shared to help the cause of the Lakota, Sitting Bull would turn and ask, "How did you know this?"

The interpreter's reply was always the same. "It was given to me by the powers."

The answer was never sufficient for the Lakota headman, but courtesy required that when a guest had answered a question to his own satisfaction, then he should not be pressed further.

The meeting lasted well into the early hours of the next day.

Shoots Straight was the cause of its ending, and the chiefs had gone away very much disturbed at the antics of the Wasichu Wakan, or the "sacred white man" as they had begun to call him.

Banyon had waited, thinking he should follow the protocol of the Lakota to the degree possible. As the night wore on, however, the former agent's patience became exhausted, and he requested the right to speak.

"We will listen to your words, Wasichu Wakan," Sitting Bull had said.

"Tomorrow we must attack Fort Peck with every warrior we can send. By the end of the day, we must have taken the fort and everything in it. The 'everything' that we are most interested in is the guns that have been sent there in the fire wagon boats."

Sitting Bull sat quietly listening, but Lame Deer interrupted rudely and railed at the white man. "An attack on the fort will cost us many young men. When a white man dies, a thousand can take his place. When we lose a warrior, there is no one to take his place."

Shoots Straight could feel a sense of urgency flowing through him as he continued through the morning to try to interest the chiefs in an attack the next day. At every point of encouragement there was a new man to rise in opposition to the plan.

With the skill of warriors of words, they parried every suggestion from the white man, urging retreat and flight to the land of the grandmother. As the morning star began to rise in the east, he had lost interest in the continued rambling of the warrior chiefs. Staring outside the now opened flaps of the lodge, he remembered that among the Sioux, as with all the northern plains tribes, the openings to the teepees always faced toward the east to honor a great man. It was said that a great leader had once come to the people and that he had taught them in the ways of peace. They also said that at the rising of the Morning Star he was always in prayer for the good of the people. At that ancient day, prayers before this star had brought peace. *Maybe in so desperate a time of need, they would again,* thought Banyon.

"When we next fight with the white men," spoke Sitting Bull, "we must do so to win something we may keep. We tire of victories with nothing to show for them but the mourning of squaws."

Shoots Straight leaped to his feet. He could feel the opportunity slipping away in the endless discussion among the chiefs. Rising to his feet, he knew, would be considered the height of rudeness. Only that, he believed, would get the attention of the bickering chiefs.

"You are all done fighting the white men. There will never be more than the smallest of skirmishes between you from now on. Only one more fight will there be between the two peoples. It will be thirteen years from now in the *Moon of the Popping Trees (December)*. It will be a band of Miniconjous under Big Foot." The tall chief raised his head immediately at the mention of his name. "It will be after the people have fled because of the killing of Sitting Bull by the white mans Indian police."*14*

The whole lodge was alive now, and the former agent knew he had an opportunity. He also knew he had taken his life in his hands again. Big Foot was watching his every move, and he knew that he would have to win now, or there would never be a better chance.

"The army will have stopped the fleeing people at the place called Wounded Knee." He turned to his friend Crazy Horse, who had stood now beside him and waited for the response of the chiefs to settle down. "This place will also be known to the people as the place where the heart of Crazy Horse will be buried."

The former agent could hear the words of Steven Vincent Benet as he immortalized the thoughts of his friend's last moments in a time line that to him was now beyond reality.

"I shall not be there, I shall rise and pass," said the writer, *"bury my heart at Wounded Knee."*

As he felt the presence of his friend beside him, standing with him against the rage and opposition of his closest associates and friends, he felt inside him the keenest resolve.

"No! No, never again!"

His words echoed through the council radiating to the listening people outside. "They will take your weapons from you, and then they will slaughter you like the cattle you have become!"*15*

There were many on their feet now, way too many for the lodge, and Banyon could feel that the people outside would soon be treated to a sight to remember if some kind of order were not restored.

---

14 December15, 1890, Omicron Line
15 The Battle of Wounded Knee December 29,1890

In the midst of the chaos, he could see Sitting Bull still sitting on the buffalo robe where he had been smoking his pipe, apparently in deep thought.

"I will attack the fort tomorrow by myself if needs be!" Shoots Straight yelled at the struggling chiefs. "I will not live another day to see the fathers of my father's father quiver in fear in a land that is still their own. When my body is brought back to the cave, I will tell the powers that you are cowards, and not worth saving. That you are men with women's hearts and should be left to be slaughtered to feed the dogs."

The former agent could feel himself being swept out of the lodge now as the chiefs all fought for a chance at this raving white man. Never in the history of the people, or in the memories of the oldest men, had there ever been such a disgraceful council as this. Never had a man had a heart as bad as this white man.

As he felt himself being pulled inexorably toward the exit, Banyon caught one last glance at Sitting Bull. The elder statesman of the Lakota was still sitting where he was. The former agent thought for the briefest moment that he could see a smile on the wrinkled face as words flowed out in a rhythmic melody.

. . .Yes do help me . . .
I love my country so
That is why I am fighting . . .

Shoots Staight felt something rising within him. It was a sensation he had known little of in his life, a sensation that, although it was rare to him, he could distinctly recognize it if he could not understand its coming. The feeling was of a new beginning, feeling of genuine hope!

Looking back at the chanting holy man of the Sioux, he suddenly joined in:

A good nation we will make live
This the nation above had said
We have given you the power to make over . . .

Chapter 12

In general, in battle one engages with the orthodox
and gains Victory through the un-orthodox . .

If the enemy opens the door, you must race in.
Sun Tzu
The Art of War

On the Tongue River
March 1877
Omega Line

The lodge on the Tongue was busy for ten days as Smiles at the People, the army Captain Hales, and Plenty Coups sat in council over the contents of the book. Sharpfish realized now that he would not be able to follow the original plan to find the Nez Perce. He hoped, however, that this new path would also help them toward a victory.

He had followed the counsel brought to him by the girl and, in spite of her unwillingness to say how she knew Rodgers; he knew the message must be true.

On the following morning, between Hales and Smiles at the People, they began to read the contents of the book to the Crow chief. The girl, who they had since learned was named Red Cherry, translated to the chieftain, both in word and perceived meaning.

Both men, however, were stunned when they had stopped for a break on the fourth day and the girl had picked up the book and begun to translate directly from the text. It was uncommon in that point of time for a native of the northern plains to be able to speak fluent English. It was almost unheard of, however, for one such person to read the written language. The former inmate had sat dumbfounded as he had watched the girl move through the chapter with the greatest of ease.

The girl could feel the former convict watching and finally, on the fifth day, she had waited long enough. "What do you want from me, Leonard? I can't imagine that you could be as dumb as all that. What do you want me to do, spell it out for you?"

He still was unable to go where she would lead so the girl gave up and shouted into the face of the dumbstruck ex-convict. "You are the reason they invented e-mail. Other forms of communication are just too slow for people like you."

Hale had his grin back in place now, and the young Lakota could not help but feel that it was directed toward him. "How did you get here?" Sharpfish asked.

"The same way you did. Only in my day they required that those who came through be a little smarter, I think, than they allow now."

Hale was laughing and Smiles at the People even thought he could see a smile of sorts on the face of Plenty Coups.

In spite of his repeated attempts in the following days, the apparently disgusted girl refused to discuss the subject further.

On the tenth day after the escape of the Crazy Horse band, the remaining Crow at the cantonment, along with Plenty Coups and the girl, left the camp on the Tongue and headed east. With them went the wounded Sharpfish who, although still weak from his injury, could ride well enough to accompany the party.

Hale mingled among them, as they got ready to leave, spending time talking quietly with Plenty Coups, thanks to the help of Red Cherry. Then, leaving those two to finish their loading, he walked over to where Smiles at the People was getting to know the chestnut gelding that had been given to him by the Crow chieftain.

The young Lakota had originally felt a great deal of satisfaction at the gift from the Crow headman. It wasn't long, however, until he was made aware that the horse had belonged to the Lakota until just after the flight of the band northward.

By the prevailing thought of the time, the horse did belong to the Crow. Horses left behind in such a situation were considered the rightful property of the man who gathered them up. Even if the man had stolen the animal right under the nose of its owner, no Indian on the plains would dispute his right to possess or to give away the animal at his discretion.

Hale patted the horse on the shoulder as he came up to his young friend. "You don't know how much I wish that you were staying, Leonard."

Sharpfish smiled weakly back at the Captain. "You don't know how much I wish I was too," he responded. "I mean; I know that in this century it's kind of expected that you take a lick like this and just keep going. But in my century, I would still have a month or two to convalesce, hopefully with a pretty girl waiting on me hand and foot."

Hale smiled broadly at the thought, and the former convict remembered again how much he had come to enjoy the friendship of the man. It really did seem there was little that could keep that roguish smile from the sharply cut face. That such as him must die without leaving the genes that produced that smile to the next generation . . .

Still, pondered the former convict, there were a lot of men just like him, each with his own set of talents and qualities. Too many of them were left in shallow graves in this place. How much was lost, no one could know. Which of they themselves, or one of their descendants, would do something irreplaceable for humanity? What idea could have formed from just the right combination of genetics and experience that somehow would have changed the future far more than any of them could have ever imagined?

Such thoughts erased the smile from the face of the Indian, Smiles at the People.

"What are you going to do about the fight at the Bear Paw, Owen?"

The grin appeared again, but behind it there was a certain something that the young Lakota thought he had seen growing in the last few days. *A certain sadness maybe*, thought Smiles at the People. "I mean, you know what is going to happen. To use a phrase from my century, 'best defense, no be there.'" The smile on the young man's face at his own humor was unconvincing.

"I don't know," answered the Captain. "I guess that there really isn't anything for me to do. Do you expect me to stay at the cantonment while my company goes out to fight?"

The young ex-con was serious now, "Yes, that is exactly what I mean! You are going to be killed, Owen. In fact, you are going to be the first one killed in that fight."

Sharpfish looked over at the gray gelding of his friend's, which was searching in an open saddlebag for loose grain. He had thoroughly enjoyed the two in his time on the Tongue. The man and the horse were so much a team, the jaunty, swaggering, army captain with his hat askew on his ragged mop of brown hair. Everywhere, without coaching or compulsion, the gray horse followed him, the man, ever into the lives of the men around him. The horse, ever into everything not tied or nailed shut!

They made quite a team, and Sharpfish mourned in advance the moment in the book where it was written that the man was shot from his saddle, killed immediately. Beside him would lay his trusty gray mount, mortally wounded.

Hale went over to get the gray out of the saddle bag and walked back to Smiles at the People talking as he went. "So let's just say that I turn my back on my men, on my oath as an officer. Heck, let's just say that I run off and hide. What happens then? My bullet catches one of my men who were supposed to live? Then what, Leonard? I'm still alive, but what *am* I then?"

"You're alive, Owen, nothing is more important than that."

The officer was looking at the ground now, and, although the younger man thought he could still see the grin on his face, it was clear that something said had struck him wrong.

After a moment he began to speak. The voice that had normally boomed out of the saucy army captain was quieter to start with as Sharpfish struggled to hear. He soon came into his own, however, as he seemed to catch the vision of what was coming out of his own head. "Do you remember, Leonard, when you told me about why the future had to be changed?" asked the officer.

"Yeah," Leonard responded, "I think I do."

"Remember you said that the problem was that 'It' didn't last?"

"Yes," the younger man replied replied, "I remember, Owen. I remember saying just that."

"Well, I've been thinking about that, and I think you were wrong. I think that '*It*' wasn't good enough in the first place, or maybe '*It*' would have survived in spite of all that "*It*" faced. If you, as a product of that time, really believe that living is the most important thing in all of this mess, then," the Captain paused for just a moment, "It *wasn't* good enough!"

"Come on, Captain," coached the determined Sharpfish, "waxing philosophical on me won't solve the problem. You are going to die, and with that death you will no longer be part of the solution."

"I don't know about that," responded Captain Hale, grinning widely now. "You don't know that one of my boys, in watching me die, won't find something inside himself that wasn't there before. Maybe that something will allow him to live his life just a little better. To be just a bit better man. You can't tell me that, somehow, the world wouldn't be improved by that."

Smiles at the People thought he could see how this was going to end now, and he fought against it. He remembered what the book had said. *My God, why do I have to go out and get killed on such a cold morning?* Hale had said that in *Omicron*, just before

214

he was killed on the first charge. Those who survived reported that the words sounded like the words of a prayer!

Sudden realization hit him like a rock. *He knew all along!* He knew with a perfect knowledge that he was going to die. Somehow in the machinations with the cave, he had been given the knowledge of his own death, and he had met it just the same.

"Owen," began the young Lakota, "I think I realize something now that I never picked up on before."

"What is that?" asked the officer.

"You aren't supposed to die on the Bear Paw site."

"What do you mean?" asked Hale. "I read about it in the book, just like you. It says very clearly what is going to happen."

"No, no," responded the younger man. "Think about it. You never had a chance. The book, I think, makes it clear that you knew you were going to die. You knew ahead of time, Owen. Maybe from what we did here, maybe some other way, but however, you knew you were going to die."

"So," responded the officer, "what does that mean?"

"What does that mean?" shouted back the animated Sharpfish. "A man who knows, beyond a doubt, that he is going to die will make no effort to defend himself or to even take reasonable precautions. A man, on the other hand, who does not expect to die, will do all of that. He will be watchful and alert, he will duck when it is time to duck, and he will take cover when that is appropriate.

"In fact, think about the whole battle, Captain. Does an army officer, knowing he is riding into an indentation in a river valley filled with the straightest shooting Indians on the continent simply call a charge and lead his men headlong into certain death? The history records, Owen, that most of those who rode with you in that charge were either killed or wounded. Think about it, man! Does that make any sense to you?

"Plus, there is more to it. If that ridiculous charge had not been made, and if the men had not been so infuriated after seeing the death of their officer, your death, Captain, then what would have happened? We're talking about what effect your death *really* had. If the charge had not happened, then the Nez Perce would have been able to affect their retreat to the north before they were surrounded and slaughtered.

"Come on, Owen, you asked me once what these mistakes were that were made, and I told you I didn't know. Well I'm telling you I know *one of them* right now. I'm telling you that the charge you will lead on the 30th of September was not supposed to have taken place. Neither you nor so many of your men were supposed to have died that day; nor were so many of the very best men of the Nez Perce.

"Remember what we said about amputating a part of our own body, Hale? Well it was on that September day that part of it happened, and the reason it happened is because you got your hands on *that* book and talked to someone from the future."

Plenty Coups had ridden up to within hearing distance while the young Lakota was yelling at the officer. Smiles at the People turned in time to see that Red Cherry was beside him and was giving Plenty Coups the translation of what he was saying.

Sharpfish did not change tones whatsoever or give any indication that he had seen them or that they were hearing what he was saying.

"Remember again, Owen. The whole thing didn't have to take place at all. After their run through the Yellowstone, they had hoped to find help from their friends the Absarokee, or the Crow; friends who had fought at their side for a hundred years and had accepted their help in innumerable defenses of their own land and lives. But those friends turned their back on them out of fear of the whites.

"Now you tell me, Captain, that it wasn't good enough. That we in the future are somehow morally inferior to you here because we think that it is important to live, while you find your honor in dying. Well let me tell you something, Mister. Regardless of what you may believe, there is no honor in dying needlessly in a foolish cause. We could give *you* a few lessons on the value of friends sticking together and standing by each other.

"I believe that principle is why our nation sends troops to protect people all over the earth. It is because we believe that *they* have a right to live. We will give all that we have, even our lives, in a 'worthy cause' for our friends."

Hale could plainly see that Smiles at the People was furious now and deep within him, he began to understand.

"I don't know where that virtue came from, but I think I have learned for myself that it did not come from here!"

To his left, Sharpfish could hear the girl Red Cherry finishing up the translation.

*

On the Missouri River, upstream from Fort Peck
March 1877
Omega Line

The following morning, good to his promise, Shoots Straight began to plan his attack on Fort Peck. He was not surprised that Crazy Horse was there with him. As he began to put together his strategy, the number around his planning area began to grow.

The warriors committing to go with the white man on his attack on the fort watched carefully as he drew out maps of the area in the mud.

"Why are we doing this?" asked Little Big Man, as Banyon worked away at the drawings. "If you want us to attack the fort, then we will attack. We are Lakota warriors. Why is it necessary to plan what we were born to do and have done many times before?"

The white interpreter had just finished up his drawing as young Black Elk came up, bringing one of the biggest horses he had ever seen!

"Hold him over there for just a minute," said Banyon, as the boy led the horse back toward the perimeter of the camp. He had learned about the horse in the early morning from the boy and his companions. It was said he had been stolen from a farmer along the Platte. He had been such a novelty that the Hunkpapa had allowed him to stay with their large horse herds, although it appeared to most that his only purpose, other than pulling the white man's plow, was for eating. Still, he was glad to see the animal estimating that it weighed well over a ton.

He watched the horse being led off and also noticed that Sitting Bull had joined the gathering warriors.

Shoots Straight directed himself to Little Big Man, starting with a statement intended to madden the surrounding warriors. "There are too many cowards in this camp; those with heart will be outnumbered by the white soldiers." His statement had the desired effect as a rumble of voices came back to him from the Lakota.

Again directing himself at Little Big Man he spoke again. "If so little a group as we, attacks the whites at the fort, what will happen?"

Little Big Man had already made it clear that he would fight along side Crazy Horse and his crazy white man. He seemed to be taking a great deal of pleasure in the situation and jumped in with vigor. "While these cowards stay in the camp with the women and the dogs, we will attack as we always have."

Banyon waited for him to continue, but he did not. "What will happen then?" he asked the Lakota warrior.

"The whites will close the gate of the fort and will shoot at us from behind their walls until we lose some brave men, grow tired, and go away."

There was laughter now from among the group, as everyone knew that what Little Big Man had described was exactly what would happen. The former agent waited for the laughter to abate; then he began explaining what he had in mind.

"What if the gate was open and could not be closed? What if there were already some Lakota inside the fort when the fighting started?"

Little Big Man spoke right to the point without mixing words. "If a few Lakota were inside the fort when the fight started, and the gate was not closed so that the remaining warriors could attack the whites inside, we would kill every one of these white men and take their guns."

"Hou! Hou! Hou! It is true!" was the response from the surrounding warriors.

"And then what would happen?" asked Banyon.

Little Big Man, as usual, was to the point. Not trying to hide his smile, he told what every man there knew would, of a certainty, happen. "The whites would hear about what we had done and send a thousand more soldiers to chase us around the country."

"What," started Shoots Straight, "would happen if we took the guns from the whites in front of their noses and left them alive?"

Little Big Man, thoroughly enjoying this fine joke, answered for the rest. "Then the soldiers would come and replace the little soldier chief at the fort and send him home as a coward. Then, knowing that we are better armed, they would sit a very long time in council before they came out of their walls again."

Four hours later, the interpreter Shoots Straight stood in front of the fort with the big plow horse at the end of an improvised halter. In front of him walked four Lakotas covered in clothing traditional to the season, i.e., heavy buffalo robes that covered their persons from shoulders to knees.

As they approached the fort, the post commander, one Lt. Gottfredson, ordered them to halt a distance from the gate and asked their business. Banyon, clearly holding a Winchester on the downtrodden looking Lakota responded. "My name is Virgil Hunter. I'm from the Bernhold agency upriver. I have a few prisoners to turn over to you."

Lt. Gottfredson looked passively at the Lakota prisoners before asking what manner of crime these men were to be charged with.

"Horse thievin'," responded *Virgil Hunter* cheerfully. "They took this here draft horse from the agency. We had just received it last fall by steamer and were gettin' ready to use it to begin to teach our Indians how to farm. Well," he continued, "he turned up missin' here about a week ago, and I found him with these gentlemen just as they were gettin' ready to eat him."

The Lieutenant seemed more than casually bored with the whole arrangement and asked *Virgil*, exactly he wanted him to do about it.

Virgil responded immediately. "Just take these characters off my hands until the first steamer comes up river next month. It will take them and the horse back upriver where we will deal with our own problems."

"I wish that you would deal with your own problems now," responded the Lieutenant. "Why should I have to feed four mouths, and a horse that looks like he could eat a house, for maybe a whole month?"

Virgil started to laugh. "Well, I guess that I can see your point, Commander. Tell you what, you lock these four in your guardhouse over night, and give me a bale of hay for the horse. I'll head them all back to Bernhold tomorrow on foot."

Lt. Gottfredson nodded his agreement and ordered the gate opened. At the opening of the gate, the four Lakota turned as if to get direction to enter from Shoots Straight. The former agent had a hard time not breaking character on seeing the look on the face of Little Big Man. The Lakota fighter was smiling from ear to ear at the agent as he told them to go inside. Waiting for the would-be prisoners to clear the inside perimeter of the enclosure, Shoots Straight let the horse follow in behind them.

As the big animal entered the swing area of the gate, suddenly, without warning, a rifle shot rang out from the trees behind Banyon.

The big horse struggled another step and then…
fell in his tracks!

Out of the corner of his eye, he could see the smoke coming from the rifle of Buffalo Calf Road standing in the trees toward the river.

Immediately, the five soldiers at the gate ran to remove the dead animal from the entrance of the fort so they could shut the obstructed gate. The horse would not move even an inch.

From the trees behind Virgil came an eruption of movement as over two hundred Lakota warriors rushed to the gate of the fort and entered.

Lt. Gottfredson turned in an instant to issue orders to his men, now emerging from the enlisted men's quarters.

Directly below him, he saw four Winchesters now out of the buffalo robes of the prisoners and pointing directly at him and the guards who, to the man, were raising their hands. In the next instant, the enclosure was filled with heavily armed Lakota, and all thought of resistance ceased.

"Virgil" stood outside the fort smiling up at the very un-amused officer. "Lieutenant, if you will just calm down a little, nobody will get hurt. We just want to do a little trading' and we weren't all too certain that you would accept our trade without a little, 'primin of the pump,' we might call it. In any event, we would like to trade a real nice big horse . . . for a few rifles!"

The valley of the Greasy Grass a.k.a., The Little Big Horn
March 1877
Omega Line

After traveling for ten days, through what Sharpfish would have described as Indian paradise, the Plenty Coups party arrived at the Crow camp along the Greasy Grass. The young Lakota was aware that the whites called the river and the valley that fed it the Little Big Horn. He was also aware that it was less than a year since the segment of the 7th cavalry under George Custer had charged into this valley. The Boy General, as he had been known in the Civil War, had hopes of destroying the combined villages of the Sioux and Cheyenne camped along its tree-lined bank. Sharpfish pondered also about the great victory that had been enjoyed by the hostiles that day. Then he thought about how, in truth, the fight had been the end of all they held dear. Custer and his men may have lost the fight and their lives on that hot June day, but they had accomplished what they had come to do, i.e., end a way of life for the last of the remaining free Lakota.

As they entered the valley from the north, he thought he recognized the hill where the three companies under the austere Colonel had made their last stand. Below that hill and across the river of the Little Big Horn, he could now see the sleepy village that was their destination.

It was worthy of note, he thought, that the Sioux were camped that fateful day on land that had belonged to the Crow for generations before the Sioux had crossed the Missouri and invaded the land of the Crow. Now driven to the westernmost edge of what had been a mighty expanse of grassland, the Crow fought beside their new allies, the whites, to save what little was left to them.

As they entered the camp, the women and children ran to receive the returning Crow warriors. After camping with the band of Lakota for several weeks, Smiles at the People was struck with how few the Crow were compared with even a single band of the Lakota.

But still, he was drawn back to his thought of the previous weeks. Although few, the Crow had held their own in a retreat that had lasted over three generations! Not just against the Sioux from the east, but also against the Blackfeet from the north and the Gros Ventre from the west, their only friends were the Nez Perce, who had stuck with them through it all. The Bannocks and Shoshone were, at best, intermittent friends to the Crow.

It was also understandable to the former convict the attitude of the Bannocks and the Shoshone. As the Lakota had pushed the Crow west from the heart of their former hunting grounds, the area that became the center of their country was progressively closer to areas claimed by those two tribes.

Smiles at the People watched as the warriors were met by their families and dropped out of the procession into camp. He also noticed that there was no sign of greeting toward Red Cherry, who continued on with him and Plenty Coups until they reached the lodge of the Crow chief.

Sharpfish was shown where he would sleep, but he was not totally certain that the thought of sleeping in the same lodge as the volatile Plenty Coups was ideal. However, he did know what he had come to do. In knowing that, he also knew that being able to have access to Plenty Coups, the man who could make the decision, would be important.

As he organized his few possessions to take in the lodge, he heard the voice of Red Cherry behind him. "So, Leonard, are you going to remember me on your own, or do I have to do all the work, like always."

The former convict turned and stared at the interpreter, smiling sheepishly. "I kind of figured I knew you from the first day. But I guess I gotta admit that, even after this much time, I just can't place you."

"What if I were to tell you that I used to bring food and supplies across the lines at night when the Feds had your sorry butt surrounded at Wounded Knee?"

Sharpfish stared, mouth agape, then looked away. "I think I know who you want me to believe you are, but that person is long dead. I don't appreciate the joke."

The interpreter reached up and slapped the former inmate lightly on the side of the head. "You never were very quick on the uptake, were you Leonard? I remember the time you came to me as the big head of security guy, asking if I was some type of an informer. I wasn't, you know. While you were asking me questions, I thought you *looked* a lot smarter than you really were. I can see that little has changed."

"Joanna?" the shocked former inmate choked. "This can't be true. Joanna Decoteau has been dead for …"

"Really?" replied the Indian woman. "How long, following that line of reason, has Leonard Sharpfish been dead? For that matter, how many years will it be until he is born?"

Smiles at the People threw his arms around the surprised woman before she could finish speaking. She pushed him away playfully, whacking him up the side of the head once again.

"Get your hands off me, you big goof. You think I am glad to see you? You are the one who got me killed in the first place, you and all your big talk and 'let's shoot at the cops' games."

The young Lakota could not stop his chin from dropping now. When Joanna's body had been found, it had been said that it had been in retribution for what had been done, an eye for an eye sort of thing. Even though he knew he had not done the shooting, Leonard had felt a great sense of guilt over what had happened to Joanna.

"You should have understood after they opened my grave the second time and could not find the body. After you went through the cave, even *you* should have put two and two together." The young woman hesitated, looking searchingly at the emotional Sharpfish. "But then, I guess I should have realized that two plus two would be high math to you."

"Well," stammered Smiles at the People, "how long have you been here?"

"Been where?" snapped an impatient looking Red Cherry.

"Here, ah . . . with the Crow!"

"Oh I have been with the Crow on and off for about five years."

"Five years? Where were you before that?"

"Before what...?"

"Before you came to be with the Crow..."

"California, for the most part, but sometimes I went back to Nova Scotia to visit my folks."

"Visit your folks?" stammered the confused Sharpfish.

"Then it wasn't you. You weren't really shot?"

"Oh yeah, that was me all right. Pretty unpleasant business, if you ask me. Hey, I never did get even with you for that. Those Feds told me they were doing it to get at you!"

Sharpfish was really confused now. "But if you're dead, then how, exactly, are you hanging out in California and going on trips back to visit your folks?"

"I got there the very same way that you got here Leonard; through the cave in the Paha Sapa!"

"Through the cave, you're trying to tell me that you just kind of go back and forth as it pleases you?"

"Yeah," responded the girl. "Something like that."

"Something like that? Well, how close am I getting to 'that'?"

"You see, Leonard, we have only recently become aware that the problem was here in this time period. Before that, we thought it was much further in the future, and we concentrated our efforts there."

"There?" repeated the incredulous former convict.

"Yes, back in what you would call our original time line. We call it *Omicron*. We did a lot of things, including seeing to it that your own precious movement had its beginning. None of it worked, though. We should have known it then, because the outcome was always the same, regardless of the many different ideas we implemented. It was just too close to the end. The ripples were too big that late in the game. The information was moving too fast, and we were too close to the culmination of the line to affect the outcome."

"Wait a minute," queried Sharpfish. "Who are 'we' exactly? I get the idea you are talking about more than just you and Rodgers."

Red Cherry seemed almost indignant at the comment. "Of course there were more that just Hergin and I. There were actually many others. Some that are still involved and many others that have been let out of the loop and are leading lives at the point of history where they were left."

"Where they were left?"

"You can't go back to where you were, obviously. If you went back, as an example, you would just be a dead guy outside of Marion Penitentiary. I, on the other hand, would be a corpse buried in a plain wooden box in a Catholic cemetery. Oh yeah, with a bullet in the back of my head…"

"But if, when we return, we're just dead, then how did you do all of those things that you say you did in the future?" mumbled the confused Sharpfish.

"Simple. They were done either before the time of my death or they happened in a different, but very similar, time line."

"Different time line, I don't think I understand?"

"Sure you do, Leonard, you're just stupid. You've always been stupid," quipped the interpreter. "With every event here, the future is changed. If you go out today and kill a buffalo, there is one less buffalo now and probably many less in the future of that time line; the time line, however, in which you do not go out and shoot that buffalo, continues on in a parallel, but very similar course. So similar, in fact, that you probably don't even notice the difference.

"I, as an example can, and have, gone back to a time just before the night that they took me out to the Badlands in the trunk of a car, and have simply stayed home and watched a good movie. The other time line in which I was killed exists as it was. The only difference, in the improved line, is that I came through the cave, so I have no actual memory of the event. All my memory of that unpleasant evening comes from the book of the main branch of the Omicron line. "Have you ever been confused Leonard?"

"Up to and including now."

"Well, we believe that confusion is a factor of the phenomena. The human brain, it turns out, is an unfailing recorder of all information that is sent to it. This information is much more than simply those items received by the sense of sight. The information received from all senses is completely and permanently recorded in the 'hard drive,' if you will. What happens then is this information, so very complicated and multifaceted in its nature, is changed in the past and, in doing so becomes incorrect to the mind."

"Confusion," proffered Sharpfish.

"Exactly! The brain has to reformat, if you please, to accommodate the new, correct information. During this time period, which can be a millisecond or, unfortunately, a matter of years, we have the 'interval,' as we call it, of confusion.

"You can see it all around you if you know what you are looking for. Old people, as an example, are unfairly and mercilessly kidded because of the confusion they experience. This is simply because they have lived much longer than those who are younger, and thus have recorded exponentially more information. For their brains to reformat takes a much longer time period. Unfortunately, some can never adjust. We refer in our feeble way to their state as a degenerative thing due to old age. We are wrong in this. It is rather because of the changes that are being performed in an unfathomably huge database.

"Some never can reach equilibrium again, and our rest homes are filled with these unfortunate beings. They are usually people that, because of their immense ability to record knowledge, have ruptured the fabric of the barrier."

"The barrier," Sharpfish queried, "What barrier?"

"The barrier that we all carry in our minds to stop just this eventuality! Do you remember being in your mother's womb, Leonard?"

The former convict blinked. "Of course I don't."

"Why? Why, if your brain is such an unerring recorder, can you not remember that most salient and satisfying time in your life?"

Sharpfish knew that whatever answer he offered would not be correct, so he just grinned stupidly at Red Cherry.

"You can't remember because of the fabric. A shield, or veil some call it that is placed in our minds to stop us from remembering everything that is recorded, to stop 'repositioning' from confusing us to death.

"A rupture of the fabric causes the mind to try to reformat an endless stream of information. It can do this, but the down time may be longer than the expected life of the person. So only a portion of what we know is made available at any one time. Your available memory is limited by the barrier to those things on the conscious side of the fabric.

"In truth, that is what education is. It is the adding of information in an orderly and systematic way, pushing back the fabric, allowing the information on the conscious side to increase in availability to the conscious being.

"That is why we were not planning to use Dan Banyon again."

Leonard was suddenly concerned. "Why? What has this to do with Shoots Straight?"

"He has gone with us too many times, lived in too many time lines, and absorbed too much. The rupture of his fabric was considered to be probable if he wasn't left somewhere to finish out his life in peace."

Sharpfish thought back to the cave where he had heard Rodgers talking to the "confused" agent. Yes, Rodgers had said something like that. He did talk about a hundred battles and of many attempts.

Red Cherry began again. "Dan had seen too many battles, been brought back to the cave too many times. His wife was always with him. She too was a great warrior, and she could steady him when the fabric was weak. But even she could not stop the inevitable."

Sharpfish interrupted, "I have never heard anything about a wife. Are you sure about that?"

"They are legend. Never were there a man and woman to compare with them. Some believed they had their beginning in the cave where all things eternal are born. Others believed that theirs was a relationship formed in the heat of battle where they had fought together hundreds of times for the future of the people.

"In his last attempt to bring the flute player, they thought they would lose him, so they brought him to *Omicron* as a child. You see; they had to start him at a very young age to erase, or at least push back, the memories of the other lines.

"However, in the line that allowed him to live, he was an orphan with no one to care for him. It was known that if there was no one to teach him, then he would be lost in the confusion of the thinning fabric that would someday find him."

Smiles at the People sat fascinated now. "You're talking about the girl, aren't you? The girl went back and became his . . .?"

"He believed that she was his grandmother. *Omicron* was his original line. He could go back as a child. She, however, was from the past and could only go across at the age she was when she went through the cave toward *Omicron*. In the age that the cave allowed her to go to *Omicron*, she was fifty years older than he was on the same time line.

"She stayed there with him until he was almost an adult. She was able to return to the cave before death took her in *Omicron*."

"Then she is his wife?"

"In over twenty of the last attempts, that is true," replied Red Cherry.

Suddenly, Sharpfish thought of Rodgers. "How does Rodgers handle all of his information? I got the idea that he had been with Banyon on hundreds of these lines and many more without him. Why doesn't he shut down from all the information?"

"It's not that difficult. We know now that some individuals can handle all the experiences and memories of multiple lines. Others cannot. It depends on the degree of insertion experience by the cave traveler. Dan has, in most cases, been the lead man. The one sent directly to the axial point. The experiences there tear at the fabric. It is at that point that endless decisions have to be made – decisions that determine, in a very real sense, who will live and who will die.

"Rodgers, as you know him, is one of those very rare few to whom the tearing and, in his case, the destruction of the fabric was not debilitating. We know there are those like Rodgers who have a mind that can handle the information of many lines without the aid of the fabric. Their minds have an unfathomable ability to store and departmentalize data. His mind also was created in an earlier time, a time before the multiple branches that have brought us to where we are now."

"Then you're saying he is not from *Omicron*, like us and Banyon?"

The Indian girl wrapped her arms around the former convict, Smiles at the People, and squeezed tight.

"He most certainly is not!"

"Well, what did you mean by *"bring the flute player"*...?

Chapter 13

We're going back to the beginning of time . . . I have no fear,
have no slightest fear whatsoever. Even if I have to face death .
. . We hold the key to eternity, where everything is everlasting
for everyone. That's where we're going. We're going home.
Wallace Black Elk

Fort Peck, Missouri River
March 1877
Omega Line

On the 14th of March 1877, six hundred and forty men,
under the command of Lt. James Baldwin, escorted the wounded
Nelson Miles into the walled perimeter of Fort Peck.

The rehabilitating Miles was made comfortable in the
officer's quarters. Baldwin thought it bore striking resemblance to
an oversized chicken coop. There, away from the unseasonably
warm weather, Miles heard the report from Lt. Gottfredson;
everyone in the fort could hear the angry yelling from inside the
building distinctly.

"Lieutenant, we spent all last fall shipping Winchester
repeaters and ammunition to your location to re-arm soldiers in
four different upriver forts, as well as my own men on the
Tongue. Then you, with over two hundred men in your command
and charged with nothing more important than protecting those
rifles, turned them over to Sitting Bull and Crazy Horse without
even a single shot being fired?"

Gottfredson, sweating through his uniform and desperately
searching for a shred of defense to help his cause, jumped on the
statement.

"No, Sir. There actually was one shot fired."

231

Baldwin, standing in the room, thought that Miles would explode at the comment.

"So then, Lieutenant, your defense is that there actually was one shot fired and that shot was fired by them! One shot to take a fort of the United States Army. And that shot killed a big . . . fat . . . horse?" Miles' voice grew louder, each word thrown at the junior officer as if somehow by the effort he could force the man to say something to give him understanding.

"Yes, Sir!"

"Well, I guess that the court martial will be able to understand your surrender, Lieutenant. I know that if someone shot a big fat horse within twenty feet of me, I'd probably surrender the whole regiment! Get this fool out of my sight before I shoot him," raged the trembling officer.

"Lt. Baldwin, I'm placing you in command of this station and every man therein, pending my recovery. If you still feel good about the intelligence you received from the interpreter, then I want you to prepare to receive an attack within seventy-two hours. I also want you to keep in mind that due to the incident with the fat horse, you will not only be outnumbered, but also outgunned; these being the facts, Lieutenant, see that there are no patrols or any other expeditions of any size over that of scouts, leaving this post until the threat of this attack is past."

"Yes, Sir," saluted the Lieutenant as he turned on his heel and left the Colonel to his fuming.

The Lieutenant had every reason to believe that within the seventy-two hours given him by his commander, he could successfully prepare his men and his position for the most decisive battle in the history of the west. Given that he had both the resources and the intelligence to do so, he had no doubt of his success.

Whatever happened, resolved the Lieutenant, no one would get inside the walls of Fort Peck. Neither would he be tricked into weakening his position by anyone, least of all by a big fat horse!!

*

The Camp of Sitting Bull west of Fort Peck
March 1877
Omega Line

In the Indian camp there was jubilation. Never in the history of the people had there been such a victory and that without the loss of a single warrior.

Every man in camp now brandished a brand new Winchester repeater and was the owner of sufficient ammunition to make them potentially the most lethal fighting force in the history of the plains.

The dancing went into the night, and there was still a segment dancing as the sun peaked above the small hills that separated them from Fort Peck. There was no concern in the camp about the soldiers at the fort coming after their rifles. There were no men so stupid as to try to take by force rifles such as these.

During the dancing, Shoots Straight sat in the lodge of Sitting Bull, in council with the chiefs. Outside, rifle in hand, stood Buffalo Calf Road. At her side was the boy, Black Elk. They were not allowed in the council with the chiefs, but *they all knew* they were part of what would now come and would be ready.

Inside the lodge there was little need of persuasion at first as the chiefs had all accepted that the rude white man was a cunning warrior and his medicine was strong.

One of the first things Banyon had done to test whether the chiefs were willing to do as he suggested, was to tell them that in four days a wall of water would come down the river, destroying everything in its path. He told them if they continued to camp

233

where they were, they would lose all they had, barely escaping with their lives.

Banyon was satisfied to see Sitting Bull give orders to a man who he perceived was the crier of the encampment. The man looked in a very big hurry as he left the lodge.

Within the hour, the whole camp was in motion toward higher ground. When they camped for the night, Shoots Straight was assured that Sitting Bull would take every precaution to save his people. He was not the type of man to wait to the last moment to do so.

Banyon felt a certain degree of satisfaction knowing that before the raging wall of water hit and destroyed Fort Peck, Nelson Miles and his men would be within its walls. He lamented the tremendous loss of life that this action would entail. He, however, found solace in the point that these men were coming after the Lakota and their allies with the intent to imprison or kill. There was no question who the aggressors were, and had been, in this war. Neither was there a question that, without firing so much as another shot, the Sioux would win the biggest and most decisive victory in the history of the plains. With such a tremendous defeat before them, he felt certain the United States Congress would end its funding for the army of the Dakotas and send out negotiators to make a treaty that would last. *After all*, he thought, *this war was reported historically to be costing the government over a million dollars a day to maintain. In this time period*, thought Banyon, *a year of such expenditure would cost over three quarters of the national budget. The whole of Montana and North and South Dakota was not worth two years of such expenditure. The politicians had to know that.*

For the Indians' part, they knew that if the Wasichu Wakan had foreseen properly, they would be rid of the pony soldiers that so plagued their lives. Possibly forever! If he had not foreseen properly, they were still better armed than they had ever imagined, and would stay and fight for their lands if any white soldiers should ever be so brave as to enter them again.

It was even reasonable to believe that those faint hearts who had given up and gone over to the whites would tie up their ponies' tails once more and join them, as the old life returned to them once again.

With the approaching destruction of the Bear Coat and his soldiers, they would own everything between the line with the land of the Grandmother and the Paha Sapa. They also knew that without the army to support the white prospectors, by the *Moon of the Ponies Making Fat*, they would ride through that sacred land and take all that had been theirs away from the white hand that grasped it.

"And when we are through pushing the whites from our land," said Sitting Bull, "we will turn on our enemies, the Crow, and drive them forever from us."

As the great holy man of the Sioux finished that statement, Banyon could feel that something was very wrong. His head seemed to spin mercilessly and then, of a sudden, stop, and then spin again. He could feel himself falling, but he was also certain that he was still sitting upright. What seemed like a hundred memories, no, messages, he thought, poured into his head.

He put his hand on the knee of Crazy Horse and tried to rise, only to fall backward. He could feel hands grab for him as his mind reeled. Then found itself for just a minute, no, a second really, a millisecond . . . yes, yes, an eternity did his mind roll and snap. Then everything was black, in a sea of dreams that haunted, and then attacked, the defenseless man.

He could hear words in a distance but he could not make them out.

"Wakan Tanka," he heard amid the deafening silence.

"God, My Father," was another phrase, and then a distant plea to the god of the Muslims and the many-headed images of the Hindus, and those who worshiped on the islands of the sea. In a moment, he realized they were all directed toward one being, and that only in name did the pleading differ.

The words went on by him as he struggled, and, finding himself unable to resist . . . he surrendered.

Women were making a bed for the fallen Wasichu Wakan as the lead men carried him gently to a nearby lodge. Not a soul missed the presence of the woman, rifle in hand, directing them, forcing the men to do as they were told relative to the fallen man.

At his head was his friend, Crazy Horse, and from the Oglala Head Man came the strangest of sounds. As the chiefs laid the interpreter on the soft buffalo robes, their eyes were riveted on the Oglala fighter. The sounds he was making were those of *the wounded bear*.

Many there had ridden with him in battle and they recognized the sounds as those, which would come from the fighter at the very height of battle. At the point where all would be won or lost, it was known that their Strange Man would return to that dream world from which he gained his medicine. On his return, so would come the sound of the wounded bear.

Sitting Bull seemed undisturbed by what was unfolding before him, although he walked alongside the fallen man chanting and shaking his rattle gourd. Some thought they could hear him saying the name of Wakan Tanka, others thought that he sang a song of his own making.

My father has given me this nation
In protecting them I have a hard time.

In the distance, the scouts could see riders moving rapidly toward them. At their head was the white man, Hergin Rodgers. At his right rode the great warrior, He Dog, who carried in his hand a wooden flute..!

Crow Camp, Little Big Horn Valley
March 1877
Omega Line

In the lodge of Plenty Coups, the night had fallen and the girl was still talking to the former convict. "You see Leonard, there is one thing you have to understand. If you go back to the future, it must be to the future that belongs to the past you are leaving. In fact, that is the only future you can go back to. For you, there is only that future."

"What about all these other futures?" asked Sharpfish.

"They do not exist for you."

"But you said earlier today that you went to see your folks in another time line."

"Yes, I did. But that was the time line that was tied to the past I was coming from and, obviously, not to the one in which I am dead," grinned the girl.

"The fact is that I probably couldn't find the one where I was dead anyway. There have been too many changes here."

"But what about the killing the buffalo thing, are you saying that buffalo created two futures, but to me there is still just one?"

"Exactly, the one with less buffalo…!"

"So if it's that easy, then why would you even be concerned over going back to that line where you are dead?"

"Because that line; is many lines in the future…"

"How do you mean?"

"I mean that you end up in a line where there is less buffalo, but that may be one of the very few differences in that line. It, unless something had been changed in the past to change that specific event, may still be a line where I am dead. The cause and effect principle is still applicable. In order for something to be or not to be, there must be a corresponding event, or lack of an event, in the past that specifically changes that future."

Sharpfish was beginning to understand what she was trying to say, but one question remained that escaped her review. "What you're saying still doesn't explain why we refer to a line as *Omega or Omicron* or whatever. You seem to refer to many lines that we call one, in name at least."

"Just exactly," responded the girl. "What you are referring to is a main branched trunk line if you think of all this as a tree. They all have the same beginning, those that you remember and many others, but they branch at a crucial point.   It is those branched points that we call axial, the place where we can make changes. From there they become what we call *main lines* and are named for reference purposes until they are completed. From that main branch many futures are possible..."

"Why, exactly," interrupted Sharpfish, "is it important for *me* to know all of this? Beyond all that, why, other than giving me a chance to live, am I here in the first place?"

"Because," started the girl, showing that her patience was growing very thin, Dan and Crazy Horse must win at Fort Peck. But we, also, must win here. Unless both victories are achieved, neither they, nor we will find the future we seek."

The young Lakota was laughing now, clearly approaching the end of his patience with the girl.

"What future is that? That is the one thing I have never understood, nor did I believe anyone in this whole crazy situation understood. What are we looking for? We are a group with many feet, pushed hard to an accelerator, but no idea where we are going. How will we even know when we find it if we cannot define what it is we are trying to create? We could go right by it and not even know we were there."

The girl rocked back, smiling at the comment. "Now, I think we are getting there."

"Getting where?" asked Sharpfish.

"Getting to understand there are many futures that can play out from the victory at Fort Peck, but only one that we are looking for. That one requires what we can do here."

"What is going to happen here?" responded Sharpfish.

"The very same thing that happened in the time line you are aware of, except there is a victory at Fort Peck. There are actually, as I said many, many futures from there. But none of them stop what will happen with the Nez Perce. This is the only place we can blend the consequences of that with what happens at Fort Peck."

Smiles at the People was certainly listening now, and the girl felt that she could get him where he needed to go. "In the history that you are aware of, the Nez Perce will come across the Yellowstone after defeating, but being badly mauled by, the troops at the Battle of the Big Hole. They have been expecting to get to buffalo country and get help from their friends, the Crow. In the history that we call *Omicron*, the Crow refuse because they will not fight against the white men, whom they have been told they must not ever fight."

"They also have been told that if they side with the white man they will be taken care of. The one individual who is unmovable in his insistence that this will be true is our host, Plenty Coups." The girl paused for a moment to gauge the young Lakota's reaction. "The same Plenty Coups who has agreed to leave with us tomorrow to visit the Paha Sapa and the cave in the Valley of the Wind."

The picture became clear to Sharpfish as he began to visualize what the chief would see in the future that at least for now belonged to him and his people

Lakota Camp
March 1877
Omega Line

Crazy Horse mounted and started out to meet the oncoming riders. Rodgers wasted no time in getting directly to the point. "Where is Banyon?"

"He is down," answered the Oglala.

"That's pretty much as I expected," returned the historian.

He Dog rode up beside his brother friend and spoke. "We must stop the killing of the soldiers at the fort."

"Stop it?" retorted Crazy Horse. "We have spent the last many days trying to make it happen!"

"I know," returned He Dog, "but we must stop it nonetheless."

Rodgers had moved on past them and was headed directly to the encampment that held the incapacitated Shoots Straight.

Sitting Bull and his nephew, White Bull, were with the fallen Banyon and the girl when the historian entered the tent. Rodgers moved quickly to his side, only to be stopped as he began to touch him by the commanding voice of the Hunkpapa headman.

"Touch this holy man and you die, white man!

Rodgers drew back, realizing that he had first to deal with the most powerful man in a thousand square miles.

"Send for the warriors in the land of the Grandmother, '*Slow*1, or we are lost." Rogers cautiously replied.

He could see a smile blossom on the face of the girl.

---

1 The Name given to Sitting Bull as a child.

The eyes of the Lakota holy man opened a bit wider, but his right hand also moved to his side and came up holding a knife with a bone handle, which he placed in his lap.

"No one has called me that name since I was a child. You will show more respect or I will teach you to show it," said Sitting Bull.

The sound of a cartridge being levered into the bore of the new Winchester was not missed by anyone; there was, however, some surprise as the rifle in the hands of the girl was directed toward the head of the chief.

"If you would not be called the name of a child, then cease to act like one!" barked Rodgers.

The Hunkpapa headman had the knife in his hand now and seemed to be tensed for a forward movement. "In what way do I act like a child, white man? Tell me quickly, before we die."

Rogers replied cautiously. They were too close now to have to start again. "It was you and your foolishness that have brought this man to where he lays. It is your senseless anger and thoughtless calls for vengeance that have brought this man and this whole nation to a point of defeat. You seem not to be able to learn that a victory is not always the way to the Good Red Road. Sometimes, we must look to those virtues that have made the people great and have them lead our actions. When you defeated and killed Long Hair Custer, you were a brave man. Your vision had led the people to victory and you were considered to be a great leader. Now, I need you to be a *wise* man and send for the warriors in the land of the Grandmother. We will need them if we are to drive the soldiers from Fort Peck."

Sitting Bull sat watching now as the white man looked into the eyes of the fallen Wasichu Wakan. It appeared that he was calling to the fallen man in the strange language of the whites. But the "Far Seeing One" did not answer. In that, Sitting Bull felt a great fear.

"This Wasichu Wakan," started Sitting Bull, "he tells us that a great flood will come and kill these white men at the fort. He tells us that we will win a great victory without firing a shot. He has shown us his medicine with a victory at the fort, in which we acquired many guns. Now comes another rude white man, and you tell me I am a child and I am not wise. You tell me that we should drive the soldiers out of the fort and cause them to live so they may attack us another day. In doing this, I know we will lose many warriors, both now and in future battles. You say that I should be wise, white man, so tell me which of these paths would be the path of one who loves his people? Is not *that* path the one of wisdom?"

Rodgers continued to speak to the unconscious Banyon, while listening to the slow, analytical musings of the Lakota headman. "Come on, Dan, we can't do this without you. Baldwin will never believe anyone but you. You have to be there to tell him about the flood!"

Sitting Bull, coming from deep in thought, began again. "I think we will follow the counsel of the Wasichu Wakan."

"Come on Dan!" yelled the Scholar. "This is your moment. This is what you were born to do. When you finish this one, you're through. When this one is finished there is no further need."

"He has told us things that only we could know," said Sitting Bull. "He has told us things that would come to pass, and they have been so. Crazy Horse, who has never lied, has told us that he can see into the future, and there he has found a way for us to walk the road of our fathers. The Good Red Road of true human beings, this is the road we seek."

"Be quiet!" yelled Rodgers at the Lakota chieftain. "I mean no disrespect. You have done and will do more for the good of your people than any other among the Lakota. You counseled wisdom when no other could see it. But it was not enough! We have tried many roads that have seemed wise. We have gone into them with good hearts and with a desire to do the will of Wakan Tanka. But our wisdom has not been enough, up to this very moment. Do you remember what Little Big Man said when this one," pointing at Banyon, "asked him what would happen if we killed the soldiers at the fort?"

Sitting Bull was silent for a moment. "Yes, I remember," responded Sitting Bull, "I was there listening with the warriors. You, white man, were not there."

"That's right," retorted Rodgers, "I was not there. But I can tell you what he said. He said that if you killed the soldiers, that a thousand would be sent to take their place and chase you all over the country."

Sitting Bull nodded his head, looking to his right at his nephew. He spoke hesitantly, "Both Wasichus tell us of things they should not know. Both claim medicine from the powers. Both say different words and counsel about the soldiers in the fort."

Rodgers became aware that Sitting Bull looked strongly to White Bull for counsel. From that awareness, the great historian went back, seeking direction from another important day.

"I can tell you who killed Pe-hin Hanska, the Head Hair Long, or Long Hair Custer," blurted the historian.

Sitting Bull stared back malevolently. "There are many who claim to know such a thing. There are many also who know that the whites have said they will hang that man, when it is discovered, of a truth, who he is."

"Then," started Rodgers, "let me tell you the story and, if that one wishes to remain silent, then it will be so between us. That warrior, who sits here with us, many years in the future, after the threat of the white man's rope is behind him, will tell this tale.

I charged in. A tall, well-built soldier with yellow hair and mustache saw me coming and tried to bluff me, aiming his rifle at me. But when I rushed him, he threw his rifle at me without shooting. I dodged it. We grabbed each other and wrestled there in the dust and smoke. It was like fighting in the fog. This soldier was very strong and brave. He tried to wrench my rifle from me, and nearly did it. I lashed him across the face with my quirt, striking coup. He let go, then grabbed my gun with both hands until I struck him again. But the tall soldier fought hard. He was desperate. He hit me with his fists on the jaw and shoulders, then grabbed my long braids with both hands, pulled my face close and tried to bite my nose off. I yelled for help. "Hey, hey, come over and help me." I thought that the soldier would kill me.

Bear Lice and Crow Boy heard my call and came running. These friends tried to hit the soldier. But we were whirling around, back and forth, so that most of their blows hit me. They knocked me dizzy. I yelled as loud as I could to scare my enemy, but he would not let go. Finally, I broke free. He drew his pistol. I wrenched it out of his hand and struck him three or four times on the head, knocked him over, shot him in the head, and fired at his heart. Hawk Stays Up struck second on the body. 1

"This warrior," finished Rodgers, looking directly at White Bull, "did not know he had killed the soldier chief, but later was told so by a relative named Bad Juice, who had spent time at Fort Abraham Lincoln and knew Long Hair Custer."

Sitting Bull was engrossed in the story, but his nephew was not.

Filled with uncertainty, White Bull spoke to the now silent white man, "This story has never been told in the counting of coups. There was no white man left alive that day to tell the story. How is it that you know to say such words?"

---

1 Most scholars believe that this account tells the probable truth of the death of George Armstrong Custer

"Because," said Rodgers, "as I told you before, later in life you told the story to a white man, who wrote down the words for those who would come after." Rodgers hesitated; looking at Banyon, then spoke again. " . . .And one other way. This one," pointing at Shoots Straight, "was there with the soldiers. After the battle, he was brought back to the Wakan cave by the very girl that holds the gun before you and there told me the story."

Both men stared incredulously at Rodgers.

"No white man left the field that day," said Sitting Bull.

"No white man left the field that day alive!" countered Rodgers.

Sitting Bull allowed his memory to rush back to the early days of his life when he had visited that Wakan cave, watching as the spirits within it made their plans for the people. He remembered the old men had said that the first six human beings had emerged from that cave to come to this world. He also remembered what they had said about the man who had beguiled them to leave their old world and come to this one. The old ones had said that he was a *trickster*.

"White man of the Wakan cave, what do you know of Iktomi the trickster?"

Rodgers sat back on his haunches and stared at the Lakota Holy Man. "Your memories are wrong, my friend. Iktomi was not a trickster he was an evil man. He was of an evil much greater than you can now imagine. He was banished from the other world for the evil things he did there. It was he, as you know, that met the first men and women to come through the Wakan cave to this world. When they were here, he told them that they must wear clothes and gave them food to eat. With the eating of food, they then had to stay in this world until their deaths. At their deaths, their spirits would return through the Wakan cave to their friends that wait in that other world.

"All save those who have not finished the work they were sent to do. These are pushed off the trail, by the powers, to finish their work. Some become ghosts and spirits who walk this world seeking that which they cannot find.

"Some; do other work . . .!

"Your people remember that the food the trickster gave them was meat. The white man remembers that it was fruit."

Sitting Bull nodded, looking at the ground. "I believe that you and this one," pointing to the inert Banyon, "are sent from the powers. Whether you were sent together or separately, I do not know. There are two types of powers, white man. Which of these sent you?"

Rodgers knew that the question itself, above the answer, was the test.

"We," making a circular motion that encompassed both he and Banyon, "are of the Sicun, or the good powers. We have come to help in answer to many prayers."

"Which prayers are these, Sicun Wasichu?" questioned the Hunkpapa.

"They are those that ask for the Good Red Road. And others, that their leader will see the truth!"

"What is this truth, Sicun Wasichu?"

The scholar began slowly, "That all men have a right to live. That the sun shines on all men. That all people or nations who will not believe this vision, in the end, must perish."

Then came the question that Rodgers had dreaded for a hundred time lines. One question that, if he were forced to tell the truth, and the truth he must always say, might make this man who needed to believe him, not believe.

"Who then are you, Sicun Wasichu?"

"I am what you call me," responded the scholar, "I am the good power of the white man. I am the Sicun Wasichu."

Sitting Bull nodded slowly. White Bull, on the other hand, gripped his knife in his lap as one ready to pounce.

"Are you flesh then, or are you spirit?" asked the Holy Man quietly.

Rodgers knew that his next answer could cause irreparable damage, but he had to tell the truth now. Only the truth would save them.

"I am both, as are you all. But the body that is mine is not like yours, or any other man's. Mine is the body of one of the dead ones, pushed off the spirit road to finish his work."

Sitting Bull began again, "Do you say that your work is to save your people, the whites?"

Rodgers could see clearer now. *Time rushed backwards, purposefully and unwavering. To the wall, to the attack, to the last day of the might of his people.*

"My people are long dead. Their bodies have been grass since before the time that your ancestors, the Black Tortoise clan, lead the serpent invasions up the Father of Waters. Before the time of the invasions of the dark-skinned ones and their war dogs, our warriors were gone. I could not save them, as they would not listen. To them, death was the only acceptable fate.

"Their descendants are the whites, as you call them, and you yourselves, if you could know all of your blood. You, I can save, if you will listen and then hear with your heart."

Rodgers could see that Sitting Bull was unaffected, but thinking. White Bull, on the other hand, stared wide mouthed at the historian. Before he could begin again, Sitting Bull reached across the inert body of Banyon and handed his knife, point first, to Rodgers.

Rodgers knew well the purpose of that act and, taking the knife by the blade, turned it and took the handle. Placing the blade end in his mouth, he bit the blade. To all present, and all those of the invisible world, he had covenanted to tell the truth.

Rodgers knew that what he would say now would be the truth, from its very beginning to its end. He knew also that, if he were to be believed *then they had won!*

"Tell us then, what we must do to save what is. Tell us what we must do to save what will come. Do not tell us only that we must save the whites. Tell us what we must do to save us all!"

"No," responded Rodgers reverently. "I will not tell you to save the white soldiers for their lives alone. I tell you that they must be saved to save the Lakota and the other tribes that will join them. I tell you to save them because, in the doing, you save us all. The Sicun powers have foreseen it; if one nation is to die, in time so will the other. In truth, we are all of one body, a body created by Wakan Tanka. If that body attacks itself, it will destroy part of what gives it life. With this, it will live for a while claiming victory, but that victory is without substance, much like your victories of the summer past. In the end, the body will die, being killed by its enemies from without or from the deep wound within.

"There is, in all of history, this truth that must be understood by all who would see their nations live. My people could not see it, and they perished. Those who conquered us were blind to the same truth and saw their armies' fall and their nation destroyed. We must all come to realize that if both live, then, together, we will find the Good Red Road."

There was quiet in the lodge as the spirit of that which searches for truth wrapped its way from that which cannot be, to that which could be.

Rodgers spoke gently now; he knew they had won the war; only the battle now and all battles are won by those of one heart.

"I will not tell you, because you already know, that if the whites hear of the destruction of over eight hundred of their soldiers, they will be angry. I need not say that they will send ten times that number as their smoking houses pour out guns and weapons of every kind to kill the Lakota. If you believe that the *Holy Road* that divides them from the people in the Grandmother country will be enough to stop them, then you are wrong. They will hunt you like dogs until there is not a free Lakota left to draw breath. The flood at the fort will win you a victory, but it will not gain you that road which you seek."

Chapter 14

When I was a boy the Lakota owned the world; the sun rose and set on their land. They sent ten thousand men to battle. Where are the warriors today? Who slew them? Where are our lands? Who owns them? What white man can say I ever stole his land or a penny of his money? Yet they say that I am a thief. What white woman, however lonely, was ever captive or insulted by me? Yet they say that I am a bad Indian. What white man has ever seen me drunk? Who has ever come to me hungry and unfed? Who has ever seen me beat my wives or abuse my children? What law have I broken? Is it wrong to love my own? ...because I would die for my people and my country?
Sitting Bull

Fort Peck
March 16, 1877
Omega Line

Within three days, the chiefs already in the country of the Grandmother had responded to Sitting Bull's urgent plea. By the morning of the sixteenth day of the *Moon of Snow Blindness*, heavily armed Lakota, Cheyenne and other allies lined the hills and the riverbank surrounding Fort Peck.

Rodgers told the chiefs that before the sun was at mid-sky, the fort, and all that was in it would be gone. At their death, he had told them there would be no hope for the Lakota. To himself he repeated other words, "The cave is closing. If the fort is destroyed with the soldiers inside, then so are we, *in six generations.*"

Rodgers rode a prancing sorrel out to the front of the fort.

Col. Miles was on his feet and, though weak, stood at the parapet. He talked with the man he remembered as the squaw man miner, who had helped them at the surrender at the Hanging Woman.

"Colonel, you have to get your command out of that enclosure immediately. There is a flood coming. If you stay then you and your entire command will, of a surety, be destroyed."

Miles stared at the man across the sharpened log uprights. "Where is your accent, squaw man? You don't sound like a prospector to me. More like some kinda eastern lawyer."

"That accent was a put on, Colonel, to help to smooth the surrender."

"Why was the surrender so important, Mister?" asked Miles.

"Because we thought it might bring peace," answered Rodgers. "But you saw to that, didn't you; attacking the camp at night after they surrendered to you in good faith?"

"I had my orders," answered Miles.

"There are no orders now, Colonel!" Rodgers' voice boomed over the plains like the knell of doom. "No one has told you to hold this fort. Get away from here and you will save yourself and your command. Stay and we will all die!"

Miles raised a hand and made a circle around the thousands of warriors surrounding his besieged command. "You think we will run because of these Indians, whoever you are? Most of us here are veterans of the late War Between the States. We have seen much larger opposing forces than these. We will hold you off until we are relieved, you can be certain of that!"

"I have no question you are right, Colonel," responded Rodgers, "but think about it. Do you really think these Indians are not also veterans of their own kind of war? They know, to the man, that attacking an enclosed fort with a closed gate is nothing less than suicide. If they did not have another agenda, then they would just ride off and wait to meet you someplace else on their own terms. *They are here to save you, Colonel, not to kill you!*

"I know it is hard to believe, but try to understand, Miles. Try to open your mind to what is happening here. They are tired of fighting. You and I both know they were not the ones who started this. It was they who were attacked and, in every battle of your recollection, it was they who were the aggrieved party. They just fought to defend themselves!"

Miles knew that Rodgers was telling the truth in this, but with all of his command listening, offered no response to the accusation. "We will not surrender a fort of the United States of America with eight hundred and fifty fighting men inside without a fight. I understand your perspective, but we will not yield, neither to your force of arms nor to your tricks."

"Is Lt. Baldwin there?" asked Rodgers. He needn't have asked. He could see Baldwin standing at the side of his commanding officer.

"I'm here," responded Baldwin.

"Lt. Baldwin, please tell your colonel why he was left alive on the trail instead of being killed."

Baldwin responded immediately. "Because my regiment had the hostiles surrounded and were commencing the attack. The hostiles, seeing their situation, offered to trade the colonel for the ability to retreat."

"You are right, Baldwin, in the superficial sense of the word. But at the very same time, you lie! What did Shoots Straight tell you was the real reason? There is a flood on its way to destroy this command, Mister, and only you telling the truth will save it."

"What I have said is the complete truth, Sir, without equivocation!"

"Tell him about the future, Lt. Baldwin. We're out of time. Tell him now!"

Behind him, Rogers could hear the sound of voices. One merging into two; the two into twenty, the twenty to hundreds... The flood was coming!!

"Do you hear that, Colonel? It's the flood. You have less than fifteen minutes to live if you don't get out of that fort. Leave now, Colonel. Save these men. Save this future!"

"These negotiations are at an end!" responded Miles as he saw large numbers of warriors moving at a fast gallop off the surrounding hills.

"Prepare to receive an attack!" shouted the Lieutenant, as he leapt from the catwalk to give a last minute inspection to his waiting troops. "They're coming, men!" he yelled as he raced across the courtyard to encourage the soldiers who were now climbing into position on the walls and the others that were preparing the Gatling guns and the small cannon that had been brought with the troops.

Outside the walls, the Lt. Baldwin could hear the beginning of incoming gun fire as literally hundreds of bullets poured into the walls of the wooded enclosure.

The return fire of the troops on the wall was like a single shot as they fired back at the Indians. The shouting from above confirmed they were going into their traditional circling technique around the perimeter of the fort. Baldwin hurried the rest of the lagging riflemen up to the catwalk as he himself climbed back to the parapet beside Nelson Miles. What he had heard from the men was correct, but nothing that was said had prepared him for the numbers that were involved in the encirclement. They had expected as many as a thousand warriors, but before him, Baldwin could see at least three times that number. The Indians were circling the fort at a distance, almost out of range of an effective rifle shot. Baldwin could see that Miles was, in spite of his wound, quite completely in command, directing fire in volleys from his position.

Then suddenly, to his complete astonishment, Baldwin noticed that Rodgers had not moved from *his* position. He had dismounted, and the horse, sensing its possible reprieve from certain death, had very sensibly left him at a high rate of speed. Rodgers, to the immense surprise of the men in the fort, now stood alone, directly in the crossfire between the circling Indians and the troops.

"Fire on that man!" commanded Miles.

Almost as a single shot, a hundred bullets roared toward the defenseless Rodgers, who went down hard. Baldwin, watching his death, blinked, feeling a great confusion overcome him for no more than a second.

Then Rodgers was on his feet again and looking as if nothing out of the ordinary had happened.

"Fire on that man, I said!" roared Nelson Miles. Again the roar was deafening as the scholar was ripped off his feet and thrown to the ground. Baldwin staggered, as did Miles, their minds reeling. First from within and then from the sight that immediately met them. Before them, out of nowhere, was the other squaw man, Banyon, standing beside the historian. *It was impossible*, thought Baldwin. There was a hundred yards of clear ground between Rodgers and anywhere that could have hidden a man. Still, he was there, standing beside the older man as they both resolutely faced the firing troops.

"Stop it, Baldwin!" yelled the younger man. "You can stop this before the flood gets here. You have to believe me, just this one last time!"

"Kill those men!" commanded Miles. "Kill those men in this moment!"

Every mind on the catwalk reeled as a murderous fire cut the men below them to the ground.

Lt. Baldwin knew then, or he thought he knew, that they were facing disaster. Banyon was right, the lieutenant said quietly to himself. The interpreter had always been able to see what was coming and had saved Miles at the confrontation on the plains and Hale at the river after telling him, personally, what would happen. Then came another volley as the young Lieutenant felt new thoughts raging through his emptied, and then so suddenly filled, mind.

"The squaw man is right, Sir!" stammered Baldwin. "These Indians have no reason to be attacking us. To do so defies understanding!"

Below them, he could see the two men standing, facing each other now. The younger man was bending over, holding his head. The older man was steadying him, speaking to him, the Lieutenant thought.

Then, from behind the two officers there was a tremendous roar as the back wall of the palisade bucked outward and then collapsed in a heap, exposing the charging Indians. The officers could see that the wall had been pulled from its founding's by large numbers of Indians on horses. They had roped the top timbers of the enclosure with their horse ropes and, at one instant, had all charged away from the frame work that held the wall secure.

Miles, fighting to focus in what now was almost overwhelming confusion, could not understand why the men who had manned that wall did not direct fire at the Indians directly under their noses. Then he realized the why of it as he saw those same men falling to the ground in a frantic mass of struggling humanity. They had been watching the events at the front gate, and, in the same confusion that had engulfed the minds of their commanders, had not been aware of the ropes of the warriors below.

The senior officer, gripping tightly the front wall of the palisade, could see that his command was doomed now and, though he could not explain the how of it, he did know exactly who had brought them all to their deaths.

"Fire again," came the order as the men who had not jumped from the walls shot at the men below the gate, they had now been joined by a woman, dressed as a warrior, who was talking desperately to the stricken Shoots Straight... The scene blinked again, and there were five men, and then over ten, destroyed by the same order.

Baldwin heard the voice of the staggering Banyon. Again, the murderous fire cut down the twenty men. "Look at us, who do you see?"

The young lieutenant could see Shoots Straight, Rodgers, and the girl before him. Beside them was Crazy Horse, and beside him, *was a little girl!* Then there were other men he did not recognize, and then, of a sudden, did. He could feel that the fighting below him was hand-to-hand, as the troops firing their rifles had decimated the first attack of the Indians. The first man to go down was a man he knew from the fort. His name was Big Crow! He was shot by the troops as he flung himself, heedless of his own fate, at the guns. Baldwin felt himself stagger as if struck. Suddenly, the Indian was gone and was one of those standing beside the white men at the front. He could see that a chief had gone down in the melee below. The name Lame Deer came to his mind from a source unfathomable to him. *Killed at the battle of Slim Buttes…*

Of a sudden, Baldwin realized that not one of his men was down. Only Indians had fallen. It seemed that as they fell, they reappeared to their front, only to be cut down by the next volley of the remaining defenders of the front wall of the fort.

Then the young lieutenant saw it. Saw the impossible. Two Lakota had a single soldier by the arms and were rushing him toward a waiting horseman. The man, thrown bodily on the back of the horse, turned to escape, only to see something at his rear that caused him to turn and clutch frantically at the waist of the warrior.

Another soldier was on horseback in the same way. Then they were twenty, then a hundred. As the horses and their double loads fled from the chaos of the destroyed fort, there arose a deafening roar upriver as all who remained suddenly realized the flood had arrived.

The officers, looking upriver, saw over forty warriors on horseback approaching Banyon and Rodgers. Behind them, they saw a wall of water, over twenty feet high, roaring down the river course directly to the side of the fort.

"They were wrong!" shouted Lt. Baldwin to Miles, who stood riveted to the scene before him. "The flood will miss us, it was all a ruse."

The warriors had Banyon now and were loading him frantically on a waiting horse. Behind him, steadying the struggling Shoots Straight was the girl. She turned to the south in a single movement as the warriors around her gained control of their frightened mounts and plunged as one in pursuit. To the front of the fleeing group, the officer could see the white man, Rodgers, following a very specific route of escape.

The cavalrymen blinked unbelieving. Rodgers was leading them into the river, into certain death, with the flood destroying everything in its path. The girl, and those whom she led, followed him unerringly into the water.

Miles and Baldwin turned to each other and began to laugh. "Lemmings to the sea," chortled Miles. The words died in his mouth as the great Missouri, the highway of the west, jumped from its course and headed across dry land, directly at the doomed fort.

The officers jumped as one man from the wall into a scene of total chaos. The shaken men found themselves grabbed immediately by warriors and lifted as if they were made of paper onto the backs of waiting horses. In a heartbeat they, and hundreds of others, were out of the enclosure and running for the high country to the north. Every man and horse fought for a better hold on the icy ground.

All around them, they could see other soldiers and dismounted Indians running for their lives. Mounted warriors swooped in from the flank to lift running men up behind them. A sudden staggering roar from their rear told them that the flood had hit the fort with the savage force of nature run amuck. The sound of the water, less than a hundred yards behind them now, told them that what had been done to rescue the command would not be enough! At least a hundred dismounted warriors, and a smattering of troops, would not make the high ground to which the horsemen charged.

"No!" The shout exploded from the Lieutenant as he reined in his horse, ordering his men to halt. Some, including Miles, continued in heedless flight toward the nearing high ground. Still, something, *something* more than just the order from the junior officer had stopped a large number of the mounted men, Lakota and troopers alike; many had their hands to their heads in obvious pain or confusion. Others seemed dazed in the saddle, as Baldwin, suddenly back to himself, screamed his order.

"Let's get them!"

The young officer, while chagrined, was not surprised that the mounted men all stared at him breathlessly. None, however, moved toward the oncoming flood and its doomed victims.

"There is time!" screamed Baldwin. "None of us would have had a chance without them! They have given up their future for us! Can we live, knowing that we could have saved them?"

Terrified horses reared and shied toward the high ground knowing what was upon them. Confused troopers and warriors fought on a double front with their terrified mounts and their crippled minds.

Only seconds had passed, but Baldwin knew they were precious seconds.

A mounted sergeant in the ranks yelled at Baldwin breathlessly. "If we go back, we are dead men, Lieutenant!"

Baldwin felt a staggering confusion as he reeled in the moment, a moment that seemed to come again and again. First they were fleeing, then they were returning for the men. He felt the flood hit them and saw the men being swept from their mounts.

Then he was on his horse again, his mind clearing, and he could hear his own laughter as his memories focused and unraveled before him.

He was leaving the lodge of the interpreter, Shoots Straight, back on the Tongue. One night after another, as he rose to go,

*the interpreter rose with him, putting his hand on his shoulder.
"There will be time, but just barely, turn to your left and you will
be safe!!"*

"Let's get them," he yelled. His horse jumped sideways,
gained the bit, and with a roar of defiance a hundred horsemen,
charged back into the path of the advancing Missouri.

Almost in a single movement, the decimated command and
its Indian allies rushed toward the doomed men.

The thunder of the horses' feet pounded at the roar of the
great river as it finished the abandoned fort. Almost as if directed
by a hidden hand, it rushed toward the fleeing men and their
would-be rescuers.

The riders were to the runners, and each man, in turning his
terrified mount, reached a hand to his fellow. No man noted
whether the man he sought to rescue was white or red, or if he
was friend or enemy. Each man offered himself to save another,
knowing they were all in the same fight. A fight they had to
believe would end in death. Still, they would not live with the
memory that they had stood by on the horses provided for their
escape as the brave men who had given those horses died.

The lines of an approaching future roiled together as the great
waters of the Missouri swept behind four hundred hooves
thundering behind their Lieutenant leader. Inexplicably, instead
of turning to flee before the raging torrent, he instead *turned left,*
to the south, parallel with the merciless wall of water.

From the lips of each man came pleading words, "Wakan
Tanka, help me!"

"My Lord, My God, help me to live!"

"Dear Father, I place my life in your hands!"

These voices charged together toward the skies of the great
American west and rose together toward a single place, along a
Good Red Road!

And then there was silence . . .

*

The south bank of the Missouri River
March 16, 1877
Omega Line

He Dog was waiting for them as they came out of the river. "Hurry! Hurry!" He was shouting to the warriors. He rushed his pony toward Rodgers as he staggered from the river. The historian was wounded badly. He Dog was not surprised by the wound and moved to his side to steady him in the saddle.

"We have done it, my brother! We have made it happen. Now we must go, there is still time to save them all if we can get you back to the cave in time."

Rodgers smiled, in spite of the great pain, as he tried to steady himself on the horse. He was hurt badly, he knew. Still, they must not make another attempt! The path was straight. They must not tamper with its course, no matter the price.

The girl was struggling, trying to keep the unconscious Banyon on the wet horse. Crazy Horse had moved to their side and was attempting to trade places with the girl. To no avail!

"I can't get him back. I am afraid the fabric is torn away. If it is, there is no hope this side of the cave!" The girl's voice was desperate.

He Dog nodded a look of intense pride on his face. The son of my daughter has gained us a great deal, now it is for us to give him the victory he has sought in so many lives. "Come, we have to move quickly or we will lose all we have gained."

Heavy rains raged at the band of warriors as they followed He Dog and the girl into the South Land. Day after day, they fought against the elements in an unrelenting plunge to the south.

The warriors ran relays of fresh mounts so those in front could keep going. By the fourth day, both of the injured men had to be moved to travois as their companions fled against hope – ever southward, ever toward the cave that had given them all life. By the ninth day, life held by a flicker.

"*They cannot die!*" He Dog yelled repeatedly to the struggling band.

The boy Black Elk rode stride for stride with the warriors. The others wondered if he was wounded initially, for he rode as if in a daze. The vision that had claimed him repeated over and over as he fought with his fellows toward the looming hills.

There was an old man sitting beside a shabby cabin, his legs folded under him. He was talking to a white man, who was writing his words on paper. There was grief there to be felt. There was pain of the soul as the vision of the people vanished. There were words. Yes, his own words, flowing from loss of hope to a generation without purpose.

"The circle of the people is broken. The sacred tree is dead!"

But then, there was a breeze coming from the north, pressing at the old man's hair, penetrating the windowless openings touching the faces of the people.

Touching the white man, as he saw what he had written disappear before him!

"They must not die!" yelled He Dog again at the failing strength of the warriors.

The boy was yelling now. The words were his, but the voice was from afar, from another day that now wavered in its very existence. "Not this time! They must finish the line at this juncture. They must close the circle of the people, and in the circle, the tree!"

On the tenth day, they entered the valley of the cave.

**

The cave of emergence, Valley of the Wind caves
March 26, 1877
Omicron-Omega path

Sharpfish and Red Cherry were coming *out* of the cave behind a fast-moving Plenty Coups, Chief of the Crow, as the rage of winter fought toward them. Neither of them had to see his face to know that the man who had counseled his people to never fight against the whites *was a very angry man indeed*.

To the north, they could see a band of about forty warriors fighting toward the entrance.

"Lakota!" spat the Crow Chieftain. He had spent his life killing these people. They were his greatest enemies and yet they were, he knew now, the last chance for his people! Untying his waiting horse from the sapling at the entrance of the cave, the Crow rode toward his oncoming enemy, chanting the brave heart song of his people. The song that had brought them north on the father of waters where they had sought a land, where *all* men could be free; in those days, remembered Plenty Coups, the Sioux and the Crow were one people. If the powers would allow it, they would be again. The circle would be complete!

"That which was one, has become many; that which is many will become one," boomed the voice of the Crow.

A good nation we will make live . . .

From the oncoming band of warriors came the reply.

This the powers above have said.

They have given us the power to make over.

Plenty Coups threw him self into the midst of the oncoming band, helping to push them forward. Forward, where the entrance of the womb of the people awaited them.

The boy Black Elk stood before the cave, now oblivious to the haste of his elders. The boy was staring at a small sapling that grew, firm and strong, just a few yards from the entrance.

"My grandson must go through first!" shouted He Dog, as they arrived at the entrance. "It is for him only to stop what will happen."

The warriors were lifting Banyon struggling for control, off the travois; he was weak. *Too weak*, thought He Dog.

The girl, Buffalo Calf Road, stepped forward, pulling his arm over her shoulders.

"Only they can enter!" commanded He Dog as the warriors reached to help. "This is theirs to do. The blood must be at their hands. No man can make this decision for another."

Rodgers lifted himself up on one elbow to watch the man and his woman stagger into the cave.

The blazer pulled into a tree lined clearing at the north end of the mound and stopped. Banyon quickly reread the last passage in the biography as he stepped out of the blazer into ankle-deep snow.

At a distance, he could see an Indian man and woman standing at the entrance of what seemed to be a cave or a large hole at the summit of the mound. The woman seemed to be supporting the man, as if he were hurt in some way. The agent thought there was something odd about the way the man was dressed, even about the way he walked that seemed out of place.

There was a familiarity in the features of the pair that, as the distance closed between them, momentarily stunned the agent into inaction.

His mind clearing, Agent Banyon reached suddenly for his service revolver. The man in the cave pushed the woman to one side and, without hesitation, lowered his rifle and fired.

The girl raised herself from the ground quickly and moved

back to her man's side as they stared together toward the body lying beside the blazer in the snow. Then, raising their hands toward The Great Professor, they beckoned him toward them. Rodgers, throwing down the pistol in his hand, rushed toward the waiting couple. Being supported by the scholar and the girl, Shoots Straight was carried back into the cave.

***

Wakan Cave
Omicron-Omega Axial Point

"Hurry," shouted He Dog, as he pulled Shoots Straight and the girl from the entrance toward the exhausted warriors.

Rodgers was supported between two men now, and they were moving him toward the cave. At the entrance, they supported him momentarily. They all knew he had to enter the cave alone. Only he could do what had to be done. Only he could finish the work!

Rodgers turned toward the unsteady Banyon and the girl. "I do not think that you will see me again. With my entrance from both sides, the cave will close here, but it will open again where we began. Your work is done! The fabric of your mind will not tolerate the remainder. Stay here and be at peace!"

With that, Rodgers stepped into the cave and there was a sound, a sound of voices in battle, and then in song. Shoots Straight thought he could understand the words, although the language was not one of his day. Still, in a distant recess of his mind, there was meaning.

Hear us wind for we are swift
Hear us rock for we are strong.
Hear us stars for we are the light
Hear our song and feel our hearts.

Yes hear us one last time
For even the Brave must die.

Banyon stood up straight, his mind now clear and strong. He put his arm around Buffalo Calf Road and pulled her to him. He looked into her eyes then kissed her softly as they shared the knowledge that at last it was finished. Here they could raise their children in peace.

In the limestone outer wall of the now silent cave, He Dog laboriously began to carve an image of a humpbacked man playing a magical flute.

"To here it is sealed," he whispered to the stone!

****

At the site of destroyed Fort Peck
March 17, 1877
Omega Line

Sitting Bull organized the surviving Lakota and their Cheyenne, Blackfeet, Assiniboine, and Yankatoni allies. Together they headed downstream, apparently following the great flood that had destroyed the soldier fort and nearly taken so many good men. Among the new allies there was a sense of confidence and direction. All of them knew they had seen something different on that day -- something that would change what was to come.

*****

On September thirtieth of that year, the newly reinforced Seventh and Second cavalry were under the command of Nelson Miles, the nationally acclaimed hero of the Battle of Fort Peck. In the morning of that day, the Shoshone scouts informed the new

Brevet General that the hotly pursued Nez Perce under Chiefs Joseph and Looking Glass were camped in a small river valley directly to their north. On the command of Miles, Captain Owen Hale positioned his men to the southeast. In obedience to orders, he charged with the entire Seventh Cavalry over a large flat plain that funneled into a V shape, leading directly into the sleeping camp of the Nez Perce. The morning was very cold as Captain Hale, mounting his precocious gray gelding, was heard to say, "My G--, why do I have to go out and get killed on such a cold morning?"

Over three hundred men strong, the Seventh formed in a single advancing line and, on the order from Hale, charged in headlong heedless abandon toward the apex of the V-shaped plateau.

As Hale felt the exhilaration of the glorious charge, he knew there was a bullet about to be fired that would end his life. He also realized there would be no purpose in that death that was apparent to anyone. Still, he had contented himself that through thousands, perhaps millions, of similarly unremembered sacrifices to cause, a great nation would be born. It would be a difficult birth, thought Hale, as the horse gained speed and he could hear the combined crescendo of his men as they yelled what, for many of them, would be their last shout of defiance in this life. They would tell the world that, though they would die, still they would die as men and pity the fools that would die as anything less!

Of a sudden, the roar of voices faltered and, just as suddenly, was still. Hale could feel riders dropping off from beside him as troopers brought their mounts to what was sometimes a sliding stop. Hale began to pull on the reins as the big gray, of his own volition, began to slow. On the surrounding hills, Hale saw first a few, and then a great number, of mounted horsemen pulling their hard run mounts to a stop.

The perimeter of the valley continued to fill with riders, pausing with their fellows to stare into the river valley beneath them, where the attack on the Nez Perce had stopped! They watched as history, like the great Missouri, carved a new course.

Hale stopped the gray and breathlessly watched, mouth agape, as what now seemed to be thousands and thousands of armed riders topped the ridges and waited. Looking behind him, Hale could see that his men had chosen the better part of valor and were moving at a trot back toward the low hills to the south from which they came. Hale surveyed the savage host to his east and north and west. In them, he could recognize the Lakota and Cheyenne, with what appeared to be fifty or sixty men dressed in cavalry uniforms. He also could see the hosts of the Blackfeet and Assiniboine. To his west, however, he was stunned to see the arrival of the Crow under Plenty Coups, dressed for war. All of them poised, prepared to attack the white troops on the moment.

From the center of the line, he could see Banyon and a girl. He could also see Sharpfish and the Crow interpreter, Red Cherry, with Lt. Baldwin. The five riders were loping their horses toward him, all smiling broadly. Behind them came Crazy Horse with a little light haired girl bouncing on a smart pinto pony, matching his every stride.

From the hilltops and the valley below them, the Nez Perce were raising from their rifle pits to view the incredible site before them.

...And on the winds of the plains, through the acts of men of good will, and the dreams of the brave, came the dancing chant of those who are the Sicun Powers.

See them dancing they come,
See them dancing, they come,
A horse nation, they come,
Behold them, prancing they come,
They come neighing, they come,
In a sacred way, behold them, behold them.

As Rodgers prepared to leave the cave, he knew they had done all they had come to do. Just to be certain, however, he went to the shelf containing the leather bound books and carefully selected the newest volume.

Time slowed momentarily in the world of man as the spirits of what would soon be, wound through the cave of the valley of the wind. In a thousand lines the sound of rejoicing reflected to its center as the man who had known them all sought for what had been done.

The printing on the page slowed and became firm. There was still a small movement at the very end that worried the scholar but the future was always such thought the historian. Everywhere that men of good heart strove together the future would change from what would have been.

Rodgers closed the book and placed it back on the shelf beside the others. "It is time to go home," he smiled.

Turning toward the outside of the cave, he could feel the sun shining a welcome. His comrades were just outside, as he had expected, with a horse saddled and waiting.

The Beginning...

Aftermath

...follow resolutely the one straight path before you, let neither obstacles nor temptations induce you to leave it; bound along if you can; if not, on hands and knees follow in it, perish in it if needful, but you need not fear for that; no one ever yet died in the *true* path . . . before they had attained the pinnacle. Turn into other paths, for momentary advantage or gratification, ye have sold your inheritance, your immortality.

George Borrow (1877)

OMEGA LINE

On the sixteenth of September 1887, the United States Congress, under extreme pressure from the President of the United States, Secretary of the Army, and the Ambassador to the United States from Great Britain, enacted the following:

"In recognition of the petition, signed and personally delivered to the steps of Congress by over two hundred Senior Officers of the United States Army, we reaffirm our dedication to enforce our obligations under the treaties ratified historically to date."

It was further established that the valley of the Walla Walla would be returned to the Nez Perce, along with hunting rights, in perpetuity as part of the great reservation established and added to by the aforementioned treaty.

It was also agreed, as additional compensation to the aggrieved parties, to establish as federal law that all American Bison remaining on the western plains were, and always would be, the property of the western tribes for their exclusive use and enjoyment.

It was, however, specified that all above referenced animals were to be removed to the above described reservations and unceded hunting areas within one year of the implementation of the agreement.

On Christmas Day of that same year, the combined chiefs of the Sioux, Crow, Bannock, Nez Perce, Assiniboine, Shoshone, Cheyenne, Arapaho, Blackfeet and Arrikara\Pawnee tribes, although reaffirming their own tribal sovereignty and lands, signed a mutual defense agreement. This agreement stated that, upon receiving notice of aggressive actions from any outside military force, all parties would send such warriors as could be readily assembled to the aid of their brother tribe.

Also, it was unanimously agreed that on any reasonable request, the combined tribes would provide men and material as was necessary to protect the sovereignty of the United States of America against all threats, both domestic and foreign.

That area described by the treaty, and all other lands described as hunting areas under that same agreement, would, from that moment forth, be described as the territory of Dakota. The Dakota Territory would be granted statehood within ten years of the date of the signing of that bill by the President.

In the spring of 1879, the greatest round up in the history of mankind began at the old Lakota campground on the Hanging Woman. For the entirety of that summer, huge clouds of dust could be seen, sometimes for a hundred miles from their origin, as warriors of the people brought the buffalo home to Dakota. Sioux rode side by side with their historic enemies the Crow and Bannock, while the Nez Perce rode beside their traditional enemies, the Assiniboine and Flathead.

It was notable that wherever the driving warriors were seen, also were seen the blue shirts of the United States Cavalry, helping their comrades in arms toward a future filled with hope. A bond had been formed in the wet sands of the Missouri that would not be broken by verbiage or policy. The fighting men of both nations had found at the destroyed Fort Peck comrades of the heart. They had found brothers of courage who would stand by them regardless of the future.

In the following year, filled with the new sense of fellowship that swept the nation, a well-meaning businessman in the east sent a letter to Sitting Bull, offering to pay for the education of fifteen Lakota young men. Sitting Bull pondered the contents of the letter as it was read to him and then dictated a response.

On behalf of my people's children, I accept your offer. We have sent other boys to your schools in times past. When they have returned, I have noticed that they found it difficult to endure strong cold. Their skills as warriors were not as developed as the boys who stayed behind. It seemed that they had become much more concerned about themselves and less about the helpless ones.

Still, we know that to walk this road, they must know of their brothers, the whites, and of their ways.

We will send you these boys and you will make them knowledgeable. Send us, in turn, fifteen of your boys, and we will make them men!

Your friend,
Sitting Bull 2

The fifteen boys were exchanged, as anticipated by the correspondence. Upon return to their families, years later, there were differences noted that were to be of benefit to each of their communities.

The young Lakota boys had become adept at the English language and were able to help drop the barriers that had, for so long, plagued the interactions between the two peoples. They also reported being treated well by their white friends and were able to communicate much of the knowledge they had gained about an ever growing and modernizing world.

---

2 Actually written, Omicron and Omega Lines

The young whites, on their return, were a marvel to their families. Not only had they been groomed in the way of the warrior bands, but also it was noticed that they took a peculiar interest in the poor among the communities. Showered with gifts from their adoring families on their return, it was seen that they gave these gifts, in a respectable time period, to those more in need of them.

As the nation, as one people, moved into the industrial age, it was found that there was a disturbing fracturing of the family, owing to the increased demand on the parents of children. Faced with the growing rebellion of their offspring, parents would send the young to their brothers in Dakota. There they would be taught how to sit a horse while pursuing a fleeing herd of buffalo. They would learn that it was important for a person to succeed in life – that there was reason behind it, beyond the acquisition of wealth. They learned that it was their responsibility to care for the helpless ones, the sick, the old, and the infirm.

They were also schooled in the virtues of the nation:

Bravery   Fortitude   Generosity
Wisdom   and   Tolerance!!!!!

***

Regardless of the virtues learned and practiced by the people of the land, the day came when its enemies were too great to hold at bay. By the year 2025 A.D., after repeated defeats on the battlefields of Europe and the Middle East, the armies of the United States and Canada were set to defend their very borders one final time.

The line, long held, finally broke along the Mexican border. Thousands of highly disciplined troops, under despot leaders, rushed through the hole into the mainland. Halting to regroup along the former borders of the state of Oklahoma, the invading army was hit from three sides by mounted horsemen of incredible ferocity.

Highly trained and well armed, the surprisingly mobile horsemen drove the invading army back upon its self. Modern weapons were unprepared to deal with the tremendous versatility of the mounted warriors. Their machines in ruins, they were driven, en masse, back across the Rio Grande.

Reinforced by the regrouped military forces, the warriors were able to surround the invading army in Northern Mexico. Most of the commanders of the invading force were certain that, on the following day, they would be destroyed. The morning, however, brought only the sound of silence. The fighting men of the nation had returned to the *land that was their own.*

No one could be certain as to the future. Indeed, neither had the ancestors of the nation known what would become of the road that lay before them. But as the word of what had been done or, better said, not done in Mexico spread throughout the world, it effected a change; a realization came that another path could be found. Even though man must always be prepared to fight and prepare his sons as he was prepared, for forever will there be evil men, an understanding had been found. Mankind might now turn his back on war and live as one people, riding as brothers down a Good Red Road.

My horses, prancing they are coming,
My horses neighing they are coming
Prancing they are coming.
All over the universe they come.
They will dance, may you behold them
They will dance, may you behold them
A horse nation they will dance,
May you behold them!

All over the universe, they have finished a day of happiness!

Author's Note

This completes the first of three or four books, which make up the tale of the Celtic Druid Amhergin, and his sons and daughters. The man himself was one of the few written historians of the conquered Celtic race, destined by fate to direct the course of mankind forever. Historically we know little of Amhergin and to be totally honest, the man haunts me.

In an age and culture where it was forbidden that those of his profession should write, he wrote!! Where the conquerors insisted that he blend, he stood out!

Surrounded by those who were resigned to the facts before them; he looked to what could be salvaged from the wreckage. I am thankful to him and those like him for the inspiration professionally and personally.

More to the point however I am grateful to those who read this and for the encouragement I have received to bring my stories to print.

I am grateful to the thousands that have listened patiently as I have practiced the ancient art of the storyteller and joined with me in all the many splendid visions of what *might have been!!*

M. Ambrose Forsyth
Dec. 2002....